Watch for Me by Moonlight

Watch for Me by Moonlight

Kirsty Ferry

Hartsford Mysteries

Where heroes are like chocolate – irresistible!

Published 2019 by Choc Lit Limited
Penrose House, Crawley Drive, Camberley, Surrey GU15 2AB, UK
www.choc-lit.com

A CIP catalogue record for this book is available
from the British Library

ISBN: 978-1-78189-437-8

Printed and bound in Great Britain by Clays Ltd, Elcograf S.p.A.

For my family, with whom I've spent many happy holidays on the Norfolk/Suffolk border

Acknowledgements

I put the finishing touches to this book in Norfolk, or, more specifically, in a cottage in Brockdish, on the border of Norfolk and Suffolk. The cottage is owned by Jackie and John Spooner, and a quick reckoning had me realising we've been coming here on family holidays since 1997. Not every year, but perhaps every two or three years on average. It's a place I love and hold very dear to my heart – and the place we brought our son for his first holiday in 2002. He was almost eighteen months old and was obsessed by the Quack Quacks on the River Waveney that runs along the bottom of the garden.

The village of 'Hartsford' is quite a bit bigger than Brockdish, which is little more than one street, and Hartsford Hall is an amalgamation of many beautiful stately homes we've visited in the past. It's mostly, I would say, Kedleston Hall in Derbyshire and Ickworth in Suffolk; Georgiana's tomb is definitely based on Mary Curzon's tomb at Kedleston. As Elodie suggests in this novel, "she had the most delightful tomb – if you could ever call a tomb delightful". Georgiana's monument also takes, in some small part, inspiration from Lady Elizabeth Nightingale's tomb in Westminster Abbey – a deliciously Gothic confection which captured my imagination many years ago, when I carefully stored it away for future use.

The character of Highwayman Ben is based on Claude Duval, who, unlike most other highwaymen, distinguished himself with rather gentlemanly behaviour and fashionable clothes. Duval reputedly never used violence, but he did have a penchant for tying people to trees as he robbed them. One story goes that he took only a part of his potential loot from a gentleman, when his wife agreed to dance the "courante" with him in the wayside.

In order to pull all these threads together and bring this lovely story to life, I have to thank the wonderful team at Choc Lit. Huge thanks to the readers who have enjoyed my previous books, and to the Tasting Panel for agreeing this one was good enough to publish with special thanks to Yvonne G, Elisabeth H, Anne E, Dimitra E, Els E, Joy S, Barbara B, Gill L, Claire W, Lizzie D, Karen M, Sheila S, Linda S and Rosie S. Also, thanks to my super editor, my fabulous cover designer and the wider Choc Lit family, who are always there for chats, rants, general despair, and providing unfailing support for one another. Last but definitely not least, I have to thank my family, without whom a holiday in Norfolk would have been a very lonely affair! I wouldn't even know about this place if my parents hadn't sourced it out in 1997, so the biggest thanks, this time, should really go to them. Thank you!

"Look for me by moonlight;
Watch for me by moonlight;
I'll come to thee by moonlight,
though hell should bar the way!"

From *The Highwayman*, by Alfred Noyes

Chapter One

None of it would have happened without the storm.

It had begun as a perfectly normal day and Elodie Bright was helping out in the Hartsford Hall gift shop. They'd just finished serving a large group of German people who'd rocked up on a bus-trip, when her colleague Margaret, a tall, bespectacled lady with a heart of gold, frowned and commented, 'Is it just me, or is it getting dark?'

Elodie looked outside. The honey-coloured Hall seemed to be standing out more brightly than usual against the sky, which was, quite dramatically, turning black. The solar lights she had stuck, porcupine-like, in the plant pots outside came on one by one, and there was a deep, ominous silence that seemed to bury everything beneath it. The first drops of rain began to fall, and, suddenly, it was as if someone up in the heavens released the floodgates and there was a complete and utter deluge.

Margaret dashed over to the window and peered out as droplets slammed against the glass. 'Have you seen that rain, Elodie?' she asked, clearly shocked.

Elodie hid a smile. 'It's hard to miss it!'

The bell on the door of the shop was going mad as the German contingent did a swift about-turn and other tourists ran inside to shelter. Most of them were shouting out the same obvious statement as Margaret.

'Look at that rain!'

'My word! That's coming down!'

'*Mein Gott! Es regnet!*'

Elodie didn't speak much German, but she understood that. She agreed with everyone and, giving up her space behind the counter, pushed forward and joined the throng of bodies at the window.

That was when she saw the lightning strike the church.

The sky split open and a dazzling, jagged fork appeared out of the seething mass of darkness. It was as if it knew exactly where to aim for. You would have thought it would have gone for the spire and the metal weather vane at the top, but it didn't. At the last moment, the fork veered and hit the roof of the Lady Chapel, illuminating the whole church like some awful Gothic nightmare. Pieces of the roof exploded outwards and upwards and rained down on the ancient building.

For a moment, there was a stunned silence in the gift shop. Elodie had never seen lightning strike anything, ever; she didn't think anyone else in the shop had either, judging by the shocked faces and the comprehensive intake of breath. Then everyone suddenly began to point and chatter, but for a moment none of the words registered. Mouths were moving and customers were pushing forwards for a better view, but she didn't notice any of it.

She couldn't think of anything except Georgiana's tomb.

Hartsford Hall belonged to the current Earl of Hartsford, Alexander Aldrich – or, as Elodie knew him, Alex. Georgiana had been one of Alex's ancestors and she'd died in 1796, at the age of nineteen.

She had the most delightful tomb – if you could ever call a tomb delightful. It was made of marble and so elegantly carved that the effigy of her took your breath away. Elodie could stare at it for hours. How could anyone ever have been that perfect? It was sometimes hard to believe – for there was surely just dust and bones in there now – that the gorgeous young woman depicted on the top, with her eyelashes brushing her smooth cheeks and her long, wavy hair spilling out over the marble pillow, was no more. Alex hadn't understood the fascination when they were children, but for Elodie, Georgiana was like the big sister she'd never had.

Elodie and Alex had known each other forever, or so it seemed. In primary school, they'd been inseparable. But because the other children thought he was special – being a viscount and heir to an earl – they had turned their noses up at Elodie and decided, jealously, to ignore her. In their minds, she was privileged and undeserving of their friendship. All because her father was the Hartsford Estate Manager and her mother had helped look after Alex when his mother had abandoned him and his sister. As a result, Elodie was sometimes desperately lonely. Alex couldn't take the place of a giggly female friend – he was utterly useless at that kind of thing. So Lady Georgiana had to do until Elodie grew up and made proper, living friends. Elodie used to creep into the church and sit cross-legged in front of the marble effigy, talking to her. She made a great confidante.

Alex just didn't get it.

And then Elodie moved to London, and stayed there, as she had sworn to do; but she was convinced that Georgiana witnessed her wedding to Piers Bingham-Scott beforehand. She had felt her nearby. It wasn't something she usually talked about – not to the bullying, hurtful children at school, anyway – but Elodie had seen ghosts and shadows all her life, unclear figures who never meant that much to her, but she knew they were there.

It annoyed her that she'd never seen Georgiana properly. Having said that, at the wedding, Georgiana's presence had left her uncomfortable and out of kilter – it was not at all like how it had been when she was younger. With hindsight, the ghost had probably been trying to tell her she was making a huge mistake marrying Piers – who turned out, sadly, to be a very wealthy playboy investment banker type, and not at all the husband she deserved. Still, the hefty divorce settlement had been welcome, and left her with a big Range Rover and a substantial nest-egg as she moved back to Hartsford.

But right now, in the midst of the torrential rain and the rolls of thunder and the forked lightning that had blown the roof clean off the church, Piers Bingham-Scott and the ghosts of her old life in London were the last things on Elodie's mind.

All that mattered was Georgiana.

Elodie had no idea how she made it to the church so quickly when she could barely see anything for the rain bucketing down in front of her eyes.

Pushing her way out of the gift shop, she ran, ploughing through mud and churned up grass, splashing through ankle deep puddles. Water was fountaining out of the drain covers like so many geysers, but Elodie didn't look down, didn't look to see where her feet were going. Her trainers would need to be binned and her clothes would probably never dry out again, but who cared? She just kept her sights on the church.

Against the shadows, she saw a tall figure running towards the place and knew instinctively who it was.

'Alex!' The wind tore the words out of her mouth and blew them somewhere towards Norfolk.

He reached the church moments before she did and stopped short at the door.

'Alex!'

This time he heard her and spun around, rain dripping off his messy dark hair and into his midnight-blue eyes. 'The roof, Elodie, it's been hit. I was in the greenhouse. I saw it happening.'

'I know!' She drew up next to him, quite breathless. 'I saw it too, from the gift shop.' She hurried past him and put one hand on the ancient bronze door handle, but Alex's hand came down on her wrist and held it in place.

'Let me go first. I don't know if it's safe.'

Elodie relinquished the handle and hovered near him as he pulled the door open.

They both coughed as a cloud of dust and plaster came out, but thankfully there was no smell of burning.

'Thank God,' said Alex, clearly expecting the worst. 'I'm still going in first though. You stay here until I call you.'

'Okay. But come right back out if it's looking bad!'

'Don't worry, I won't hang around if it is.' He disappeared into the building and Elodie peered anxiously in after him. After what seemed like an age, he called out to her. 'It's pretty grotty, but safe enough I think. The Lady Chapel got the worst of it. You can come in if you're careful. But if it's too much for your asthma, go straight back out.'

'I will. But the poor Lady Chapel!' Her heart pounding, she hurried into the church. As she stood there in the dark with the modern-day emergency lighting glowing in the rafters, and tiles smashed beneath her feet, and one of the beams hanging at a crazy angle from the ceiling to the floor, and one candle still miraculously lit and flickering wildly in an alcove near the altar, Elodie fought back the worst feeling of dread she'd ever experienced in her life.

'Oh, my God!'

The Lady Chapel, which housed Georgiana's tomb, was behind the fallen beam and rain was streaming down as if someone had aimed a garden hose through the roof. If anywhere in the place had suffered the worst from the lightning strike, it was, as Alex had said, that area. It had been built on to the church especially for Georgiana's monument and never seemed to be quite fully part of the old building. The storm had obviously decided that the time had come to sever the connection completely – and it just felt all wrong, somehow. Damn.

'I have to check Georgiana!' Elodie scrambled over the rubble and crunched her way towards the Lady Chapel.

'You're not going over there on your own! God knows what it might be like. I'm coming with you.' Alex tossed some bits of wood out of the way and followed her. With difficulty, they climbed over the beam and choked their way through the plaster cloud, the rain still hammering down and bouncing off the stone floor, but doing little to dampen the dust. Elodie felt the tell-tale tightening in her chest that warned of lungs that weren't particularly happy in that sort of environment, but she had other things to think about and tried to ignore it.

She'd never forget what she saw after that – Georgiana's beautiful marble tomb was split, right down the middle. It was as if the lightning strike had come straight through the roof and pierced the heart of the monument. It was all sort of broken in half and the place wasn't filled with plaster dust; it was more like a mist of marble fragments. There were shards of the stuff scattered around and huge parts of the figure were shattered too. Even Georgiana's lovely face was cracked from forehead to chin, yet she still looked so, so peaceful. And with the rain flowing over her cheeks, it seemed as if she was crying.

'Oh, Georgiana!' Elodie whispered and reached out, touching her hair.

There was an ominous creaking and groaning – then, 'Look out!' Alex grabbed hold of her arm and pulled her towards him as the whole tomb collapsed in on itself. The side fell off and Alex yanked Elodie out of the way. She lurched into him and automatically buried her head in his sopping wet chest. Then there was a horrible silence and all she could hear was the rain pounding on the wreckage of the tomb and Alex's heart beating.

The silence was broken by Alex swearing.

'Where is she?' he asked. 'Where the hell is she?'

'Who?' Elodie pulled away from his chest and turned to face the mess that had been the tomb. His arms were still around her, and, seeing what she saw, perhaps it was just as well.

Amidst all the mess that had been Georgiana's tomb, there was no Georgiana. There was no actual body inside it. There wasn't even a trace of a body ever having been there. No ragged cloth that might have once been a beautiful gown; no bleached white bones rattling across the floor; no long, wavy hair spilling out. Elodie had a sudden memory of someone telling her about Lizzie Siddal, the artist Dante Gabriel Rossetti's muse. Lizzie died and it was said that when they exhumed the body, her red hair had filled the coffin and her body was still well-preserved.

At that moment, Elodie felt quite sick. She didn't know what would have been worse – getting an eyeful of Georgiana's hair filling the coffin and the mummified remains of the girl grinning at her, or the fact that she had been filched from her tomb and nothing remained of her. Which was odd, because she'd seen so many ghosts in her life that the idea of simply seeing a skeleton shouldn't have been that repellent. But it was.

'Grave robbers. It has to be.'

'Don't be ridiculous.' Alex broke away from her and splashed and crunched his way across the floor. It was just as well it was made of stone flags – any sort of wooden floorboards would have been ruined by now, thanks to the rain still streaming into the place. Elodie followed him closely and he didn't bother to tell her to stay back.

'Grave robbers didn't come here – surely!' He frowned, his dark blue eyes troubled. 'I mean, I know in Scotland and London and what have you they were rife … but here? No. I suppose there could have been an opportunist …'

He turned to her and pushed his wet hair out of his face. His expression was one of bafflement and she didn't blame him. 'Where is she?' he asked, again. 'Where the hell is Georgiana?'

Elodie felt torn between feeling sorry for him, horrified for Georgiana and sick to her stomach at the thought the girl hadn't been there. At all. The whole time she'd sat and talked to her – she wasn't there, physically, at least. Bloody hell.

She felt as if the world, not just the church and the

monument, was being washed away from under her feet. Nothing made any sense. She couldn't even speak to answer Alex, so she just shook her head.

'Is the tomb just built *over* her grave?' she suggested eventually. 'You know, as if she's ... down *there*.' She jabbed a finger towards the floor. 'In the crypt or something?' She looked up at Alex hopefully.

'No, she's not. There's nobody down there. We had work done before we opened the Hall to the public, to strengthen the foundations. I insisted they use geophysics to check what was underneath the crypt floor before I let them start. I wanted to avoid ...' It was Alex's turn to jab his finger floorwards and then towards the tomb. '... *this*. I wanted to avoid this. I didn't want them disturbed.' She knew he was thinking of his father who was now in consecrated ground outside, over by the wall and traditionally under the grass where he should be. 'They didn't find anybody,' he continued. 'Nobody at all. Whoever is buried at Hartsford Hall is in the graveyard or—' His hand waved expansively across the area of the church. '—or in here. In the tombs.'

There were two or three other square tombs in the place and Elodie looked around with fresh eyes. 'So what about Alexander who died in 1172?' she said, remembering one particular stone in the floor.

Alexander, Earl Hartsford – Mortuus in Gloria MCLXXII (or 'died in glory, 1172' for those who didn't speak Latin) had always been Alex's favourite memorial. The stone made up part of the original church floor and Alex would often boast that he had been named for this old Earl.

Alex shook his head. 'Not here. Not underneath the floor, at any rate. He might be in the cemetery hidden away without a stone, or even on a battlefield somewhere but we'll never know. Elodie—' He turned to look at her and she saw confusion in his eyes. 'What the hell is going on here?'

Chapter Two

Alex had grown up with a sense that Hartsford Hall had some secrets – it couldn't possibly *not* have any, being so old – but never in his wildest nightmares did he ever think that the corpse of one of his ancestors would be missing.

Why on earth would someone have broken into the church somewhere between 1796 and today and taken Georgiana's body? It made no sense and he couldn't even think of a reason good enough for that to have happened. Elodie's theory about grave robbers was ridiculous, but at the present moment in time it seemed the most feasible.

'I wish I'd checked the tomb properly before all this happened,' he said. 'Maybe there was a sign there – a crack or a join that showed someone had been inside. I know the chap who made it would have sealed it all up properly. She was supposed to have just been put in it. Placed in her coffin and sealed in the tomb. How hard can it have been?' He stopped talking then, conscious that he was in danger of cursing and swearing about it all. That wouldn't do. He was the Earl of Hartsford now. Competent. In charge. Respectable.

Not that Alex really expected an answer from Elodie – it wasn't her problem after all – so he wasn't disappointed when she just shook her head. Her blonde hair wetly slapped the sides of her face like rats' tails, and she folded her arms.

'Do you think we can find her?' she said at last. More of the slapping hair as she shook her head again. 'I know. We can't. I'm stupid.'

Alex shook his own head. It would be an impossible task to find Georgiana. Where on earth would she be?

'Do you have any records up at the Hall about her?' Elodie stared at the mess before them. She took a couple of steps towards the tomb and ran her fingers down Georgiana's cheek. 'Anything about her burial? Or her life?'

The rain continued to splash down and it was ricocheting off the marble and bouncing up around Elodie in a constant series of dull thuds, but she seemed oblivious.

'There's nothing that I've ever seen.' Alex shrugged. 'We have one picture which might be her. It's in the attics, but the canvas is rolled up and it's in a terrible condition. We've never done anything with it. We – I – needed to prioritise. I had to get the house and the gardens ready for visitors.' He smiled wryly. 'Public liability insurance took priority over restoring a cracked old painting, and I always thought it would be the very devil to prise it out of Cassie's grip anyway.'

He knew his younger sister Cassie had spent many hours in those attics as a sad little girl, perhaps wondering what it would be like to grow up and be as beautiful as her ancestor, whilst waiting for her father to notice her and her mother to come back for her. Their father didn't know how to spend quality time with his children – books, academia and horses were much more absorbing – and although he loved his children, a few pounds tossed their way for ice-creams or an affectionate ruffle of their hair as they scurried past was, to him, perfectly good parenting.

As for their mother, she had left them when Cassie was only six months old. They hadn't seen or heard from her since. All they'd been told was that she had remarried and now lived in a castle in the Dordogne with her new husband, a wine merchant.

Alex's father may not have been much of a hands-on parent, but he'd been overly generous to everyone else. He was so generous he just kept giving and giving and spending and spending and investing in one crazy scheme after another; and then, when he'd died four years ago, the money was all gone, along with the race horses and most of the estate lands.

Hughie, Alex's old pet carthorse, was the only horse left in the stables by then. The racers could go, but to give the old Earl his due, he'd never tried to get rid of Hughie.

Cassie had just started University when the old Earl died and Alex hadn't wanted to disrupt her studies, so he'd tried to take on the running of Hartsford Hall and everything else by himself. How hard could it be?

He'd soon found out it was very hard. Very hard indeed.

Elodie nodded now, still staring at the tomb. Her fingers rested on Georgiana's face, then traced the crack on her forehead. 'An old cracked painting, eh? Well.' She sighed and turned back to face Alex. 'I wish I'd known. I've got a friend who might have helped. Do you think Georgiana had any diaries or letters then? Young ladies *always* had stuff like that.'

'If they were educated enough,' he agreed. 'But yes, Georgiana should have had something. We never found anything. It was like she never existed. Makes it all the more crazy, when she isn't even in the bloody tomb. Dad had some old family papers and genealogy charts he tried to show me once when he mentioned the end of their family line and the start of ours. He never said anything about finding any diaries or letters from Georgiana herself though.'

He ran his fingers through his hair and stared around him. This place was going to cost something to repair. He sincerely hoped the insurance company would pay up and not, ironically, class the lightning strike as an Act of God.

'But why would anybody build a tomb and leave it empty? Sorry – I know you don't know the answer to that. Forget I asked.' She bent down and peered into the mess of shattered marble.

'Elodie, there's nothing there.' Alex held his arms out, ready to receive her again if she perhaps still felt emotional, but she bent down even further and then poked her fingers through a space in what had been the wall of the tomb.

'Alex! Look!'

It was the work of a moment for her to thrust her hand all the way in and pull something out. He heard her exhale as if she had been unsure what she was going to get hold of, and then she hurried over to him. 'It's a locket, isn't it?'

Sure enough, in her hand she held a grubby-looking silver oval on a heavy chain.

'You're right! May I have a look?'

She hesitated, standing in front of him like a statue. Her eyes took on a faraway look, as if her mind was elsewhere, and her hand was shaking a little.

He remembered the obsession she seemed to have had over this ancient relative of his. 'Earth to Elodie?'

But it took her quite a while to respond.

As soon as she stood up with the locket in her hand, Elodie had a sense that the world was shifting. She was no longer in the church, she was in a coach, and she could feel the gentle motion of it as the horses pulled it towards home; towards Hartsford Hall …

Her brother Jasper was rather drunk. He was slumped against the side of the seat, singing a bawdy song, quite off-key, that he had learned in a tavern somewhere. Georgiana was torn between laughing at him and feeling a burning shame that she had had to ask two footmen to help escort him back to the coach after the Duchess' birthday party.

'Jasper, I do hope you sober up before Father sees you!' She squeezed his hand.

'Ah, he cannot complain about me, Georgy. Have you seen our dearest Mama recently? Why do you think she decided to stay at home tonight? She's sleeping it off, you see. Sleeping it off.'

He grinned at her, that cheeky, lopsided grin that was irresistible to anyone of the female persuasion.

'I suggest you sleep it off too, Brother,' she teased, 'and wake up before Mama does and then tiptoe around her as we always do when she's had an episode.'

Jasper rolled his eyes and lolled his head against his sister's shoulder affectionately. 'There's only you and I, Georgy, who are the sensible ones in this family. Lucy is sly and spoiled and grates on my last nerve at times.'

'I must concur with that,' agreed Georgiana vehemently. 'She argued over her ribbons being the wrong length last week and cried until I set them right for her.' They looked at each other and they both laughed.

'As I say, it's you and I against the world. I do think—' He swore, as the coach bucked and stopped abruptly. A shot rang out in the darkness beyond the coach walls and a scream bubbled up in Georgiana's throat as the silence was broken by the coachman's shout and pleas.

A strong, confident voice cried out, making her want to shrink inside herself and hide.

'Oh, be quiet. I have no argument with you. It is your passengers I wish to see this fine evening. Now, Mesdames and Messieurs, would you be so kind as to hand me your valuables this very moment, and please, make no noise, for if you do I will shoot you dead. And tragically so.'

This man sounded faintly amused and entirely bewitching. This was no vagabond; no thug or ruffian. His accent was very much like her own: aristocratic and well-bred. He was not to be disobeyed.

Georgiana stared at Jasper. 'It's a highwayman!' Her fingers gripped her brother's convulsively.

'It's a damnable heathen!' roared Jasper. 'I'll see him swing for this, I'll see him—' He staggered to his feet and lurched across the coach, making it wobble. His hands grappled for his pistol, missed, then strayed to his belt, trying and failing to unsheathe his dress sword instead. He threw open the door and stepped outside; then he misjudged his footing and slithered down the steps landing in a messy heap at the bottom of them, entirely unconscious.

'Oh, dear Lord!' Georgiana began to shake. The coach door remained open and she was beyond terrified. The stark moonlight shone down on a scene she had only imagined from engravings and news articles. The coachman was being held at gunpoint by a man sitting astride a huge black horse with a white flash on its forehead. The man was staring at her brother and shaking his head slowly, still pointing the gun lazily at the coachman.

'By God. The lad cannot hold his wine. What a poor, poor specimen. I feel for him, I most certainly do.' He raised his head and the moonlight glinted in his eyes. Georgiana saw them flare then soften as they settled on her. 'I did not realise the coach contained such treasure. Step into the light and let me see your face properly.' The lower half of his own visage was covered in a black kerchief, a black tricorne hat pulled far down over his forehead; but Georgiana could tell he was smiling as he spoke. 'I won't harm you. I promise. Come.'

Elodie was stunned. The images had come to her so clearly, she could even feel the rocking of the coach as Jasper strode across it, hear the thud as he landed at the bottom of the steps. The highwayman's eyes were imprinted on her mind and she knew if she closed her own eyes she would see his sparkling straight at her again.

The chill of the night had, for a moment, enveloped her and her breath had come in small puffs of mist in the cold air as she panicked and looked around helplessly. The velvet of the cushions had crushed beneath her fingers as she grabbed at them; her heart pounded as the fear made her shake. It was as if she had lived through it and she knew, without question, that Georgiana had done just exactly that.

She looked down at her hand. It was trembling, just a little, as she released the locket into Alex's palm. Alex closed his fingers over the silver, brushing hers for a split second and she jumped as if she'd been stung.

She balled her hand into a fist and stared at the top of Alex's head dumbly as he bent to examine the necklace. That little scene in the coach was something she hadn't anticipated seeing when she fought her way through the rubble of the church to the tomb. She didn't think it was something she should share with Alex just yet either; not when the Lady Chapel lay in ruins. Instead, she tried to push the memories out of her head and forced herself to concentrate on the here and now.

Alex didn't blame her for jumping. He'd done the same – something like a tiny electric shock had shivered up his arm when he'd brushed her fingers. He looked up and they stared at each other for even less than a split second; then both of them looked down at his hand, which was now curled into a fist around the locket.

'Do you think it's hers?' asked Elodie. Her voice was a little shaky and she sounded breathless.

He looked up, worried that her asthma was going to get the better of her. 'Are you okay?' he asked. 'D'you want to get out of here?'

'No. It's fine. I'm fine.' She shook her head. 'Is it Georgiana's?'

He looked down and opened his fist. 'I'm not really an expert on jewellery, but it looks pretty old.' He turned the locket over and over, and could just make out some engraving on the face of it. 'Very ornate in its time. The catch is damaged so we'll have to be careful. We'll try and open it later, at home.'

'I wonder if there's anything else?' Elodie dropped to her

knees in front of what was left of the stone sarcophagus and peered inside.

He came up behind her, just close enough to hear her swear under her breath.

Then she raised her voice and spoke again: 'Yes. Yes, there is.' She sat back on her heels, turned to him and looked up. 'I can see something else in there. But it's definitely not a body.'

There was certainly no body, but there was something else. Well – three somethings.

Elodie reached her hand in, and she knew she was screwing up her face and holding her breath. After all, the tomb had been sealed up for over two hundred years. That was over two hundred years' worth of spiders, spiders' descendants, desiccated spider corpses, spiders' horrible cobwebby homes ... and so on. Yuck. But the worst thing was not the spiders; it was the musty, dank, fetid air that was seeping out of the tomb. If she hadn't felt sick enough beforehand, she did now.

Plus, there was the small matter of kneeling in a puddle with a steady stream of water gushing onto her back through the hole in the roof, which made her shiver and shake. She leaned further into the monument and made a conscious effort to relax and breathe, trying not to think about the fact that she was now inside a tomb, which was something she'd never anticipated doing while she was still alive. Her fingers closed over the square edge of an object and drew it out slowly.

It seemed to be a leather-bound book and her heart began to beat faster. 'Maybe *this* is her diary?' she said, more to herself than to Alex, but as she brought it into daylight and wiped her forefinger over the front, she saw the gold blocking that declared it to be a Bible.

'Careful with that!' whispered Alex. 'If it's been sealed

up for years, the air might make it disintegrate. We need something to protect it. Hang on.'

Elodie wasn't quite sure what to do, so she thrust it back inside the tomb, just in case, and watched Alex over her shoulder. He looked around, and his eyes lingered on a walnut and glass display case housing a Victorian altar cloth. One of his great-great-somethings had embroidered it. Elodie couldn't remember the relationship, but knew the lady had a pretty name.

'Sorry, Polly.' Alex did this incredible karate sort of roundhouse kick that brought his foot down on the glass, crushed the table and let the cloth tumble out. He did look rather impressive. Margaret had told her he'd done some martial arts training during the period when Elodie lived in London, but this was the first time she'd seen him in action with it. She regarded him with renewed respect.

Alex caught the material before it hit the floor and hurried back over to her. He shook it out to get the dust and little cubes of glass off, because, apparently, it was a special sort of glass that didn't end up in shards. The little embroidered angels looked like they were fluttering. 'Put the Bible in here. We'll wrap it up and hope for the best.'

'I hope wrapping it up *is* enough! I've never had to do anything like that before.' Her voice was muffled as she leaned forward and explored the tomb again. 'Here. There's something else on the bottom.' She came into contact with an object that resembled a small pen, about the size of the ones you put in your handbag. It was freezing cold, and as she gripped it more securely, she felt an intricate shape at one end.

'It's a key!' She pulled it out eagerly.

'Interesting! Wonder what it's for?' Alex took the key and laid it gently on Polly's altar cloth, then hunkered down next to her. He peered inside the tomb, his head close to hers, blonde and dark hair tangling together. It felt curiously nice and she could feel the warmth coming from his body – which was very welcome as she was still kneeling in an ever-deepening puddle and was half inside a cold, empty, marble tomb and her chest was beginning to hurt. She shifted position so she was leaning against him a little and he didn't complain.

'I'll see if there's anything else, then I'll have to get out of here.' Elodie swept a hand around the void. There was nothing until she placed her hand on an item that was hard and cold and metallic. And lethal.

She felt the colour drain from her face and the rain was forgotten as her stomach knotted and she began to shake.

'Alex.' Her voice was no more than a croaky whisper. 'I think I've found a gun.'

At first Alex couldn't believe what he was hearing.

'A gun?' he asked. 'In there?'

'I think so,' she said and leaned back. Then she sort of wobbled, lost her balance and sat down fully in all that water. She didn't even flinch, but as her face was the colour of the marble she was surrounded by, he shouldn't have been surprised. 'I don't want to touch it again.'

He squeezed her shoulder. 'Want me to do it?'

She nodded and shuffled out of the way. 'Please.'

It was Alex's turn to lean into the dank interior and he didn't enjoy it much. There should have been a body in there, and if Georgiana, or what was left of her, wasn't in plain sight, had she somehow been washed out the back? He paused. A couple of hundred years ago, up in Newcastle upon Tyne, the cemetery walls of All Saints church had collapsed. The rumour was that there were coffins tumbling out onto the main road and bodies were littering the streets. It was not a scene he particularly wanted to replicate at Hartsford Hall. The tourists would certainly want a refund then.

The back was off Georgiana's tomb anyway and, cursing under his breath, he leaned out and peered around the back.

But, thank God, she wasn't there.

He cast a glance at Elodie, who had dragged the altar cloth onto her knees and was wrapping everything up tidily. She looked up and caught his eye. He was rewarded with a little smile.

'Did you get it?' she asked.

'Not yet. I just had a horrible image in my mind that she had escaped the back way.'

'Ugh!' She shivered.

Alex had to agree.

Then he reached back in, grabbed the gun and brought it out. 'Got it!' He turned it around carefully in his hands.

It was very definitely a gun – no, a pistol – and it had something that looked like ornately carved ivory on the handle. And as he held it, he knew that not only did it look like ivory, it was ivory. And if he could look inside the barrel with a magnifying glass it would have something else distinctive in there too.

'It really *is* a gun!' said Elodie in a whisper, as if it was somehow sacrilegious to acknowledge that in the church.

'Not just any gun. It's a duelling pistol. Eighteenth century, ivory handle, wooden barrel. And it'll have scratch rifling in the barrel – spiral marks on the inside to stabilise the spin on the shot. This would have been one of the most accurate duelling pistols out there.'

'Gosh. I'm impressed. How do you know that?'

'Because the other one from the set is at the Hall, but we never knew where this one was – Elodie? Elodie! Are you all right?'

Chapter Three

Georgiana knew, strangely, that the man on the horse spoke the truth – he wouldn't hurt her. Her heart pounding, she did as she was bid. She imagined doing anything he desired, if he asked her to do it in that exact voice. As she came out onto the top step of the coach, the man dismounted. He walked over to her, and she looked into his eyes, their faces almost at the same height; he was much, much taller than her. An imposing figure, who held his black-gloved hand out to help her. His pistol was still trained on the coachman, and Jasper was still insensible. The horse whinnied softly and Georgiana paused, looking over to it.

'Blaze won't hurt you either. Come.' The man bowed low as her fingers connected with his, and something ignited deep inside her, an explosion in her heart, and she started. The man's eyes flared again and she felt the warmth of his hand through his leather gloves and her kid ones. His gaze never left hers as she stepped onto the ground.

'Now, pray tell me who this young man is. He seems rather tired.'

The man looked down at Jasper and the corners of his eyes crinkled in the golden light of the coach lamps. Georgiana guessed he was smiling. She dipped down, ostensibly to check her brother was still breathing. Her fingers brushed across his pistol, briefly considering whether she should take her chance and snatch it, firing a round off at the highwayman; but as if some power other than herself was guiding her, she decided against it.

'That's my brother, Sir. Jasper Kerridge, Viscount Somersby. Our father is—'

'The Earl of Hartsford. I know of him. However, what I

have heard is not, I am afraid, very complimentary. So you are Lady Georgiana Kerridge? It is common knowledge that he has the prettiest daughter in the county. I would have guessed that you – please, stop right there, Sir!' The man directed his attention to the coachman who was trying to slide unnoticed down from the driving seat. 'I told you that you need not fear me, but should you persist in moving around in such a fashion, I shall have to take action. Come over here.'

'No!' Georgiana grasped his hand tightly. 'Please – don't hurt him!' The coachman was one of the nicest men in the stables, always happy and with a kind word for Georgiana and Lucy.

'I won't. I'm simply going to ask if he would step inside the coach and wait.'

'I'll do whatever you ask, Sir.' The coachman glanced at Georgiana. 'Just please, I beg you, don't hurt the lady.'

The highwayman lowered the gun. 'She is very safe. Now, if you wouldn't mind – thank you, my good man. Thank you so much.'

The highwayman waited until the man was inside the coach, then closed the door firmly. He turned the handle and, jamming it shut with a branch, ensured the coach door was locked. 'Usually, I tie them to a convenient tree, but in this particular instance, he's safer here. He's old. Your brother will be the one I tie up this evening.'

The man leant down and took hold of one of Jasper's unresponsive wrists. He produced a piece of rope from around his own waist and briskly tied Jasper up, binding his arms to a coach wheel. 'Hopefully that will keep Viscount Somersby in one place long enough for me to make your acquaintance properly. Let us take a walk.' He indicated the moon. 'It's as bright as day, don't you think?'

Georgiana put her hands behind her back and shook her head. 'I don't want to leave them.'

'I understand, but we won't go far. Look, there's a clearing up ahead. Please, would you do me the honour of a moonlit stroll, Lady Georgiana?' He bowed again, and, spellbound, she found herself curtseying back. He offered his arm and she took it. Then they walked the few paces towards the clearing. 'Here, I can see you fully.' He indicated the lack of branches above their heads where the moonlight was flooding through. He studied her face. She was so close to him, she could feel the warmth of him through his cloak, smell the outdoors and the frost on him, see the dark lashes which framed his eyes.

'You're shivering,' he murmured. 'Please – take this.' He shed his cloak and placed it around her shoulders. 'Such a perfect treasure should not feel even the smallest chill and I believe it is beginning to snow. But I must demand one thing before I leave you. Would you dance with me? An Allemande, I think. Then we shall go our separate ways and I will not detain you any longer.'

'An Allemande?' Georgiana blinked. 'Here? But there's no music.'

'No, not that we can hear. But we have our own music.'

Georgiana hesitated, just for a moment, then took the man's hand. She believed him, she truly did.

'Close your eyes, if it helps,' he whispered, leaning towards her. 'Feel it in the earth beneath our feet, in the skies above our head. In the light that shines upon us from the heavens.'

'But if I close my own eyes, I cannot see yours.'

'Ah, but then I can study you and remember the curve of your cheek, and every curl that escapes from your hair.'

'Very pretty words indeed.' Georgiana smiled as the man began to trace out the steps, leading her in the dance. She had spent an entire evening in a ballroom, but this was different. Every dance before this midnight one faded into insignificance; every flirtatious comment seemed insipid and forced. This was dangerous and mysterious and yes, she could

feel the power of the earth and the heavens, and magic she had yet to discover, embracing her and wrapping her up in sensations she had never felt so intensely or so deeply before.

'I've never danced with a stranger,' whispered Georgiana, entranced by the presence of this man. His shirt gleamed white in the starlight and his eyes reflected the constellations a thousandfold. The snowflakes began to fall faster, like whispers, and they settled around them and on them as they danced, and she felt they were like angels' kisses.

'Neither have I.' There was that smile again in his voice. 'This isn't how I envisaged spending my evening. I should have been on my merry way by now, my pockets loaded with your family gold. However, I cannot lie. This is far more preferable. In fact—' He stopped talking, his face and his lips very close to hers as the dance brought them towards one another. She leaned forwards, arching towards him, her eyes closing and—

'Unhand my sister!' Jasper's voice penetrated her world of dancing and moonlight.

The stranger pulled away from her and shouted back. 'Do I look as if I am harming her? Rather, I think we are both enjoying the melody.' He kept his face turned away from Jasper, guiding Georgiana to move with him.

She was unable to look away from the highwayman. There was a connection as old as the earth itself, drawing them together; the ancient magic which lingered in the woods was there, in her very spirit, that evening. Twin souls who had been lost and were now found again, brought together by something beyond her ken.

His eyes sparked. 'Do you feel it too?'

'Yes. Yes, I do.' She raised her hand tentatively and tugged at his mask. He didn't resist. She pulled it free from his face and it was as if she was staring at her very heart. He was as handsome as she had dared to believe; his nose straight, his *mouth sensual, his eyes black in the moonlight and framed with those long, dark lashes. His cheekbones were sharp, and his face clean-shaven. She reached up and removed his tricorne hat, still looking into his eyes. His hair was dark and tousled and tied back with a black ribbon; one lock fell across his forehead. When she replaced his hat, her hands trembled, and she couldn't help but move the lock away from his forehead as she did so. He smiled; and there was a sense of recognition there that she couldn't fathom.*

Before she could process this thought further, Jasper's voice broke the spell, louder this time: 'I said, unhand her, you damnable dog!'

Then a starburst of light pierced the night and a sharp crack shattered the silence.

Georgiana screamed as the smell of gunpowder penetrated the air and a plume of smoke whispered up towards the tree tops.

'Dear God!' That was her brother, sounding startled and shaken. Jasper was still sitting by the coach wheel, but his pistol was some distance away; the weapon was bent and destroyed by the highwayman's bullet.

'How could you? Thank God you missed!' cried Georgiana. 'Oh, Jasper!' She turned to run to him, but the highwayman still had hold of her hand and he held her firmly.

'I didn't miss. I aimed for the pistol. I told you, I mean none of you any harm. I simply wanted to stop him harming me. You can't blame a man for that! I've heard your brother is partial to a duel.' He raised her hand and kissed it, then released her. 'Go – he's quite safe.' He whistled and Blaze whinnied in response, then came trotting over to him.

'But ...' Georgiana stared at him, still wearing his cloak.

'I'd delope before he shot me in a duel!' called Jasper. 'I swear I would. You devil!' He meant, of course, that he would deliberately shoot away – into the air or into the ground, thus

ending the duel before it even started. It was a technique Georgiana knew meant that the opponent was beneath his notice. But there was a hint of admiration in Jasper's voice. He was blustering, that was all. He was as impressed as he'd ever been.

The highwayman laughed and mounted Blaze.

'Your cloak, Sir.' Georgiana took it from her shoulders and handed it up to him.

'Ben. Please, call me Ben.' He leaned down and took her chin in his hand. He tilted her face up to his and kissed her. 'May I see you again?' he whispered. 'I'm often this way on my travels. Work, you know.'

His eyes glinted with mischief, and Georgiana found herself nodding. 'Yes. When?'

His voice dropped even further. 'Watch for me by moonlight. I shall come to you and I shall find you.'

'On the next full moon?'

'Yes. If I can wait that long.' He smiled down at her.

'Where?'

He sat up and gazed across the countryside, towards Hartsford Hall. 'The Faerie Bridge. At midnight. Be there?'

'I promise.'

'As do I.'

He pulled his mask back on and dug his heels into the horse's flanks; as if it knew it had to look as impressive as possible, it reared and pawed the air, then leaped off into the night.

Georgiana watched him disappear.

Her lips burned where he had kissed them.

All Elodie could do was stare at Alex. She could still smell the gun powder and hear the sound of the horse's hooves.

'I think I need to get out of here after all.' She knew her voice was faint.

'Of course. Come on. I shouldn't be sitting here talking about pistols. D'you want to come back to the Hall with me and get dried out a bit?'

'Yes. I'd quite like to leave, if there's nothing else inside?' She looked back at the empty tomb and shivered. She was soaked to the skin and the church wasn't the healthiest place to linger. Her lungs were threatening to break their tentative peace treaty anyway. 'I wish we had seen her in there, you know? That would have been better than not knowing where she is.' The image of the highwayman flashed across her mind again and she blinked, feeling faint. Alex's voice seemed to come from a long way away – it was like he was talking to her from another world.

'Would you really have wanted to see her like that?'

'No, you're right.' Elodie pulled herself together long enough to reach up and touch the marble face again. 'I wonder if we'll ever find her.'

'Who knows where she might be, but I don't think I like what images I'm conjuring up.' Alex looked down at the pistol. 'Can we tuck this inside the altar cloth?'

'Sure.' Elodie waited until he had put it inside the cloth and folded it up again. 'I don't like the images I'm getting either.' It was probably closer to the truth than she cared to admit.

'Come on, then.' He stood up and held his hand out to her, hauling her out of the puddle.

Once she was on her feet, clutching the bundle to her, Alex looked around the church and shook his head. 'I don't even want to think about the cost to repair this place. I need to lock it up and keep people out for now.'

There was a steady stream running in through the hole in the roof, but it seemed more like water from a drainpipe now than rain.

'I think the rain's stopped though,' Elodie commented.

'Perhaps. Come on. Let's get going. Are you okay with the bundle?'

Elodie nodded. 'Yes. Let's just – go.'

She didn't linger to make sure Alex was behind her. She walked as fast as she dared out of the church into daylight and fresh air and closed her eyes briefly. The strange visions she'd had in there were something altogether different to ghosts and shadows and she didn't quite know how to deal with it.

Chapter Four

The place was slowly starting to come back to life again. Visitors were peeling away from whatever shelter they had managed to find, and shaking umbrellas and stamping boots whilst they shook their heads and did the very British thing of discussing the weather with a complete stranger.

Alex was mentally assessing the damage and the cost of it all as he waded back to the house with Elodie by his side. She was, however, a bit too quiet and he wondered if the whole Empty Georgiana Tomb thing had affected her more than he thought.

'At least Georgiana wasn't disturbed when the tomb broke. That's good,' Alex said, trying to make light of it.

'But we still have to face the fact that she's buried somewhere else, and it would be nice to know where.' Her next words took him by surprise. 'Georgiana's brother was called Jasper, wasn't he?'

'What? Yes, he was.' They passed the stone fountain which was created solely, it seemed today, out of incontinent cherubs, and Alex noted the water overflowing the bottom tier and running down onto the ground. The grass surrounding the fountain was now like a bog, but thankfully the cherubs all seemed to be in one piece.

'So what happened to him again?' Elodie seemed oblivious to the cherub overflow she was squelching in. On a normal day, she would have giggled about that. Today was clearly not normal any more. 'Remind me. It's a long time since I heard any tales about your ancestors.'

'He got into a brawl and died. There were a few more romantic rumours that it was a duel over a woman, but I think the plain truth was he was a drunk young man with more money than sense and thought himself untouchable. The men who attacked him obviously didn't see it that way. I think old Jasper was flashing the cash in a coaching inn if I remember correctly. That or gambling. The rumour is he almost lost his inheritance before he'd even inherited. Poor guy never got it in the end anyway.'

'But I'm sure someone told me he'd died in a duel? Forgive me. It's just with seeing the pistol …'

'No. Jasper didn't die in a duel at all. It's one of those stories that the family made up to cover the truth. A duel would be more honourable than a basic brawl, so that's what they put about. He was renowned for his duelling skills, so it would have made sense. But there are too many eye-witness, contemporary accounts of it for his death to be anything more than the result of a bar brawl. I do believe his own father put an advertisement in *The Gentleman's Magazine* to try and save his son's reputation. Anyway,' Alex said, pushing Elodie gently, hoping to make her smile, 'I guess it worked. At least you believed the story. That's good for the family, eh?'

'Hmm.' Elodie didn't seem convinced.

She hoped she hadn't been too obvious with her line of questioning. Maybe Alex would think she had genuinely brought Jasper up because of the pistol, and that had jogged her memory of some old family tales that Alex's father had shared with them. Another of the Earl's passions had been genealogy and every so often, when he remembered he was supposed to be rearing the heirs to Hartsford Hall, he would chatter about his ancestors.

But she couldn't help it. The image of the angry, drunk young man tied to the carriage wheel haunted her. 'His monument's in the corner, isn't it? The big one? How old was he when he died?'

'Jasper? He was twenty-two. He went a few months before Georgiana. The three of them – Jasper, Georgiana and Lucy, the little one, all died young. Lucy survived just long enough to see the end of the French Revolution in 1799 and died at the turn of the century, but she was the last one of that branch of the family. That's how the original Hartsford line ended. It's about the only piece of information I found interesting enough to retain.' He added, 'Lucy's under that little stone angel by the lych-gate, and Georgiana was *supposedly* in the chapel, while Jasper is in the corner. I never understood why they were so scattered. It just seemed a random thing, like nobody had really given it much thought.' He shrugged. 'My lot are descended from someone else, the chap who took over the title. Some French cousin that appeared after the Revolution and Waterloo. Dad tried to teach me but, you know. All I remember is he had the surname Aldrich.'

Elodie nodded as she picked her way through the mud. All around her was the sound of steadily dripping rainwater running off the trees, but alongside that was birdsong, as if the feathered residents of the parkland had quite enjoyed the rain and were chattering about it. Two peacocks ran in front of her, the sun glinting off the droplets on their bluey-green feathers.

A third bird, a silly little peahen, darted out after them and caught Elodie off guard. She stopped quickly to avoid trampling on it, but a sudden halt, trainers that were slick and done-for and a muddy lawn did not work well together and she slipped, landing hard on her bottom whilst trying to save Great Aunt Polly's altar cloth.

'Elodie!' Alex stopped, just as suddenly, almost slipping in the mud himself. 'D'you need a hand?'

She grimaced; it hurt. It was also very embarrassing and tears sprang to her eyes. 'Stupid mud!'

She thrust the altar cloth bundle at Alex. He took it,

then hauled her up with his free hand. Despite the horrible predicament she was in, Elodie was astonished at how firm his grip was – those martial arts must have toned up more muscles than she thought. It was a long time since they had held hands properly – in fact, it was possibly when …

Her cheeks burned at the memories. And suddenly it was all too much; the mud and the hand-holding and the weird images and the damage to Georgiana's tomb – it had all shaken her more than she cared to admit. Elodie turned back towards the house and a sob caught in her throat. She couldn't stop the messy snivels that came after it.

'Oh, come on. It's not that bad, is it?' Alex looked down at her and his voice was so nice and so sympathetic, she wanted to cry even more. She was exhausted and wrung out. 'Let's get you back home. You need more than just a drying out now.' Alex took her elbow, regardless of the mud that now caked it, and steered her away from the little path that led to her lovely cottage; in his mind, of course, "home" was the Hall. But, oh God – that was another thing. What if her own house was floating away across the walled garden as they spoke?

'My house—'

'Forget it. It's the landlord's problem if it's leaking, not yours.'

'But you're my landlord!'

'And I'm insured. It comes with the territory. Nobody said being the Earl of Hartsford would be easy. Look, I'm taking you back to the Hall. At least I know my wing is waterproof and Cassie has some stuff left in her wardrobe, so we can get you clean.'

She half-smiled through her tears. 'When we were at school, you would have laughed your socks off at me in the mud.'

'That was a long time ago. People change.'

I know, she wanted to say. *But what if it's too late and people have changed too much and they suddenly realise they've lost something along the way?* But instead, she said nothing and just let him guide her home.

Hanging onto Elodie was like hanging onto a seal. The mud had made her slippery from head to foot and Alex couldn't really get hold of her properly. He thought she might end up on her backside again if he let her go, so they sort of shuffled and slipped their way across to the Hall.

'Wait,' she said at one point, and stopped to take off her shoes. 'My feet are sliding out of them anyway. What's a bit more mud in between my toes?' She dropped them into the nearest bin, but at least having bare feet gave her a bit more purchase as they walked around the side of the Hall to his front door.

When they reached it, however, Alex didn't hesitate to scoop Elodie up and prepare to carry her into the house. 'Good grief, have you been packing away too many of Delilah's scones?' he teased. Delilah owned Coffee Cream Cupcake, the tea shop in Hartsford village, which also supplied the Hall's little café with treats. Elodie worked at Delilah's a few days a week when she wasn't volunteering at the Hall, and was rather partial to a cake or two.

'I have not! I'll have you know, I weigh next to nothing.' Alex laughed and shouldered the door open as Elodie demanded to be released. 'Alex! Put me down. This instant!' At least she had stopped crying and was laughing with him now.

Alex started up the stairs. 'No way. You think I'm letting those feet anywhere near my carpets? Think again.'

He took her straight up to the bathroom and made her stand in the bath.

She slipped a little and he caught her arm. 'Take as long

as you need. There's not really any bubble bath but Cassie swears by her rose bath salts. Use those, she won't mind. There's a clean towel on the rail and I'll get some of my sister's gear for you. I'll leave it on the landing, okay? Actually – no.' He assessed her as she stood in the bath. 'Cassie's fairly straight up and down. You're not. She's, what, five-eleven, six feet? You're five-three, five-four? Her stuff won't fit, will it?'

Her eyes narrowed to slivers of aquamarine. 'Did you just call me short and fat? Again?' There was no malice in her voice.

'No, you're anything but!' He grinned and switched on the underfloor heating – the bathroom was huge and a bit chilly, especially since he'd left the window open that morning and the damp from the storm had crept in a little. 'But trust me. I'll find something. See you later.'

He left the room and shut the door just as he heard the taps turn on.

Elodie ran the water and rinsed the worst of the mud off her feet and down the plughole, then when she felt she could walk without leaving stains all over the grey and white tiles, she stepped out of the bath, and shed her sodden clothes. She put them in the shower cubicle and turned her attention back to the bath. It was huge – one of those old-fashioned ones that sit in the middle of the room and you had to climb up a couple of steps to get to it. She put the plug in, left the hot water going and headed over to the open shelving unit on the wall. She gratefully located a bottle of unisex supermarket shampoo and the rose petal bath salts. They smelled divine.

She stripped off her underwear and, joy of joys, the floor was actually heated underfoot, so she simply laid her bra and knickers on the tiles to dry out a bit and stepped into the bath. Lying back, she let the water slowly fill up. She hadn't realised how damp and uncomfortable she felt, so the water was soothing and very, very welcome. The warmth washed over her and she closed her eyes, drifting off into a rose-scented dream …

It was the first full moon since that night. She waited and watched by moonlight, as she had promised.

A cloak was wrapped around her body, but still she shivered. A blanket of fog wreathed the Faerie Bridge, boiling up from the River Hartsford, rushing sea-wards beneath her. A lantern, stolen from the stables, was placed by her feet, out of sight of anyone who might be watching from the Hall. She thought the fog was heaven sent; it hid her while she strained her eyes to see into the woods. All sound was muffled around her, and she listened hard for the pounding of hoof beats. Her fingers were frozen and stiff as she clutched the balustrade of the bridge. The dampness crept into her hair and drove it into ringlets around her face.

There was a noise along the pathway leading back from the village and she tensed, her heart hammering. It was a song; a bawdy song, sung off-key as a young man appeared through the mist, holding an imaginary woman in his arms as he danced by himself, spinning and turning and bowing exaggeratedly.

Georgiana recognised Jasper and exhaled. He stopped at a fork in the path and debated which way to turn. She prayed he would take the path straight to the Hall, and her prayers were answered. The bawdy song started up again as he disappeared into the mist and faded as he stumbled away from her.

Georgiana smiled, filled with love for her well-meaning, if misguided and at times reprehensible brother. He had a new pair of duelling pistols, and had talked of nothing else for days. She was sure he had one tucked into his waistband tonight. He was so proud of them – bought to replace the one Ben had ruined with his shot. She only hoped he'd never have cause to use them. Blowing on her fingers, she flexed them to keep them warm and looked into the woods. She wasn't sure what time it was now. She didn't even know if she should wait much longer.

Then the clouds parted and the moon shone more brightly, and she saw him coming through the trees. She saw the big, black horse and was frozen to the spot. He paused in the clearing and looked, it seemed, right at her. She watched him dismount and stride towards the bridge. His cloak billowed out behind him, his boots made no sound on the soft earth.

She stood on the cusp of the bridge as he approached. He wore no hat, no mask tonight. He saw her and his face, his beautiful face, the face that was as familiar to her as her own, split into a smile.

'Ben! You came.'

'Lady Georgiana.' He took two more steps and he was beside her. 'I always will.'

And she was in his arms, enveloped in them, breathing in his scent, completely certain that she had found the other half of herself. Completely certain that she would never, ever let him go. And absolutely sure that he meant every word he said.

'I didn't know – I didn't know if I should wait.'

'I'm pleased you did.'

'I don't even know your name, beyond the word Ben. Who are you?' She stood away from him slightly, searching his face for answers. 'Why do you do – this?'

'It pays well.' He dismissed it with a wave of his hand. 'Mostly. And once, the treasure I found was worth more than gold.' He smiled down at her. 'Believe it or not, I'm from a fairly high-ranking family; not quite as grand as yours, perhaps, but I suppose as the second son I was never meant to uphold the family name quite so much.'

Georgiana couldn't help but giggle. 'You were destined for the church or the army, then?'

'I'm more of a devil than an angel, and I'm not terribly fond of being shot at. It was never going to work. No, my vocation is in the arts. Which doesn't help me much at present, as I tend to travel around at night when it's too dark to write or paint or sculpt or do anything worthwhile. I fell into some – interesting – company, and I won some money from them. Then, as I began to lose to these people, I found that this profession was a less risky alternative. You don't have someone wanting to kill you every night, when you do this. Just some nights and that, Lady Georgiana, would be a very unfortunate night indeed.'

'But what about your family? Don't they wonder about you?'

'As far as my family is concerned, I'm on the Grand Tour and unable to communicate with them. Damn tragedy. I might even be caught up in the French Revolution and lying low. Who would be able to confirm that? Or, I could very well be in Germany, learning to dance an Allemande.'

'Is that where you learned it?'

'It is.'

'I won't tell anyone your secrets, Ben.'

'I know, Georgiana. That, my love, is why I'm telling you …'

Chapter Five

Elodie's eyes flew open and she sat up in the bath, confused. All of a sudden, she was back in her own life, in Alex's bathroom, and she wanted out of that big, echoing room and to have some human companionship. Her heart was thumping and she could still smell the cold and the frost coming from the man who had taken her in his arms and claimed her heart ...

She quickly washed, then scrambled out of the bath, her hair still dripping, and slithered across the warm tiles to the towels. Finding a huge black one, she wrapped herself in it and hurried over to the door, cautiously opening it and peering out into the corridor. There was a neat pile of clothes on the floor, exactly where he'd said they would be – a clean white t-shirt, a blue checked short-sleeved shirt and a pair of faded denim shorts, all smelling familiarly of his fabric conditioner. And he had even included a big leather belt. He must have known the shorts wouldn't stay up without it.

As it was, the shorts came down to below her knees and still flapped ridiculously around her thighs, but she was grateful to him. And even more grateful that she'd waxed her legs the other day.

She opened the bathroom door and stood in the corridor, trying to get her bearings. She'd never been upstairs in his house since the wing had been privatised and couldn't quite work out where she was. The layout had changed considerably since her childhood when the three of them – Alex, Elodie and Cassie – had free range around most of the Hall.

He'd swung her around a couple of corners when he was carrying her upstairs, so she headed in the direction they'd come from. If she found a staircase on her travels, she would simply walk down it.

However, the first staircase she found headed upwards and there was a sound of scraping and banging coming from the top of it. Elodie paused at the bottom, trying to peer up into the darkness.

'Alex?' she tried after a moment. 'Are you up there?'

She really didn't know what she would have done had he answered her from behind and left the upstairs occupant a mystery, but luckily the scraping stopped and his familiar voice came floating down the well-worn wooden stairs.

'Yes, I'm here. Come on. I left the door open for you!'

'Right.' She placed her hand on the railing. Then she paused. 'Are there spiders?'

'Some Daddy long-legs,' he shouted and she shuddered, 'but no spiders yet.'

'O-kay.' She headed up the steep little flight of stairs. Goodness only knew what she would find at the top. 'Weren't we going to look at the duelling pistols though?'

'We can do that later. I just thought I'd check this out while you were in the bathroom. You might find it more interesting.'

The steps came out into another corridor which turned right, but it wasn't half so welcoming as the one Elodie had just left. She knew from her stints as a tour guide that she was in the servants' quarters. In the main house, the night nursery, playroom and school room were up on the third floor – but here the metaphorical green baize door, which was kept locked and inaccessible to the tourists, opened from the children's rooms onto the servants' corridor. The servants had to share their part of the house with the attics, and it was in one of these, in the first room on her left, that she discovered Alex.

He had propped open the attic door with an old chair and

there was a great deal of dust swirling around, the motes catching in the washed-out sunlight that was coming through the small lead-paned windows. He too had changed out of his wet clothing, but the new trousers and the clean t-shirt were already looking slightly grubby.

'Hey.' Elodie coughed, her lungs reminding her they objected to dust. 'Found you. You're "it".' Twenty years ago, this would have been perfect for a game of hide and seek.

Alex laughed, sat back on his heels and gestured to the items in front of him. 'Close the door if you want. I just left it open so you'd find me more easily. Then you can come over here.'

Elodie moved the chair and the door swung shut. A large, battered travelling trunk was open in front of Alex, and it had all sorts of treasures spilling out of it: there were, amongst other things, embroidered, yellowing petticoats, a riding crop and a broken parasol, and even a 1920s style feather boa irrevocably tangled with a string of what might have been real pearls or simply white paste beads, snaking down the side of the trunk and pooled on the floor.

'This would be a *wonderful* resource for the next Living History weekend,' Elodie said. Living History weekends were something Hartsford Hall was becoming famous for. Elodie had worked in West End theatres as a costume designer, and had been used to dealing with everything from diva to disaster. The weekends had really taken off when she had come back and it was one of her favourite jobs on the estate. She knew those events were something she could do, and do well. She could be in control again. Living with Piers and having her life unravel as it had, in a knot of his extra-marital affairs and his petty power-games, had chipped away at her confidence.

Alex had seemed to know instinctively that she needed to take ownership of something to make her feel valued again. She was very grateful to him for coming up with the Living History idea – he had decided that certain weekends throughout the year could be themed, for example as a Victorian Christmas, or a Georgian market, or as The World of Jane Austen. The staff dressed appropriately and the event always incorporated all sorts of wonderful historical elements, and Elodie loved them.

Elodie dug her hand into the trunk and pulled out a hideous little animal's head, complete with sharp teeth and evil eyes. 'Well, most of it would be a wonderful resource, apart from the fox fur. Disgusting thing.' She screwed up her face and dropped the dead animal on top of the feather boa. It looked like it was in some horrid, raggy little nest and she turned away, slightly sickened.

'There's some nasty stuff in there, that's for sure.' Alex bent over the trunk and dipped his hand in, searching for something. 'One day, I'll let you loose in the other attics. I could lose you for days; get some peace from you trying to boss me around for a bit. Okay – here you go.' He handed her a hat adorned with a dead bird. Its one remaining beady eye glared at her and she shook her head.

'Keep it. I'm talking "living history", not "exploiting taxidermy".'

Alex laughed and placed the hat on top of the fox fur where the bird continued to glare at Elodie until she moved the angle so it fixed its gaze on Alex instead.

Alex remained unfazed. 'Interesting though Cassie's dressing up box is, it's not the clothes I want to show you. It's this.' He held up something that looked like a rolled-up canvas. 'It's been in there forever to protect it from the damp or the mice, just in case. I'm glad it seemed to survive. Cassie was obsessed with it. I kept finding her up here with it flattened out in front of her. I wanted to make sure it was okay. Because this, you see, is potentially Georgiana.'

Elodie's stomach did one of those lurching things, like a tumble dryer shifting its load about. 'Georgiana?'

'Yes. It's really fragile though – be careful with it.'

Alex came closer to her and unrolled the canvas, spreading it out on the floor in front of them. He placed one hand on the edge nearest to him, then gestured for Elodie to do the same so it wouldn't curl back up.

He was right. The paint was cracked and dirty, the dark background coming away from the canvas in tiny flakes that made Elodie worry about the rest of it. The portrait itself showed the head and shoulders of a girl, her curled, pinned-up, fair hair and exposed neckline suggesting she belonged to the late eighteenth century.

Unfortunately, she was in such poor condition that it was well-nigh impossible to see any of her features and Elodie touched her hair lightly, feeling the rough paint under her fingertips.

'It would be nice to know for sure,' said Alex. 'God knows what Cassie imagined she looked like, because I'm damn sure I can't see her very clearly.'

'We'll never know what she looks like, not if she stays in this state.' Elodie sighed. 'But, like I said, if you're happy for me to let my friend's husband have a look at it, we might get somewhere. He works in the Tate and he's done some art conservation. I could ask him?'

Alex shook his head. 'And like *I* said, it's all about prioritising. The roof's off the church now, Great Aunt Polly is probably out to haunt me ceaselessly for ruining the altar cloth and I've got a collapsed marble tomb to deal with. And that's the stuff I know about. I think Georgiana will have to be put away for another few years. She won't come to any harm up here.'

'But do you really want her hidden away in that trunk? Look, Simon owes me a favour. I loaned him some Pre-

Raphaelite costumes from the theatre for some work he was doing, and he said just to let him know when I wanted something in return.'

Elodie *knew* Simon would do it. He was cheerful and good-natured – just like his wife Cori and their six-month-old baby, Kitty. Cori had done some web-design work for Elodie, when Elodie worked at the National Theatre. The theatre had run an exhibition alongside the costume collections at the V&A, and Elodie had been in charge of it all. Elodie and Cori had hit it off pretty well, and it was a big contract for Cori. That, coupled with the costume loan for Simon, had quite cemented their friendship. All Elodie had to do was ask them. And then maybe everyone could see Georgiana properly.

She looked at the picture again, and then more closely. In fact, she peered at it so her nose was about a centimetre away from it.

'What's so interesting?' Alex leaned over, and again they were close together, staring at something that had caught Elodie's attention.

'A locket. Isn't that a locket around her neck?' she asked.

'Possibly. I daren't try to rub the dirt off, though. Here.' He pushed his hand in his pocket and brought out the necklace they'd found earlier. 'I grabbed it to have a closer look before I came up here. What do you reckon?'

Elodie tore her gaze away from the painting and held her hand out. Looking at Alex's profile and the way the rays of sunlight caught his hair, it was somehow strange to equate the man next to her with the boy she'd grown up with. Alex had certainly improved with age and she wondered, not for the first time, why he'd never married. Alex had a lot to offer really.

'Have a look. See what you think.' He smiled up at her and dropped the locket into her hand.

She metaphorically shook herself as she closed her fingers around the silver oval. *Yes, he has a lot to offer, but you're supposed to be over him, remember?* One misguided moment after the Prom. Two eighteen-year-olds, high on life, with the world open to them. One moonlit night with the warmth of the summer in the evening air and the stars twinkling like fairy-lights. Too much cider at the after-party and a kiss in the woods that led to something more …

'I love you. I think I really love you.'
  'I think I love you too.'
  'Shall we …?'
  'Do you think we should?'
  'I know somewhere we can go …'
  'Then let's …'

What could possibly go wrong? Too much. That was what could go wrong.

Elodie forced the memories back where they'd sprung from. One thing she couldn't shake, however, was that image of the highwayman's smile. She tried to imagine Alex with his hair just a little longer, wearing the outfit that man had been wearing.

Good grief. The thought was disturbing in a very strange way. She stood up quickly and headed over to the window before he saw that she'd blushed the colour of a ripe tomato.

'Where are you going?' Alex was still kneeling on the floor. He stared up at Elodie in confusion, clearly wondering why she'd disappeared when they had discovered what might have been that very same locket around the girl's neck.

'I just needed some air. It's a bit dusty.' *Alex, in a loose white shirt and tight breeches and riding boots …*

She needed more than air.

Especially as the locket seemed to burn her palm and the attic started going all wavering and fuzzy, and the trunks and things disappeared before her eyes …

Instead of the faint sunshine outside, it was suddenly dark again and the room was lit by a cold, silvery sheen that could only be moonlight.

Ben knelt before her, his hands in hers and he was looking up at her with such love that she was quite taken aback.

'I didn't know you felt so strongly about me,' she said, her gaze travelling over his face and his loosened hair. His hands were rough but strong, the callouses worn there by too many nights of riding his horse.

'Georgiana, I do believe I am finally lost. You have bewitched me. You fill my waking moments and ensnare my dreams.'

'Pretty words yet again, Ben.'

'But I mean them!' He smiled and stood up, still holding her hands; one step closed the gap between them. 'I thank the good Lord above that he has provided me moonlight to see you by, for this is no life otherwise.' He raised his hand and stroked her hair away from her face. 'I wish that we could be lovers in sunlight as well. I would that I could offer myself to you fully as a husband, yet the decent part of me – whatever is left in there that is decent – knows you should not take me.'

'Why not?' she asked. 'What would stop me?' She moved closer to him, pressing her body against his. It was dangerous but she yearned to find out more; her senses cried out for it.

'The fact that you are you and I am me,' he said softly. 'Oh, Georgiana.' He leaned forward, resting his forehead on hers, and closed his eyes. His lashes brushed her skin and she clung onto him more tightly. 'Would that I had met you sooner, when my family name still meant something to me.'

'But I don't care what you are,' she whispered. 'I don't

care about your profession and I wouldn't have cared about your family name. I care only for you, Ben. My twin soul.'

'You'd care if you married me and I took you away from here.'

'Not if I could ride beside you as your wife or even, God forgive me, as your lover. I'd gladly leave everything here to have that.'

'And then when they found me and hanged me at Tyburn?' he teased. 'What then? Would you come back here and expect all to remain as it had been when you left?'

'I would not let them hang you. I swear it to you. Why, we are joined as one in here,' she said, indicating the locket, 'as we would be in life or in death. And as such, I will protect you with my life.'

He laughed and she felt his forehead move against hers as he shook his head. 'Pretty words, as someone once told me. I—'

'Georgiana! Are you in here?' The bang as the attic door slammed open startled her and she gasped. Ben pulled her closer, and in one swift movement drew his pistol and aimed it at the bearer of the voice.

Lucy, ten years old and promising great beauty even at that age, screamed. Her hands flew to her face and she squeezed her eyes shut. She stood in her white linen night gown like a sturdy little ghost – a very noisy, sturdy little ghost.

'Lucy!' Georgiana hissed, breaking away from Ben and hurrying over to her. She slammed the door shut and dragged her small sister over to the window, shaking her hard as she continued to keep her eyes shut and make that wretched noise. 'Lucy!'

Lucy took after their Father in the fact that she had pale, reddish-coloured hair and hazel eyes, but in her nature she was like their Mother: weak-willed, mindless and easily excitable. Georgiana would hesitate to say it to anyone else, but her sister also possessed a spiteful side which was utterly unpleasant.

45

Jasper and Georgiana were quite the opposite; in countenance, they resembled their mother, fair-haired and blue-eyed – but they were like their Father in temperament: headstrong and outspoken.

Georgiana gave her sister one final shake and Lucy looked at her at last. 'Georgiana! I heard noises in the attic.' She sniffled and fixed doe-eyes upon her. 'I was scared. I didn't know what it was. I was in the night nursery and I was sleeping and was terrified that someone was in the house.'

'If you were truly scared,' Georgiana snapped, 'and indeed sleeping, you would not have come up here alone.' She glared at her and Lucy's wide-eyed, innocent, hazel gaze slipped slyly to the side.

'Well, all right,' she admitted. 'I may not have been asleep and I may not have been as terrified as all that. But I did hear noises. And I was desperately curious.' She moved closer to Georgiana as if for protection and stared at Ben. 'And who exactly are you?'

'Lucy! How rude!'

'I'm sorry.' Lucy dipped a pretty little curtsey, exactly as her mother had taught her, and looked up at Ben. 'I'm Lady Lucy Kerridge, Sir. Please may I enquire who you are?'

'You have dreadful manners, little sister!' Georgiana said.

'Perhaps,' Lucy acknowledged. That sly look again. 'But I'm not the one hiding a man in the attic at night time while I'm just wearing my shift.' She folded her arms triumphantly and glared at Georgiana.

'The young lady has a point,' said Ben, a smile in his voice and his pistol now hidden again. 'I'm a friend, that's all you need to know. There's no reason to be scared of me.'

The answer, evasive as it was, seemed to satisfy Lucy for she nodded. 'Very well. I am Georgiana's sister. So I suppose that makes you my friend as well.'

'I suppose it does,' Ben agreed.

Lucy hitched herself up on the window seat and began to swing her legs back and forth, her bare heels knocking on the wooden panelling. 'Do you want to see the Priest's Hole?' she asked. 'I can show you it if you like.'

Exasperated, Georgiana opened her mouth to reply but Ben answered first. 'Not tonight. I have to go. But there is something you could do for me, if you don't mind?'

'What is it?' asked Lucy eagerly.

'I think my horse shed his shoe somewhere down by the lake. If you happen to see it, will you keep it safe for me?'

'A horseshoe? Of course, I will!' Lucy jumped up as if she was going to go down there right now, but Ben raised his forefinger to his lips and stilled her with this motion of secrecy.

'It's a special horseshoe,' he whispered. 'In daylight, it will turn into a silver coin. That way nobody can ever find me, because they don't know where I've been, you see. So if you find a silver coin there, that's the horseshoe and you must keep it safe for me.'

'Will it turn back into a horseshoe at night?' asked Lucy, her eyes even wider.

'No. Once a coin, always a coin. It holds a special wish. But it will only work like that if you never tell anyone you met me. Do you understand? If you tell, the silver will be carried off by faeries. Do you like horses, Lady Lucy Kerridge?'

'I do.' Lucy nodded, obviously entranced by the lies Ben was telling and almost preening at the fact he had called her by her full title.

'Well, if the bad faeries find out I've been here, they will take the coin and they will find my poor horse and make him work for them. And it's no life for a good horse.'

'I see! Very well. I shall search tomorrow and I won't tell a single living soul ever that I met you.'

'Good girl. Now, goodnight, little princess.' He put one

hand on her shoulder and steered her gently towards the door. 'Let me see you safely along the corridor before I take leave of your sister, then in the morning you must see if you can find the horseshoe for me.'

'Oh, I will! I promise you!' Lucy ducked away from his hand and hurried over to the door. She turned back to them and smiled. 'It's all right. I'm not scared any more. I can go back to my room alone.' Suddenly seeming to remember her manners, she dipped another curtsey and ran out of the room.

Georgiana dashed after her, watching to make sure she had disappeared. A sliver of white vanished behind the connecting doorway, then the door shut and the corridor was in darkness again.

Georgiana went back into the room and leaned against the door, staring at her lover. His shape filled the window and her stomach lurched as she realised just how badly she wanted him and exactly how dangerous those last few minutes had been.

'A singular child.' Ben walked over to her, a lazy smile on his lips; then he leaned past her and shot the bolt. 'Now. Let me take my leave of you properly, as I promised.' He drew her towards him. 'I think we were just about here, were we not?' He led her towards the window and turned her so he could see her face clearly.

'Beautiful,' he whispered and leaned over to kiss her. She closed her eyes, offering herself to him with everything she had, and longed for the day when she could give herself up to him properly.

The door banged again and Elodie blinked.

'Hey you guys! What are you doing up here?' asked Cassie.

And Alex and Elodie were both exactly where they had been when Georgiana and Ben arrived in the attic ages ago. Time hadn't moved on at all.

Chapter Six

The slam of the door startled Alex and he twisted round.

'Cassie!' He jumped to his feet. 'I could ask you the same thing. We're just having a look at some old stuff up here. Elodie is quite taken by Aunt Amy's fox fur.'

'Cool.' Cassie smiled. 'I decided to come home this weekend. Trust me to bring the storm with me!' She shook her head. Her long, dark hair did that flicky thing that shampoo retailers want girls to emulate. 'I was stuck in the village the whole time the storm was going on. I had to park my motorbike up, throw myself on Delilah's mercy and hope for the best. Then I had to direct some guys in with deliveries to the Hall as well, because they needed to dump some stuff and get back on schedule. So that's all in the spare room – in case we had a flood, you know, it'll be safe up there. Oh – and the river burst its banks down by the Faerie Bridge, so you might want to check the lake … sorry.' She pulled a face. 'It's probably not what you want to hear right now. And Margaret said she's called the water people out to sort the drain as well.'

The river that ran beneath the Faerie Bridge was a tributary of the Hartsford Hall lake. Or maybe it was the other way around. One ancestor, many years ago, had decided to divert the river into the estate and created his landscaped lake out of that. It was a wonderful idea, but he didn't seem to have considered how it would flood every time the river burst its banks. Alex didn't really want to consider it either at that moment – he was just pleased the livestock were up the hills and away from it.

And he was also pleased there was a ha-ha in front of it, which would at least prevent any tourists from being too close to the water. The last thing he wanted was a lawsuit, even if they had gone down there at their own risk.

'No, it's not really what I want to hear today. Did anyone tell you about the church yet?'

'The church?' asked Cassie. 'No, what's happened? Oh, don't say that beautiful stained-glass window broke.'

'Worse than that. The roof's damaged and Georgiana's tomb is wrecked.'

'No!' cried Cassie. 'That lovely statue!'

'It's not just the tomb.' Elodie came over to them. She looked a bit pale and her voice was a little shaky, but she still smiled a welcome at Cassie. 'Tell her what we found inside it, Alex.' She looked at him, her eyes a little unfocussed – then she seemed to regain her self-control and stood there, folding her arms across her body as if she was self-conscious of something.

'We found nothing,' Alex told Cassie.

'Well, there were *some* things in there. Just not a body.'

'Yes. Just not a body,' Alex conceded. 'We found a key. And a Bible. And a duelling pistol – the one that's missing from the Long Gallery. And, the best thing, I think, was a silver locket. It looks like it's rusted tight shut though, so we can't open it. But I think it's the same one as on this picture. See? Around this girl's neck.' He pointed at the portrait.

Cassie knelt down beside Alex and reached out her own finger, quite possibly with the intention of trying to rub at the paint, but Alex knocked her hand away before she could touch it.

'No. Best not. It's too delicate.'

'It's not like I've never touched it before! But point taken.' She took her hand away and instead leaned forwards, very close to the painting. Cassie was a yoga fiend and it still surprised Alex sometimes how bendy she was, considering her height.

'I'd need to see the real locket before I could make any judgements. It was more her face I used to study.' Cassie smiled, a little ruefully. 'I used to think she was listening to me. I never really noticed her jewellery.'

She sat back on her heels and looked at Alex. With her big, brown eyes she looked exactly like Horace, the estate spaniel, and Alex found himself giving into her the same way everyone gave into Horace. The dog was actually Margaret's. He came to work with her every day and usually amused himself by wandering around greeting tourists. He was even allowed into the house and it wasn't unusual for visitors to say they'd seen him sprawled full length on the rug or the bed or the sofas.

And, as if Horace was sitting there begging Alex for a chew, he looked up at Elodie. 'Will we let her see it then?'

'Oh – of course. But Cassie, can I just ask you something?' That was Elodie, her voice still a little wobbly.

'Sure. Have *you* got the locket?' Cassie was obviously determined to see it, just as soon as humanly possible.

'Yes. But how did you know we were up here?'

'Oh, easy. I came past the gift shop and Margaret said she'd seen you heading over here. Alex's clothes suit you, by the way,' Cassie added impishly. 'Then I saw you both standing at the attic window, so I knew you must be in here. I only hope I wasn't disturbing anything.'

'Why would you think that?' Alex glanced across at Elodie. Her skin had gone a greenish shade now and she looked a bit sick. And indeed, why shouldn't she look green? Alex had known Elodie forever. There was only ever that one time after the Prom which hadn't exactly ended brilliantly ...

'Here? Are you sure?'
'What's wrong with here?'
'Nothing.' A giggle. 'It's just Hughie ...'

A soft laugh as he buried his nose in her hair and sniffed the perfumed curls: that floral scent that was forever Elodie. 'Hughie won't care.'

She pulled away. 'But I care. Isn't there anywhere else ...?'

Alex crushed the memories. 'You can see there's nothing going on up here,' he told Cassie, a little too abruptly.

'That's not what it looked like from down there,' she said, obviously unconcerned at his tone. She folded her arms and nodded. 'I saw you two – hugging each other in that window. Don't lie.'

'I'm not lying!' Alex stared at her. What was she on about?

'No,' added Elodie. 'He's not.' She wasn't green any more, she was white with big pink splotches on her cheeks.

'Oh,' said Cassie. She considered it for a moment then seemingly dismissed the thought. The idea of the locket was clearly more interesting than what might or might not have been a trick of the light. 'Come on then, I'm waiting.'

'Okay.' Alex also dismissed the idea for what it most likely was – Cassie seeing Elodie at the window and the rest made up from her imagination. 'Elodie – shall we let her see it?'

'Of course.' Elodie handed it over. 'Here you go. Sorry, it's going to be well-nigh impossible to open it, but never mind. We think it might be the same one as the picture, but I'll be honest. We didn't really get a chance to study it properly.'

Cassie took hold of the necklace and cupped it in her hands. 'This is incredible. If it's genuine, it's got to be Georgian or Regency or something like that.'

'I would guess Georgian if it's related to Georgiana,' Alex said. 'Regency was a little later.'

'Of course.' Cassie nodded. She hadn't been brought up in the Hall without knowing the difference between Georgian and Regency, considering the house was a mish-mash of architectural styles and an even bigger mish-mash of previous residents. 'I could try and clean it.' She turned it around in her hands. 'Some warm soapy water should do it if I'm careful and if I use a soft cloth. Or maybe some silver polish and some oil on the hinges. It might at least bring it up a bit. That's what I did with this, anyway.' Cassie lifted her arm and a silver bracelet dangled from her wrist. 'It's Grannie's antique one. I used to have it in that old dressing up box over there, then when I got a bit of sense I took it out and decided to wear it. It's far too pretty to be hidden away.'

She was right. It was a beautiful Art Deco design, right out of the thirties. Alex could remember Grannie wearing it. He'd often wondered where it had disappeared to and now he knew. Cassie the Magpie had clearly struck again. Despite owning a monstrous red and black motorbike and having a penchant for roaring off on road-trips at every opportunity, Cassie had a definite girlie side and did like her jewellery.

'Well if you think it'll work.' Alex shrugged.

'I'll try it,' replied Cassie confidently.

'Will you be very careful with it?' asked Elodie. 'It's probably really delicate.'

'Elodie, you *really* don't look like yourself.' Alex stood up and went over to her. He put his hands on her shoulders. 'Is it the dust up here? I never thought.'

'No. No, it's not the dust. It's just Georgiana, and whatever might be hidden in that locket. It's all a bit overwhelming.'

Elodie sat down on a stool, before her legs gave up on her. Alex's hands had burned through the thin cotton of the shirt and she could still feel his touch. A traitorous bubble of lust had sprung up from somewhere deep inside her and she couldn't quite shake the idea of him being dressed like Ben now – as well as still seeing the smile on his face that those latest memories had presented her with.

'Look,' she said, pointing at the floor, just to try and

shift the attention away from herself, in case her thoughts showed too clearly on her face. 'The picture's all rolled up again.' In actual fact, it had probably been rolled up a while, but it was as good a distraction as she could muster at that point.

Alex swore and knelt down. From here she could see the top of his head and the way his hair kind of fell over his forehead a little and curled around his collar, and the fact that beneath this latest t-shirt was a fine collection of muscles on his back and on his shoulders, shifting and undulating as he moved around, trying to flatten the canvas.

Oh, God. Where had her quiet, pliable childhood friend gone? What had happened when she'd been in London? The changes were subtle, but they were there.

In that moment, Elodie was lost.

Alex. It was over long ago, wasn't it? Over before it really started …

'Isn't there anywhere we can go apart from here? Look. Hughie's staring. How about the woods?'

'Well yes, there's the woods.'

'Or the shed? Or the greenhouses?'

'The folly?'

'The folly sounds good.'

'You look good.'

A giggle. 'So do you.'

'The folly's a long way away and you really do look good. The Faerie Bridge might be better.'

'It might be …'

Elodie closed her eyes in a vain attempt to stop the images.

Of course, the reasonable side of her suddenly said, *this might all be just because of Georgiana.*

Yeah, right, the non-reasonable side of her said rather

sarcastically. She opened her eyes and looked again at Alex kneeling on the floor.

'Come on down here, Elodie, and have another look at this locket,' Cassie's voice interrupted her thoughts.

Elodie didn't have a good reason not to kneel beside them, and Cassie bunked over to one side so Elodie was forced to squeeze in between her and Alex. He was so close she could feel the warmth of him and she clenched her fists, ramming them into her thighs so she didn't suddenly grab him.

'It might be the same one.' Elodie's voice came out surprisingly steadily and she studied the painting. 'It'll be so wonderful if you ever get the painting cleaned up, though. Then at least we could see her properly.'

'Ha! That won't happen,' said Cassie with a laugh.

'How come?'

'Because I don't want her to leave the Hall. She'd have to leave the Hall to get cleaned up, because I doubt anyone would come and do it here.' Cassie leaned into the portrait and smiled at it. 'She was my heroine growing up. I used to want to know all about her and make up stories. In my daydreams, she was my best friend.' She looked up at Elodie. 'Some people have imaginary friends. I didn't. I had her, and she was very real to me. I was a very weird child.'

'No, I don't think you were.' Elodie smiled. 'I used to do the same with the tomb. Alex always teased me about it.'

'That's because you would chatter away to it as if Georgiana would answer you back!' said Alex. He hadn't taken his eyes off the painting either. 'It would be very wonderful, but Cassie's right. It's not going to happen.'

'I told you, my friend would do it!' said Elodie. 'He really would. But yes. I'd maybe have to take it to him.' She frowned, considering it. 'I wouldn't feel right asking him to come all the way up here. But if she can't leave the Hall...'

'And there's your problem,' replied Alex with a grin. 'I

wouldn't like to try and talk Cassie into letting her leave the Hall. My sister can be very fierce when she wants to.' He sent Cassie a teasing glance, then made as if to touch the painted girl's cheek, but his fingers hovered a few millimetres above her before he seemed to decide against it. 'But playing match-the-locket is the least of our problems. Remember Georgiana herself is actually missing.'

Maybe just physically! Elodie wanted to say. *I'm pretty certain she's popping in and out of my reality and I don't feel I can talk about it with you guys right now.* Georgiana had apparently made it her business to show Elodie her memories, for whatever reason, and perhaps the locket was part of it. But Alex was right; the locket really *was* the least of Elodie's problems at the moment.

Cassie gathered up the necklace and Elodie hoped that she really would be careful with it. It was clearly special; otherwise why would she have supposedly been buried with it?'

Her mind replayed the scene she had just experienced, and she thought there was maybe one way to prove if any of it was real and Georgiana had come back to the Hall briefly. Well maybe there were *two* ways to check it out.

One – she could get the painting cleaned up and see if it matched the face of Georgiana's effigy, but she'd have to take it away from the Hall and go down to London for that – and she wasn't sure she wanted to risk Cassie's wrath to do that. The second way to check was if she could find any records of highwaymen being hanged at Tyburn with the name Ben.

Then she realised how ridiculous that was. Even if she could find a Ben who was hanged, all it proved was that a highwayman called Ben had been executed. And there could be dozens of them – it must have been a fairly common name. It didn't prove it was Georgiana's Ben. Based on the way he had swept Lucy up into the secrecy, he was clever and quick thinking. He was probably a very good highwayman – and if that was the case, would he even have been caught?

Elodie cast a quick glance up to the window and realised now how the moonlight in those memories made sense. Georgiana had never shown him to her in daylight, because Ben himself wouldn't have risked being seen other than at night. If the highwayman was in love with someone like Lady Georgiana Kerridge, there was way too much to lose.

Elodie blinked as the sun broke through the last of the clouds, pretty sure that she saw a shadow flit past the window and block the sunlight out again very, very briefly.

Chapter Seven

Elodie eventually got out of the attic. She made some comment about checking the duelling pistols and Alex shrugged, tidied the canvas away and stood up.

'We might as well go down and check,' he said. 'That's if you don't mind being seen in public wearing my clothes.'

'Ah.' How could she have forgotten?

'Ah.' There was a wicked twinkle in his eye and she swallowed a groan. She wanted that wicked twinkle to mean more than just a teasing joke. 'I thought that might change your mind. We should really wait until the place is closed, don't you think? If we start raiding the cabinets and taking the guns out with visitors there, you know they'll want to talk about them and handle them. How about we do it later tonight?'

Elodie knew the comment was perfectly innocent but she felt herself colour, and had to hide her face by concentrating intently on the stool she scraped back across the floor into the corner. *How about we do it later tonight?*

'Whatever.' She tried to keep her voice even.

'That's quite good, though,' chimed in Cassie. 'It gives me time to clean up the locket.' She touched Elodie's hand lightly. 'Tell you what, I'll leave it for you to open.'

'Thanks. I know you'll do your best with it.'

'I will. I'll be careful.'

'You'd better be, Cass, or you'll have me to answer to as well.' Alex stared at the trunk and tapped the lid. 'That's Georgiana tucked away. So, we've got a Bible and a key to investigate now.' He shook his head. 'And the pistol of course, but I'm pretty certain it's the twin from downstairs. The mystery is, of course, why it was in the tomb.'

'Oh, look.' Cassie ducked down and picked up something from the floor. She handed it to Alex. 'This must have fallen out. Unless you brought it up here with you?'

Alex glanced at what he held in his hand and shook his head. 'No. That's not from me. More likely, it's fallen out of the trunk. Goodness knows what's in the pockets of those old clothes.' He laid the item down on top of the trunk and turned away. 'Right. I really have to go and survey the damage.'

Elodie watched him head towards the door, then fussed a little, pulling things around until Cassie spoke up.

'Come on!' She was waiting by the door, holding it open.

Elodie cast a quick glance at the trunk before she headed out to join Cassie. Alex had put a small, silver disc on top of it and she hesitated. It looked, from where she stood, a lot like a silver coin and her stomach lurched again. *Once a coin, always a coin. It holds a special wish.*

'Hang on!' she said. 'I just want to check something.' Hoping it was really just an old 10p piece, Elodie went over to the coin and picked it up. Her stomach turned over. It wasn't. It was a silver coin, definitely, but it showed the face of a man with a rather pronounced nose and long hair tied back. The words embossed on it were difficult to read, but they seemed to spell out GEORGIUS.III.DEI. GRATIA.REX. The date stamped on it was 1796. She dropped the coin as if it was burning hot and watched it bounce onto the floor and roll away.

Her heart pounding, she wiped her hand down her shorts and looked, almost guiltily, at Cassie standing by the door.

'Are you coming?' Cassie asked.

'Yes. Sorry. I thought it was something exciting, but it wasn't.' She smiled and, if her expression looked anything like it felt, it would be obvious that it was completely fake.

'God knows what's in here,' said Cassie and grinned back. Her expression mustn't have been that obvious then.

'Yep.' Elodie took a deep breath and forced herself to turn away from the coin. Instead, she made herself think of Alex and the portrait. He had really seemed to be taken with the picture. If only she could get it restored for him. Surely, he deserved *something* after all the hassle he was going to have to deal with after this storm?

As she followed Alex and Cassie along the corridor and back to the top of the steps, she thought she had potentially devised the perfect plan. It would mean getting Cassie on her side as well, though, which might be easier said than done.

'Alex, if you need to do some surveying, I'll head back to the cottage. I'll get changed, check my own damage and then come back. I'll even lock up the Hall after closing if you like, to give you some more time outside. Then we can see the pistol.' And if she *could* get Cassie on her side, if Elodie locked up this evening, she could perhaps get the painting today, and take it down to London, ask Simon to restore it and bring it back …

'Would you really lock up? That's so kind. Thank you. I'll head over to your cottage with you.' Alex looked over his shoulder and smiled as he held the door at the foot of the steps open for her. 'It'll give me a chance to see the lake and check the bridge over your way.'

She was very aware of him just behind her as he stood back to let her pass, and it was completely ridiculous that she was having palpitations over his closeness. This was the same man she'd buried her feelings for years ago. She was beginning to think the storm had stirred up more than just the weather, especially when she made the mistake of looking up at him and caught him watching her.

'Is that all right?' he asked. 'Or will I be in your way?'

'No! No, that's fine. No problem,' she answered, far too quickly. 'And I'll still come back later on and do the lock up for you. I want to see the pistol.'

'Yes, that should work. I need to get around the estate and see what it's like, and you locking up would be a great help. Cassie, are you coming over with us?'

'No thanks.' She patted her pocket. 'I have this little beauty to sort out. I'll see you later.'

She turned away and disappeared down the corridor towards Alex's kitchen. Elodie knew she was off to find the biggest bottle of silver polish she could lay her hands on.

Alex headed off towards his front door, which was really at the side of the Hall. 'I just hope the storm damage isn't too bad.' He paused on the step and looked out. There were still visitors milling around and he pulled a face. 'Actually, I might wait a little while until things settle first. Let the tourists sort themselves out.' Then he looked down at her and smiled. Her stomach somersaulted. 'Wait with me?'

She nodded. She couldn't find a reason to say no.

Alex walked around to the main steps of the Hall, which gave a better view of the estate. He stood, hands on his hips, staring around at what he could see. Even Elodie could tell it wasn't brilliant news, but it could have been a lot worse.

The lake looked suspiciously full and the ha-ha was flooded, but it didn't look like the water had reached the public areas. There was the church, of course, and the wooden summerhouse in the dip looked as though water had crept up the steps, so it appeared to be a little island floating around – but seeing the waterline and the bit where the stray twigs and leaves had stuck to the building's walls, Elodie could tell that it was already receding and draining back into the ground. One of the manhole covers had popped off in the turning circle at the side of the house where the disabled guests could park and water was spouting out of that, which was obviously the problem Cassie had mentioned, but Elodie didn't know if there was anything else further through. No doubt Alex would find out.

She could see, however, that there was a big tree down in the parkland – an oak tree, one of the old ones that had stood in a clearing on its own. Margaret had once told her it was on a ley line and it was a magical pathway, but it definitely didn't look magical now. At the moment, it was lying down, split into two pieces with its roots out of the earth and the tips of its branches crushing a couple of younger trees.

'Ouch.' Elodie stared across at it. 'That doesn't look good.'

'What? The oak? I'm bloody pleased it's down,' said Alex, frowning. 'I hate it.'

'How can you hate a tree?' she asked, surprised. The street where she'd lived in London had only been leafy because of the trees in people's front gardens. It had boasted a few spindly saplings in the pathways and proper, climbable trees within a couple of metres which were one of the things that Elodie had missed the most when she'd been there. Not that she'd climbed a tree for many years – but she would have liked the option to do so if she wanted to.

'It's just that one. Somebody told me the roots go down to Hell and it stuck with me. I think I was about eight at the time.'

'Who told you that?' Elodie was shocked that someone could be so thoughtless to a child.

'It was a labourer my Dad employed to do some forestry for us. He was a proper traveller, I think – at least, to me, as an eight-year-old, he looked like a traveller and he talked like I'd imagined a traveller would talk. He was probably just someone who had worked outdoors all his life.' He frowned, as if bringing the man's features back into his vision. 'He had shaggy, black hair and dark eyes. His face was brown, really tanned, and leathery looking. He walked with a kind of stoop and always had his axe over his shoulder. Oh – and he limped, because he told me that one day he'd dropped his axe and chopped his toes off.'

'Ugh!' Elodie stared at Alex. 'Really?'

'Well, he did have a limp, but he'd lied about his toes. I saw him with bare feet when he had his afternoon break under the oak, the last day he was here – it was a really hot day and he'd taken his shoes and socks off. And he definitely had the full complement of toes on each foot. So I asked him how his toes had come back, and he told me that the oak was magical and it had gifted him the toes out of some old twigs. Then he wiggled them and said he hoped the stiffness wouldn't go all the way up his leg, as if it did, he might end up wooden and stuck here like the tree. I'm not kidding, I ran back to the house screaming!'

'What a horrid old man!' Elodie felt indignant on eight-year-old Alex's behalf.

'I think he was more than likely just an old boy with arthritis that liked to spin a yarn. Some kids might have taken it with good heart – I didn't. My father thought the whole thing was hysterically funny.' Alex grinned down at Elodie and then looked back at the fallen oak. 'So yes. I bloody hate that tree and I'm pleased it's gone. That'll be my first job tomorrow – getting someone up here to turn the damn thing into logs I can sell off.'

'You're the boss,' Elodie replied and he laughed.

'I am that.' He gazed out over the parkland. 'But not forever. All I'm doing is being a guardian for the place. Trying to keep it going for future generations.'

Elodie felt a moment of panic. Future generations?

'For *your* children?' she asked, before she could stop herself. She wished she could have thrown herself into the lake at that point – how snipey she must have sounded.

'Or Cassie's. Whoever has mini-Aldrichs first, I guess. Oh!' He looked at Elodie and his eyebrows went up into his hairline. 'Sorry – did you think I was having an illicit affair or something? With somebody you know nothing about? And planning mini-mes?' He laughed and folded his arms. 'No.' He stared off into the distance again, shaking his head and making his fringe flop around. Elodie couldn't take her eyes off it and felt her jaw slacken.

Her jaw came back together with a snap when she realised those clear, midnight blue eyes had glanced back at her. 'No. There was only ever one girl for me. And I think I blew it. There was lots of rebound stuff – but nothing lasted. So no. I have no immediate plans for marriage or children.'

'I'm sure it wasn't your fault.' Elodie tried to keep the words light. In a way, though, she was pleased. It might help this silly, sudden crush disappear if she knew he was lusting after some woman.

'Nah, it was definitely my fault. But it's fine. Well – it is at the minute,' he clarified. 'Things could change. Anyway. Let's get to the cottage. I'd hate to think of the place floating down the river.'

'What, and me not floating away with it?'

'Something like that.' Then he winked. 'Joking! Come on. Let's go.'

Yes, he'd blown it, all right.

Even as they began to walk towards her cottage, so many years later – with poor Elodie keeping to the grass, still barefoot – he cringed, remembering Prom Night. Why on earth had he thought the stables were an appropriate place to take her? Especially knowing how she felt about horses – she was terrified of them …

'Do you really even want to go all the way to the Faerie Bridge?' he had asked, a last-ditch attempt at pouncing on that immediacy, teasing her, running his fingers down her

64

face, settling his thumb under her chin and raising her face to his.

'I don't know.' A little catch in her breath as she moved closer to him. 'Now you come to mention it, even the Faerie Bridge is quite a long walk ...'

Alex didn't want to remember. 'Oh, look. Your cottage is still in one piece.' He exhaled carefully as they rounded the corner. The red-brick cottage with its thatched roof and two first floor dormer windows looked as sturdy as ever.

'Oh, I hope so!' she said, everything surrounding that previous conversation apparently forgotten.

Elodie hurried on ahead – surprisingly quickly for someone without shoes – and she pushed the white door open, disappearing inside the cottage. Alex, a few moments behind her, stood on the doorstep. She had left the door swinging wide, but he wasn't about to just barge on in there.

'Everything okay?' he shouted, leaning in as far as he dared. The place smelled of Elodie – that floral perfume she wore and the Linen Fresh scented candles she favoured, merging with freshly ground coffee.

There was also a welcoming aroma of some sort of casserole, stewing away in the slow cooker. Elodie was always organised with her meals, probably because she had lived such a hectic life in London and had never been sure when she was coming home or when Piers or Paulo or whatever the idiot was called that she had married was going to be around. Old habits died hard, even here in Suffolk – but at least, she had said laughingly one day, she would never starve.

Alex was completely the opposite. He'd forget to eat or be too busy to prepare something, but luckily Margaret and Delilah were observant ladies. They'd often bring him slices of pie or servings of lasagne or neatly plated up roast dinners, claiming they had simply made too much for tea.

Sometimes, Alex worried that he was going the same way as his father – too wrapped up in other things to think about real life. Mostly, he found himself wandering up to the stables of an evening, especially when Cassie was away at her university and he was alone. He'd climb onto Hughie, heedless of a saddle, and take him out for a canter around the estate, holding onto nothing more secure than the horse's mane. He'd ride around the woods, and across the Faerie Bridge and wonder what had gone wrong. Being with Hughie outside the confines of the Hall was sometimes the only way he could escape from the fact he was Alexander Aldrich, Earl of Hartsford, and all this was his responsibility.

Sometimes, he'd pull Hughie up onto the hill where the folly was and he'd look down on the parkland and resent his father for dying and leaving him to deal with everything.

Elodie's little coach-light might be on outside her door and he'd look across and see her perhaps moving around behind the windows, or the TV flickering. Occasionally, he'd see her out in the little garden weeding away. And once, he'd seen her sitting in the upstairs window. She was perched on the sill, her legs dangling outside. She was leaning back, her hands on the window seat behind her, her face upturned to the evening sun as it dropped behind the horizon.

He had determined to call in on her on his way back, but she was gone by the time he reached her cottage, so he just kept going.

It was as he was thinking these thoughts that he heard Elodie pad down the creaky, wooden staircase. He turned his attention to her and once again was struck by how natural and pretty she looked with the sunlight slanting through the landing window and spinning gold into her hair.

Once again, he felt like punching that stupid ex-husband of hers for doing what he had done to her. But then, she would never have come back here and he would never have seen her coming down those stairs and she would never have had a bath in his house …

'You still have bare feet,' Alex said.

But it didn't seem enough, really.

'They're not bare. They're covered in mud again.' Elodie looked down at them. 'Which means I've tracked it through the house. Never mind.'

And in that moment, the spell – whatever spell there had been, because there was definitely something that shifted – was broken.

'There's only a little leak,' Elodie told Alex. 'Why are you looking at me so strangely? Did you not want to hear that?' For Alex was, indeed, looking at her strangely.

'What was your ex called?' he asked.

'That's a very odd question! Where did that come from?'

'It's just that I couldn't remember his name for a minute. Piers or Paulo?'

'Piers.'

'Okay.' Alex nodded briefly and gestured to the hallway. 'May I come in?'

'Of course.' She stepped to one side. He brushed past her as he walked through the door – it was a very narrow doorway and he had to stoop a little as it was also very low – and she got the zingy thing going on up her arm. Hoping he wouldn't notice, she shook her arm to try and get rid of it and followed him to the bottom of the stairs.

'It's on the landing. The window at the back. It's just on the sill. I think perhaps the window wasn't closed properly. These houses were built to withstand all sorts, it seems.'

'That's good news at least.' Alex paused on the stairs and

turned back to look at her. 'I think you're right. Those old builders definitely knew what they were doing.'

'Indeed.' She followed him up the stairs because it seemed the appropriate thing to do.

They paused on the landing and Alex poked around the window frame until he was satisfied. 'One less thing to worry about. You get a good view of that tree from here, don't you? I never really stopped to look. The previous tenants were in here so long, they just got on with it and did their own bits of maintenance. And Margaret and your mum came to get the place ready for you moving in.'

'They did a marvellous job.'

'They *are* marvellous. I hope Margaret's made too much food again tonight. I'm starving. And Cassie won't find anything to cook with if she's looking.' He grinned and patted the window sill. 'Okay, I'll get on my way if you're happy enough to leave everything as it is?'

Elodie wasn't *really* happy, because she was dreadfully aware of how close they were to the bedroom and at the back of her mind the Prom Night debacle was threatening to erupt again. Seeing Georgiana and Ben – or rather *being* Georgiana, as she felt she had been, albeit briefly – had brought the whole train of memories hurtling back, but she found herself nodding dumbly. 'I'll still come over at closing time and lock up the Hall for you, after all the visitors have gone.' Then, as an afterthought, she added, 'And I'll bring some food as well, so don't worry about Margaret providing for you tonight. She might have enough to do once she gets home. We don't know what the village is like, remember? I'll call my parents' neighbours and ask them to check their cottage out too. I can imagine the storm swept through all the villages hereabouts, and the neighbours can pop in quicker than I'll be able to.'

After her father retired, Elodie's parents had moved out of the tied cottage Elodie had grown up in, and now lived in a nearby village. They usually spent the summer in her mother's old family property in France, where her mother had, in her turn, grown up. After devoting their lives to Elodie and the young Aldrichs, nobody begrudged them their adventures, although Elodie did miss being able to pop in and see them regularly.

'I hope Hartsford's not too bad,' Alex said, nodding out of the window, 'because there's Kate from the Folk Museum sneaking out the back way. She'll quite possibly end up in three feet of mud if she climbs that wall today.'

Elodie took one big step and was at the window, staring out. 'Kate?' She laughed. Kate was great friends with Cassie and often clambered over the boundary walls as a shortcut.

'Yes. Did you think I'd spotted the ghostly horseman?' One of the Hartsford legends told of a shadowy man on horseback who wove through the trees on moonlit nights. Elodie had always dismissed that tale. The only shadowy horseman she had seen was Alex, riding out there when he thought nobody was around. She wondered now if there was a little more fact to that legend than anyone had thought.

'Oh, there he is, speak of the devil. I just saw him through the trees.' He pointed in mock horror.

She shivered despite the warmth on the landing. 'Oh, don't be silly. He's just a legend!' Maybe she was trying to convince herself as well. 'And if he is a ghost, a bit of rain won't harm him.'

The window let in a lot of sunshine and it was always a warm spot. In fact, if it hadn't been for the puddle of water on the windowsill, she really would have thought the whole storm that afternoon was a dream. Or a nightmare. She shivered again, remembering the empty tomb and the objects they'd found inside it. She remembered also the painting and her plan to restore it for Alex. She sneaked a look at his watch and saw that the Hall had half an hour left of opening.

'Look,' Elodie said, 'you go and get your surveying done, I'll get changed and then sort out some food. Then I'll pop over to the Hall and get the closing-up routine sorted for you. Just take your time.'

'All right.' Alex smiled at her, and she hoped she could pull the painting restoration off. It would be worth it to see that smile again, directed right at her.

Then Alex surprised her by bending over and brushing her cheek with a kiss. 'You look bloody good in my clothes,' he whispered, teasing her. 'No need to change on my account.' He turned away, heading down the stairs and out of the door with that long, loping stride he had.

She just stood there like an idiot on the landing watching him go. She pressed one hand to her cheek where he had kissed her, and it almost burned.

Chapter Eight

Elodie gave it twenty minutes before she left the cottage. It took her that length of time to wash her feet and change into a long, floaty skirt, sandals and a strappy top. She also called her parents to report the good news that their house was undamaged, and the only issue seemed to be that their front garden had developed a bit of a pond in the middle of the lawn. She spared them the more horrid aspects of the incident at the church, and just told them the roof had been damaged.

'Poor Alex,' her mother had said, worried about him as always. 'As if he didn't have enough to do!' Elodie agreed, and was doubly pleased she hadn't told them about the tomb.

It would normally be a five-minute walk to the Hall, but she had to carry a bowl full of casserole this afternoon. She'd filled a huge dish and hoped the lid was a good enough fit to stop the stuff spilling over her. She'd also managed to roll up the latest copy of some interior design magazine that she'd subscribed to in London. She didn't need it now, of course, as the cottage was perfect. But she still liked to read it and see what the latest trends were. It was also useful for her career, she told herself. The mere fact that she had no real desire at present to return to costume design was incidental. She liked the pretty pictures. And the magazine was large enough to conceal a certain portrait.

It was, to be truthful, more like a salad sort of evening now the storm had passed over, and it was warm but muggy when she headed across. The air was heavy with the scent of grass and soil and lavender and carnations – and, it had to be said, beef. Elodie wasn't that fond of a salad when she knew she had some estate-reared stewing steak in the refrigerator. And neither, she knew, were Alex or Cassie.

The door to Alex's wing was standing open and she shouted through to announce herself before entering.

'In here!' called Cassie from the kitchen. 'I've been working on this locket.'

Elodie followed her voice and found her friend sitting hunched up at the breakfast bar, rubbing at the silver oval. It still looked a little grungy, but it certainly wasn't as bad as it had been.

'Are you hungry?' Elodie asked. Cassie, for all she was a stick of a thing, could certainly put away her food.

She nodded without looking up, giving the locket another rub. 'Alex has absolutely nothing to eat in here. I've cleaned out his biscuit barrel but my tummy is still empty.'

'Would you like some of this, then?' Elodie opened the casserole dish. Cassie spun her head around so fast she truly thought it might fly off.

'I love you Elodie!' she said. 'Ohhhh, that smells good.' She closed her eyes and gave a deep, satisfying sniff. 'You're staying as well, of course.' It was more of a statement than a question.

'There's more than enough for three of us. I always over-estimate.' Elodie looked ruefully at the casserole. 'That's why Delilah hates me dishing up food in the café. Especially cakes. I can make a cake that should feed twelve, feed six.'

'I'll get the plates, then.'

Cassie hopped off the bench and Elodie took the opportunity to peer at the locket. 'Is it ready?' Elodie indicated the piece of jewellery and Cassie followed her gaze.

She sighed. 'No. I'm going to rub it gently with cotton. I'll go and find some soon, and then I'll look for some oil in the garage.' She checked the clock, which was a replica of one from Paddington Station. 'I'd best go and close up the Hall, anyway. Alex has disappeared somewhere assessing damage.

I'll throw the tourists out and then I'll come back and deal with this.'

It was the perfect opening.

Trying to keep her voice steady, Elodie said, 'Don't worry. You plate that all up, and give me the keys. I told Alex I'd lock up for him, but you'd dashed off along the corridor from the attics by then with the locket, so you probably didn't hear me. And at least if you're in charge down here, we should all get an even amount of dinner.'

'Oh, really?' Cassie grinned. 'You trust me with this stuff? It would be *splendid* if you could lock up tonight. Do you know what you're doing?'

'Of course. I know which route to follow, I've done it plenty of times for Alex.'

'Thank you. You really are very wonderful.' Cassie turned and deftly unhooked a huge bunch of keys from the hook behind the door. 'You know they're all in order, right?'

'I do.' Elodie smiled. Her heart was beating so loudly she felt sure Cassie would hear it. But apparently, she didn't, as she handed her the keys and turned her attention to the casserole.

'Oh. Just one thing,' Elodie said.

'Hmm?' Cassie had the plates warming in the Aga and turned around quizzically.

'You know that old picture in the attic – the one of Georgiana?'

'The one we weren't allowed to touch?' asked Cassie wryly. 'No matter all the times I touched it before.'

'That's the one.' Elodie smiled and twitched at her skirt. 'Is it okay if I sort of borrow it?'

'Borrow it?' Cassie looked astonished, and Elodie thought with a stab of horror that her plan could go horribly wrong.

'Yep. Just for a little while.'

'For what? I'm not sure – like I said, she belongs here. I

know the tomb is shattered and all that, but the painting won't help repair her face. Not yet, anyway.'

'Ah – and there we have it, in the word "repair".' Elodie smiled, she hoped, engagingly. 'Like I said, I have a friend in London who could clean her up for us.'

'And you were serious?' Cassie's eyebrows rose. She was always intrigued by Elodie's tales of theatre-land, but this was something she mustn't have heard before today. 'You really have friends who do that sort of stuff?'

'Well, one friend. Simon. He's married to Cori, remember?'

'Oh! Cori. Of course.' Cassie nodded. She'd heard of Cori. 'And he's said he'll do it? Really?'

'Well not yet – but I know he will.'

'Gosh. I don't know.'

Elodie played her last, desperate card before she had no option but to turn to theft. 'To be honest with you, Cass, I want to do it for Alex. It's going to be a surprise. He's had a rubbish day, and I want to do something nice for him. But it's fine, I'll leave it.' She crossed her fingers behind her back. She wasn't going to leave it at all.

'For *Alex*? Well why didn't you say so?' Cassie smiled suddenly. 'Take it, by all means. There's not many reasons I'd let that portrait leave the premises, but if it's to make my brother happy, then you can take it, with my blessing.' Cassie looked down, and her face shadowed. 'He gave up so much to come back here, you know. He moved back from Oxford and he'd made a life down there. He had a great job, and a lovely house, and a girlfriend, although I didn't rate her much and it fizzled out before long. And he came back. It was only going to be temporary – he was going to get the estate sorted, get things tidied up and leave it ticking over until one of us was ready to come back permanently.' She shook her head. 'It didn't work out like that at all. Once he saw how many debts there were, and how much had already gone, he knew he had to sell this place or open it up to the public.

'He had to let so many staff go, he felt terrible – but they'd been whittled down to the bare bones anyway. Your Dad did what he could, but of course he had retired by the time things reached breaking point – the new guy, one of my own father's so-called racing friends was as much use as a chocolate fireguard. I swear he gambled half the money away on horses. I would have signed his dismissal papers myself, if I'd had the chance.'

Elodie had heard the story before, of course, but it seemed different coming from Cassie, rather than as gossip from the village. Elodie's father hadn't even talked about it – he simply refused to get involved in the gossip and had always remained loyal to the Earl and to Alex, despite the way things had turned out. He was lucky though – when he retired, Elodie's parents had at least managed to buy their little cottage.

Other people Elodie knew, from hearsay, had their rents raised or simply lost the tied cottages and had to get jobs and move elsewhere. The impact of the estate's collapse on such a small village was horrible, and she still felt ill on Alex's behalf if she let herself think about it.

'He's never told me that much about it,' she admitted to Cassie. She certainly hadn't heard about the girlfriend.

Cassie looked up at her. 'No, well he wouldn't. I only found out because I saw his computer on and poked around the files. He wanted to protect me, I think, so I never told him I'd seen anything. He had a few demons when he came back – he was very bitter and very angry and wouldn't open up to anyone. He drank too much and he was never *happy*, you know? In fact, he only started coming out of it when—' She closed her mouth, as if she'd already said too much.

But Elodie wanted to know. 'When what?' Her heart was

pounding; it was as if she already knew what Cassie was going to say.

'When you came back,' Cassie finished softly. 'Sorry.'

'No need to be sorry. I *do* care for him, despite – well – everything that's happened. I hate to think of him hurting.' Cassie could interpret that how she liked; she might choose to think it was because of Elodie's failed marriage and the fact that she too had returned to Hartsford under something of a cloud. Or she might not. But she wasn't going to go into details.

'I know you care, it's plain to everyone who knows you. And getting the portrait restored for him is a lovely thing to do. Thank you, Elodie.'

Elodie's face burned. Was it really so obvious how she felt about him?

But Cassie had decided it was time to change the subject slightly. 'I think he might go off on Hughie after he's seen the damage – especially if he knows we're around to close up the Hall. He'll just want to escape real life for a while. You nip up and get the picture, and we'll say nothing to him. But don't bump into any ghosts up there!'

'Thanks.' Elodie smiled, almost sagging with relief. For all of her grand schemes, she wasn't really a thief and didn't know how she would have slept, let alone looked one of the Aldrichs in the face afterwards. It was hard enough looking at Alex at the moment anyway, as the image of him in Ben's black clothes seemed to have haunted her since that morning. 'I think I'll be fine up there. It won't be anyone I haven't seen before.' And that, at least, was true.

Elodie left Cassie to it with the plates and the Aga and the casserole, and hurried towards the connecting door along Alex's corridor, to enter the grand space of the Hall. She loved the Hall near closing time. It was like a sleepy old duchess settling her skirts around her for a snooze. You knew she was still there, imperious and ever-watchful, but this was the time of day you could slip past her and not have her attention on you.

Cassie's words were still playing on her mind though – had her return really been the thing that dragged Alex back from the brink? She certainly knew that when her life fell apart in London and her health began to fail so drastically, his face was the one thing that kept her going. It was him she wanted to see when she was in hospital on a ventilator – not Piers. There was too much unfinished business between them, and she fought so hard to pull her life together afterwards, simply because she had to see him one last time to make it all right again.

And when she was stronger, and she felt a bit silly and dramatic about it, she still knew that she had to leave Piers and everything that he represented. She could have gone anywhere, really. There were theatres in towns all over the world that would have taken her on with only a cursory glance at her CV. But no. It was Hartsford, always Hartsford, where she wanted to be. Where she *needed* to be. Her confidence had gone, her health was following suit and she just wanted to escape.

Yet when she got back, just being near him seemed to be enough, and the urge to sort the past out didn't seem so important any more. Because she was still with him and he was in her life again and it was *safe*.

With those thoughts spinning around in her mind, Elodie headed down to lock up the kitchens first, then came back up into the service corridor. She quite liked the pictures of animals and landscapes along here; there were so many dreary family portraits hanging up elsewhere on the walls that she sometimes felt watched in the Hall – but she wasn't intimidated by any of them, apart from Georgiana's father who glared out at everyone from his perch above the fireplace in the dining room. Elodie always averted her eyes from him. She had once asked Alex where the portrait of his wife was, and Alex had shrugged and said he didn't know, but from what he'd heard, she was a hideous woman anyway so it was maybe better that she was missing.

Alex called the dining room the Christmas Room. They had always had Christmas lunch in there when he was growing up. In latter years, however, he'd gone to Margaret's house and, seeing the room like this, as it was this evening, all mellow with the parkland golden and green beyond the huge windows and the sweeping driveway heading away from the Hall, Elodie thought it was such a shame that it might not be used like that again unless Cassie ever brought her future mini-Aldrichs over.

Because she still refused to think of Alex meeting anyone and producing small people any time soon. Elodie had a sense of possessiveness over him that she knew, deep down, was unfair and unwarranted. She'd moved away as soon as she could, then got married – what was wrong with Alex marrying? Surely she should be pleased if her old childhood friend found someone to make him happy? She knew, however, that she herself wouldn't be happy at all. Whoever he married probably wouldn't want her hanging around the Hall, despite the fact they'd grown up together.

Her cheeks burned as she remembered Prom Night again …

'So say we just forget about going to the Faerie Bridge and stay here?'

He had leaned down and brushed her lips with his and it was the first time she'd been kissed properly. Her knees wobbled and she clung onto him, half of her thinking it was the most wonderful thing in the word, and half of her wanting to run away screaming because, my God, this was Alex!

'Alex, what if anyone finds us?'

'They won't. Who'll be in the Hall stables at this time of night?'

The Prom had officially finished an hour ago. It had been hosted at a marquee in the Hall grounds, and most people had drifted away from around ten o'clock.

'I don't know. Cassie?'

'Cassie's in bed, you dolt.' His words had been affectionate, a smile on his lips as he brushed hers again. 'Where we should be.'

Her legs had wobbled again, and she'd clung to him as she felt his hands snake around and undo the zipper at the back of her sea-green prom dress ...

'Urgh!' Elodie cringed and hurried through the dining room from the service corridor, refusing to look Georgiana's father in the face in case he could read her mind with his arrogant, all-seeing eyes.

A couple of straggling visitors were chatting to a tour guide as Elodie passed through the main hall and locked the library door behind her – but as that was the first and last place on the tour, Martin would be ushering them out rather swiftly. Fourteen clipboards were stacked up on the oak desk where they stocked the guidebooks, and Laura in the corridor was clutching the fifteenth. They only had one per tour guide so there were no guides in the house anymore and therefore no tourists.

Martin nodded to Elodie and managed to take the guests outside, closely followed by Laura, and Elodie quickly locked up the main door, loving, as always, that satisfying *clunk* you get with old locking mechanisms.

She worked through the rest of the house; she *clunk*-ed the drawing room, the music room, the Chinese parlour, the ballroom and then walked up the wonderful cantilever staircase that terrified people with its gravity-defying design.

Hurrying along the gallery, she locked all the bedrooms and bathrooms. Then up she went onto the third floor. She secured the nursery, and wished "Goodnight", as tradition demanded, to any little spirits that might be playing in there. Just outside the door, however, Elodie paused for a moment. It seemed busier than usual up there, but she couldn't put her finger on it – the atmosphere was heavier, more unsettled. It might, she reasoned, be something to do with the storm. It was a nursery though – she shook herself. Nothing to fret about, they'd calm down before long. 'It's fine,' she whispered, into the empty room to try and reassure the little spirits inside. 'It's all fine.'

From there, she moved along the corridor and shut up the servants' rooms. Then she saw the connecting door back into Alex's wing. Taking a deep breath, Elodie steadied her nerves and leaned into the door, listening hard to establish if anyone was roaming around behind it in the private quarters – and then decided that Alex, if he had returned, would be consumed by the promise of casserole and probably wouldn't have got further than the kitchen anyway.

And if he was, by any remote chance, in the corridor by the attics, Elodie's excuse was that she was simply taking a short cut after her business of locking up.

Still, she opened the door as quietly as she could and stepped through it. There was a funny little shiver as a draught swept past and she remembered little Lucy, hurrying back here after encountering Georgiana and Ben in the attics. Putting the thought out of her mind, she shut the door firmly behind her.

All she had to do now was creep along there and get into that attic. Thanking her lucky stars for the emptiness that pressed around her in that corridor, she climbed the short flight of stairs, reached the room and tried the handle, and the door swung open easily. Now she just had to get the picture, hide it in her magazine, get back to the kitchen, sit and have dinner without Alex realising, look dutifully at the pistol – and then escape.

It seemed an awfully long time until that part of her plan would be complete. But it was pointless thinking that far ahead at the moment.

She eyed the trunk that Alex had so carefully shut and hunkered down by it. A quick fiddle with the catches released the lid and it opened with an overly-loud creak in the silence of the attic.

It was the work of a moment to find the portrait, put it inside the magazine and roll it all up. Exhaling, she sat back on her heels and let her heart rate return to something close to normal. Casting a look around to make sure she'd left no trace that Alex could find, she saw the little silver coin that had rolled onto the floor. Something clicked into her brain, because it *had* rolled onto the floor, hadn't it? And it wasn't there anymore. It was on the window sill.

There was that draught again, and it curled up around her, sitting as she was on the floor beside the trunk, and she stood up hurriedly.

Then she felt the tiniest of pushes. She stumbled and turned around, a cold sweat breaking out and making her strappy top feel too constricting.

'Who's here?' she asked, looking around the room. There was, of course, silence. Elodie looked at the window sill again and the coin glinted in the sunlight. Another push and she took another lurch towards the window sill.

She swore at that point. 'Look, whoever's in here, stop it! If you want me over there, I'll *go* over there. Why not just show me who you are and ask me? It would be much easier for us both!' And before anyone could shove her again, she took two strides and was there, reaching over to pick the coin up.

'See, I found the coin!' Lucy was standing next to her, dancing from one foot to the other. Her lemon satin gown danced in the light with her, the skirt sticking out with the extra petticoats underneath, the way she always liked to wear it. 'It was exactly where he said it would be. Down by the lake. I'm clever, aren't I? Do say I'm clever, Georgiana.'

Georgiana looked at the coin in her hand. It was just a silver penny, but to Lucy it was clearly more valuable than any amount of rubies or emeralds.

'Remember his warning, though,' Georgiana said, thinking quickly. 'You mustn't tell anyone he's been here. Think of his poor horse, having to work with the faeries if you do.'

'Oh no, I won't breathe a word, I swear,' said Lucy, 'but now you have to promise me something.'

'I have to do no such thing! You're just a child.'

'I might be just a child,' said Lucy, her hazel eyes narrowing, 'but you're hiding something and I don't know what it is.'

'I beg your pardon?' Her face flooded with colour. 'I don't know what you could be talking about, Lucy Kerridge!' She moved slightly, standing over the floorboard she had just replaced, moments before she heard her sister racing along the corridor from the nursery. It creaked tellingly, but Lucy seemed unaware of it.

'I want you to promise me that you'll show me what you keep in that locket.' Lucy jabbed her forefinger at Georgiana's bodice. 'I know you're hiding something in there. I want to know what it is.' She stood still then, folding her arms in a singularly annoying fashion. 'And I shan't leave until you show me.' For good measure, she stamped her foot.

Chapter Nine

The attic came back into focus around Elodie and she stood staring at the spot where Lucy had just been, demanding to see what Georgiana kept in her locket.

For the first time, Elodie was annoyed that the memory, or the flash or whatever it was of Georgiana's life, had cut off. She wanted to see what was in the locket as badly as Lucy did. She dropped the coin onto the window sill, then she looked at the floor and wondered if the floorboard was still loose.

There was only one way to find out.

She knelt down and felt around, pressing down until one of the old wooden boards wobbled under her fingertips. Her heart pounding, she poked until she got the edge of it. There was a tiny knot hole half way along, and she wriggled her finger into it. The knot hole was just big enough for her to hook her finger underneath the board and prise it out. It gave her a strange thrill to think that Georgiana might have done exactly the same thing with the same piece of wood.

A waft of dank, dusty air hit her in the face and she coughed, then choked as she fought to breathe again. *Not now!* she begged her lungs. She didn't have an inhaler with her and really didn't want to collapse up here. It had been embarrassing enough when Alex had found her in the old squash courts last year, half-dead in the corner. She'd not had an attack like that for months and had managed to keep it all well hidden from him until then.

'Sorry,' she'd gasped. She'd fumbled for her inhaler when the attack had started, then dropped it. It had rolled away, and become wedged beneath some display boards. They were too heavy for her to move, and she began to black out, panicking.

Alex had burst in, just as she'd started to despair, and through some frantic form of sign language, she'd managed to communicate enough for him to retrieve it for her. Then he'd sat next to her, his arm around her, looking into her not-so-blue-anymore face in horror as she began to calm down. 'Asthma. Can't – breathe.' She'd struggled badly to speak.

'Asthma?' Alex had snapped. 'Since when do you have that?'

'L-London.'

He had sworn and called Piers something vile and stayed with her until an ambulance came, then gone with her to the hospital.

He'd been lovely, actually.

But now, after she'd sat still for a few moments to let her breathing catch up, she bent down to the floorboard again. She reached in and felt around, trying not to think of spiders. There was something horribly cobwebby down there, which made her gag, then she felt something tickle her hand which almost made her scream. Finally, she got it: the corner of a piece of paper.

She moved her hand carefully, trying not to catch the paper – or her hand – on any old nails that might be down there, and brought it out gently. Pieces of paper had survived for centuries under floorboards; shopping lists and notes had been found in other stately homes around the country and it was quite nice to think that she might have something exciting here. Or, of course, it might have been one of Cassie's old drawings from when she used to play up there.

Elodie grimaced. She really hoped not.

As she eased the paper out, her heart jumped. It was no drawing. It was a yellowing, brittle piece of paper, with faded ink on it.

I know what he is because he has a beautiful horse and

They have horses like that. I know he is a Bad Man and he lied to me about the silver pennies. I will tell Mama and Papa you are friends with him and you were angry with me when I asked to see your special locket. They will be cross and you will be sorry you did not let me see it.

'You spiteful little child!' Elodie said out loud, shocked. 'You awful, awful little girl!'

The letter was clearly from Lucy – God loves a trier and this child was obviously one of those. The comment about the locket must have stung, together with Georgiana's attitude towards her. She must have seen the loose floorboard after all and perhaps stuffed her own message in the space. Georgiana had clearly kept something in there that she wanted hidden away and Lucy had found out about it – and it was the perfect place to hide this little blackmail note. Elodie had a moment of surety where she thought it probably wasn't the first or the last note she'd sent either. The child seemed tenacious.

'Good grief.' Elodie tucked the letter into the magazine with Georgiana's picture and replaced the floorboard, stamping on it to settle it in place. She would tell Alex about it and—

Of course, she couldn't tell him, could she? He didn't know she had been up here, let alone poking around the floorboards.

She sighed and stared out at the parkland, thinking of the best way ahead. She saw a man on a horse, weaving through the trees. He was in the shadows and Elodie leaned closer to the window, trying to see him properly. Then he rounded the path towards the clearing where the oak tree had fallen and disappeared into the darkness of the forest.

It played on her mind that she seemed to be reliving Georgiana's memories, falling through some safety net that separated the two realities. For those times, she *was*

Georgiana. The eighteenth-century girl wasn't a ghost, otherwise Elodie would be seeing her move around and do things, just as she *always* saw ghosts do. She'd be removed from it; an observer like she normally was. No. This was different. She was in the girl's body, in her mind. There was no conscious choice from either of them – Georgiana's life just happened, and Elodie remembered it happening. It was entirely possible her memories and emotions had stained the atmosphere, for good or for bad.

She looked out at the woods again and saw the horseman come back into the clearing. It was Alex, of course, riding Hughie bareback as he always did when he needed to touch base. She pressed her fingertips gently to the glass and watched the man she'd happily give her life up for canter across the parkland on that great, galumphing, stupid animal of his. The thought should have startled her, or brought her up short at the very least. But it didn't. It was as natural as breathing.

Her mind wandered as she watched him and she remembered another man, another black horse that cantered through the parklands under the lattice-work of tree branches where the moon broke through.

His dark hair was loose, and she had hastily wound a length of red ribbon in her own fair hair, trying to tame it after he had tangled his fingers in her long tresses. And after she had undone his shirt and run her hands down his muscular chest and around to his back.

Stray curls hung loose about her shoulders as he pulled her close and kissed her again, more gently. She was bidding farewell to him just inside the church. The easiest way for him to leave was through the lych-gate at the back. From there, he could disappear into the woods and he would be safe. Nobody would disturb them here and the vicar himself only came on a Sunday morning.

'Don't fret, my love. You know that I can look after myself.'

'But I worry about you! I never know if I'll see you again and I'm afraid that something will happen to you. I'd die for you, I would!'

He shook his head. The shafts of moonlight that pierced the stained-glass windows gave him a silvery halo which, God knew, he did not warrant. She believed that was why she loved him so much.

'Georgiana, my sweet.' He lifted a curl away from her cheek and tucked it behind her ear, then ran his finger down to her chin. 'In this moonlight you are the very image of an otherworldly being.' He lowered his face to hers and brushed her lips with his. She closed her eyes, shivering beneath his touch. 'And as I keep telling you, I will return. I have been kissed by an angel, and that is enough.' She heard him laugh softly and opened her eyes to see him shaking his head. 'However, I must go. I have work to do.'

'But Ben—'

'No, my love.' His eyes were midnight blue and warm and she knew that, despite what he was and what he did, she would never have need of another man in all her born days.

'Do you regret anything?' Georgiana asked suddenly. 'Anything about your life, or your work, or about meeting me?'

'Some things.' He quirked that smile that made her heart gallop. 'But you – you, my love – I could never regret meeting you.'

He leaned in to kiss her again and she closed her eyes, ready to welcome his lips …

Elodie's world returned and she found herself at the attic window, her fingertips pressed to her lips, her heart pounding. Alex was still weaving through the woods. He dipped his head and leaned forwards patting Hughie's neck, and dug his heels into the animal's flanks before they disappeared around the corner towards the stables.

She leaned in to the glass, not sure if the pull her own heart felt towards Alex was real or just a product of Georgiana's memories.

It terrified her as much as it burned her up inside with desire, and she couldn't move or think properly for quite some time.

'You couldn't possibly have cooked that,' Alex said to his sister. He nodded towards the Aga where a delicious smell was wafting out from behind the doors. He'd just come back, the ride around the estate making him feel almost human again.

'Why ever not?' asked Cassie, offended.

He shrugged. 'I didn't have enough food in. So you had no ingredients. And besides, Elodie told me she was bringing us dinner.'

'Caught out!' She swung her long legs off the high chair next to the breakfast bar and wandered over to the Aga, where she proceeded to pull three plates out. 'Elodie's joining us. She's been gone ages though. She must have been throwing visitors out as well as locking up. It happens.'

With the plates out of the oven, the casserole was even more tempting and Alex wasted no time in going to the cutlery drawer and clattering knives and forks onto the breakfast bar. 'Is the locket nearly done?'

'I think so.' Cassie came over, balancing the plates, and nudged the necklace towards the end of the breakfast bar where clearly none of them were going to sit. 'I need to give it another rub with the cotton duster, but I've wiggled it and the hinges seem looser. I promised Elodie she could open it.'

Alex nodded. 'She'll appreciate that. Where is she? I said I'd take her back through to see those pistols.'

'Yes. She went ages ago.'

'I said I'd take her back through to see those pistols when everyone had left. What a bloody day, eh? Empty tombs, a broken church, a fallen tree and a flooded ha-ha. Not to mention the drains.' He ran his hand through his hair and sat back in the chair. He could have gone on about all the other minor things he'd seen that would need attending to, but what was the point?

The door clashed open just then and Elodie walked in with the keys jangling and some fancy designer magazine rolled up under her arm.

She started a little as she saw him, then put the magazine down and drew up a chair in front of one of the plates. 'Did you enjoy your ride?'

'I did. There's a lot of tidying up to do, but Hughie was splendid and he didn't mind going a little slower tonight so I could check everywhere.'

'That's good.' Elodie reached for the glass of red wine Cassie had poured and took a couple of sips without seeming to give it a thought. Piers had been something of a wine aficionado, Elodie had confided one night when she was pretty drunk on something cheap. He had refused to drink anything but the best and, she said, drinking cheaply was just one of the little ways she was rebelling out of London and back up here.

Alex leaned towards her and whispered, '£5.99 at the post office, *vin du courrier royale*.'

'It's nice. I'll have to get some myself.' She cast a glance up at him and her cheeks flushed as she looked away and tucked a curl behind her ear. She concentrated on eating her dinner for a little while, then, seemingly abandoning her meal halfway through, she pulled the locket towards her. 'Is this ready now, d'you think? Can we get into it?'

'You can give it a go if you want,' said Cassie. 'Might not be quite ready, but you're welcome to try.'

Elodie nodded, then she took hold of the necklace, and cupped it in her hands.

Before, when they had pulled the necklace out of the tomb, Elodie had been jittery, worrying whether they would find bones or something inside it. Now, when all she held in her hands was a simple yet heavy locket, all she could think about was the memories that seemed to tinge the attics.

Ben still had Alex's smile and Alex's dark blue eyes, and, although his hair was longer, he seemed as familiar to Elodie now as Alex did. To be truthful, when Alex had leaned into her and whispered about the wine, she'd had a hard time stopping herself from grabbing him and dragging him upstairs to one of the bedrooms.

And that really confused her, because she still didn't know if it was Georgiana's feelings for Ben, or her own feelings for Alex that had come to the surface.

'Are you going to open it then?' Alex's voice interrupted her thoughts.

'Like I say, the hinges might need a little more work.' That was Cassie, through a mouthful of beef swimming in gravy.

'I think the hinges will be fine.' Elodie's voice was steadier than she thought it might be. Alex moved closer and she could sense the excitement in him as well. She could also sense his breath tickling her skin. *Oh, God!*

Elodie closed her eyes briefly, then opened them and dug her fingernail into the little gap where the two halves of the locket came together. She gave it one little wiggle and it sprang open. If she had expected to see two miniatures in there, one of Georgiana and one of Ben, she would have been desperately disappointed. But what she did see, against a background of black velvet, were two locks of hair – one fair and one dark, plaited together with a red ribbon.

She put her hand up to the nape of her neck, thinking

for a moment she was still wearing Georgiana's red ribbon. Then she saw Alex make a little movement and dragged her attention away from the locket – just long enough to see his hand go to the nape of his neck the same way as hers had.

He was staring at the locket, and then, seeming to sense that she was looking at him, he turned his head towards Elodie and fixed his gaze on her.

And she found it impossible to drag her eyes away from his.

'Oh, that's interesting!' Cassie said. 'I wonder who hid that away. Perhaps Georgiana had a secret lover, all this time.'

Elodie was vaguely aware of a clatter as Cassie pushed the high stool away from the breakfast bar and jumped off it. She padded around and leaned in between them to see the locket more closely. 'Well, which one was Georgiana's hair? Is she blonde or dark? See, that's another mystery we need to solve. How exciting! She's blonde, I guess, if that's her painting upstairs. I just hope she's *this* blonde, a nice, bright shade, like yours, Elodie; not a dirty, grubby, dishwater blonde like she looks up there. I mean, I know she's all flaky and everything at the moment, but still.'

Elodie opened her mouth to reply, but Alex answered instead. His voice was quiet and Cassie, bless her, probably didn't even sense the undertone there.

'Georgiana was blonde.' He was still looking at Elodie. 'Don't you think?'

'More than likely,' she replied, carefully. He simply nodded and at last the spell was broken. He looked away and made a big fuss of standing up and collecting the plates and taking them all to the dishwasher.

'Coffee?' he asked, with his back to them. 'Or perhaps more wine?'

Elodie cleared her throat. 'Not for me thanks. I'll have to get back to the cottage.' She reached out and snaffled her magazine, her heart pounding to think of what she had concealed in it.

'But weren't you going to see the duelling pistols?' asked Cassie.

Elodie shook her head and stood up. 'No, it can wait. I think I've had enough excitement for one day. I'm just happy to have seen the locket open. Don't worry about that casserole dish, I'll get it next time.'

'When will that be?' Alex's head was bent over the counter as he rubbed away at a splash of gravy with the corner of a cloth. He still, it seemed, was refusing to look at her.

'I don't know. Not tomorrow. And not the day after as I'm with Delilah. It'll be after that some time.' It was the world's woolliest answer and she knew it.

'Okay.'

'Okay.' Elodie tried to smile at Cassie but she knew it didn't reach her eyes. 'I'll leave the locket here, it's a shame to take it away from everything.'

Cassie was staring at her. 'What have I missed?' she asked, looking from Elodie to Alex and back again.

'Nothing,' they both said together. Elodie could feel herself colouring, and she turned away, heading towards the door. 'I'll see myself out,' she called over her shoulder.

She wasn't really surprised when nobody answered her.

Chapter Ten

When Elodie had opened that locket, Alex had no idea what to expect inside it. He'd wondered if there was perhaps a watercolour of Georgiana or pictures of her parents, or even some of those silhouettes that were very popular around that time.

He had never imagined there would be two locks of hair plaited together, nor that one would be blonde and almost the identical shade of Elodie's hair, and one would be dark. And he definitely hadn't known they would be tied with red ribbon.

So how on earth had he remembered handling those two locks of hair, and tying the ribbon around them?

He somehow knew he'd taken a pair of scissors and cut a curl from underneath a girl's loosened hair, and the girl looked a hell of a lot like Elodie. And then he'd seen her take the scissors and lean into him with a smile on her face. He had felt the cold edge of the scissors against his neck and heard the quick *snip* as she took a piece of his hair and held it out to him to inspect.

'Now, may I take your ribbon?' he'd asked her, his eyes mischievous.

'Of course.' She pulled the red ribbon out of her hair and handed it to him.

'And now the scissors again, please.'

'What are you going to do?'

'What are we going to do, you mean? Watch me.' He grinned and straightened the ribbon out. 'I'll hold it taut, if you cut a piece off the end. And this is where I need your help. We need to plait them all together – the ribbon and our locks of hair. Bind them tightly, my love.'

Georgiana giggled and between them, they twisted all three items together and he tied the final knot, raising it up and kissing it before handing it back to her.

'Why did you do that?' she asked, smiling.

'So my love will always be entwined within it. It's a love-knot, you see.'

Her eyes sparkled and she handled the bundle tenderly. 'I have the perfect place to store it.' She drew a silver chain out of her bodice, and attached to the bottom of it was a silver locket. 'It will hide in here until I can tell the world I'm yours.'

'My sweet Georgiana.' He tilted her chin up and kissed her gently. 'I would fear for you if our secret was discovered as we are now. I have some money put aside, and as soon as I have enough to help us disappear, I shall come and fetch you.'

'Will you come for me under cover of the stars?' she teased. 'As you always do?'

'I'll come for you by moonlight. And I'll lift you off your feet and seat you before me on Blaze. Then we'll ride away together and nobody will ever find us.'

'I can't wait for that day.' Georgiana moved towards him. 'But until then I will at least have part of you close to my heart.' She lifted the locket up and he opened it and placed the love-knot inside. It closed with a tiny snap and she covered his fingers with hers.

'You don't have part of me close to your heart,' he whispered, 'you have all *of my heart.'*

'You have my heart too. And yet, I wish you had something tangible as well.' She frowned, then smiled. 'I know – here – take the rest of this ribbon and cut it in half. It's more than long enough. Then you'll have something to keep as well and I shall be happy knowing that part of me is travelling with you.'

'Very well.' There was a snip as the ribbon fell into two

pieces. Georgiana reached up and fixed it in his hair, tying it back at the nape of his neck; his skin tingled with her touch and he could feel her soft breath as she came closer. 'Let me do the same for you,' he said.

Georgiana moved closer to him, but instead of reaching behind her, he took her face in his hands, the ribbon dangling from his fingertips. He leaned down towards her and her hands snaked around his waist. She began to tug his shirt out of his breeches, and slipped her hands between the waistband and his skin, giggling softly against his kisses. Her hair was still loose, and the ribbon was soon forgotten by both of them ...

When things appeared to be getting *very* interesting, Alex found himself sitting at the breakfast bar, staring at Elodie, and both their hands were at the nape of their necks, as if they were feeling for a ribbon, or touching the part where a lock of hair had been cut away and plaited together over two hundred years ago.

What the hell was that all about?

Elodie had always been a bit – well, he wasn't sure how best to describe her – weird? Strange? Psychic? All Alex knew was that ever since they were children, she'd seen things that no one else had.

She didn't talk about it much. Even in a small village like Hartsford, there were bullies and kids who wanted to be unkind to others. Elodie very much wanted to avoid singling herself out for that one, already having the stigma of being best friends with the heir to Hartsford Hall. She had, very wisely, kept quiet most of the time. Alex only knew because she asked him once who the children were in the nursery, and why one of them wouldn't play.

They'd been about seven years old at the time and it had been about four o'clock in the afternoon, one dreary spring day when the sun wasn't quite warm enough to tempt them out for too much longer. Elodie had fallen off her bicycle and grazed her knee. They were closer to the Hall than they were to Elodie's parents' cottage, so they'd gone inside the Hall to search out a sticking plaster. By the time they found one, it had, inevitably, started to rain and they decided to stay in.

There was a selection of puzzles and games and books and things in the old nursery, as well as a scalextric track, a train set and Alex's great-grandmother's old dolls' house. They had free rein throughout most of the house and automatically gravitated to that big, airy room at the top of the stairs.

Elodie had pushed in front of Alex, but then she had come to a sudden halt in the doorway of the nursery room. She stood for a moment and tilted her head to one side as if she was watching something or listening to someone.

Then she turned to Alex, her face full of fury. 'Well I'm afraid I don't think that's fair, do you, Alex?'

'Think what's fair?' He peered into the room over her shoulder.

'That horrible girl playing with the dolls' house and ignoring me. I'm afraid,' she said, turning back to the room, 'that Alex is here, and as he will own this house in the future, you have to let us play. It's the law.' There had been another pause, then she had nodded her head graciously. 'Well that's all right, then. I understand.' She turned back to Alex. 'The other children said we can play with them. They said that other little girl isn't usually here and she mustn't know you.' She stepped to one side and pointed at him. 'See? Everybody *else* here knows that this is Alex, don't you? We can all play together nicely, can't we?'

Then she had ushered him in and he had skulked in a corner well away from the dolls' house, hoping that "they" wouldn't bother coming anywhere near him.

So, knowing that and knowing that look on her face when

they had been sitting together, Alex had no option but to assume that she had seen at least some of what he'd seen just now.

It was either that, or God knows what kind of mushrooms she had put in that casserole.

'So let me get this right,' Cori said in her lovely Northumbrian accent. 'You stole that painting from Alex's attic and brought it down here to London under cover of darkness?'

'I didn't really steal it,' Elodie defended herself, passing little Kitty some horribly garish toy. 'Cassie knew, so that makes it okay.' Kitty's hair was as bright as Cori's – that gorgeous shade somewhere between gold and auburn that people who have it hate, and people who don't, want.

Cori bent over to retrieve a ball and her hair tumbled in a beautiful red curtain over her shoulders, half-covering her face. Elodie had had her own hair bobbed to mark a new start when she moved back to Suffolk and had bitterly regretted it. It was shoulder length now, but it would be a little while before it would tumble like Cori's again.

Cori rolled the ball back across the floor to her daughter and sat up. She sank into a mound of cushions on her squashy sofa and picked up her coffee cup. Then she looked at Elodie and shook her head, trying not to laugh. 'And may I ask why you stole it in the first place?'

'I didn't steal it! I wanted to get it restored as a surprise. The estate was a mess after the storm and I wanted to do something nice. I don't mind how much it costs, but I thought Simon might …' she trailed off, looking at Cori hopefully.

'I'm sure Simon will, but I don't know how long it'll take him.'

'Thank you.' Elodie smiled and, matching Cori's position, sank back into her own seat. Cori had a slight obsession with cushions and nothing in her enormous mews house in deepest Kensington had matched anything else for as long as Elodie had known her. But strangely, that seemed to suit her.

'Are you staying down here for long, or was it a whistle-stop tour just to fence the goods?' asked Cori.

'Whistle-stop,' she admitted. 'I'm heading back now. I'm at work tomorrow.' Elodie pulled a face. Delilah would know for sure there was something going on when she saw her the next day in the café. She often told Elodie she had "one of those faces". 'It'll take about three hours to drive home, so I need to get off.'

It was Cori's turn to pull a face. 'I don't envy you the drive,' she said, 'and I don't like you calling Suffolk "home", either. I got too used to you being here. Do you think you'll come back? I'm sure the theatre company would have you back like a shot.'

'They would, but I don't know if I'm ready to uproot myself again. I'm just getting established back in Suffolk, you know?'

Cori nodded sagely. 'After *how* long? Well, I'd like to ask what he's called, but I won't. You'll tell me when you're ready to. Though I suspect it begins with an "A".'

'Hmm,' replied Elodie, noncommittally. She didn't want anyone, even Cori, to know what was going on until she knew for certain herself. The thought of that broken and empty tomb was still haunting her, and not in a way she was used to.

Elodie drove home to Suffolk via her old house near Wandsworth Common. Well, maybe it wasn't technically on her way – in fact it was a long way *out* of her way – but she made it her business to ensure she went past it.

The street was part of that wonderful grid that someone had imaginatively christened the Toast Rack. She'd loved it, but she didn't miss it. She went slowly past the house, which she knew would be deserted at that time of day, and parked up opposite. She had never really known her neighbours that well. There were some stay at home Mummies and some workaholics and as she never fitted into either category, their paths tended not to cross. So she knew nobody would really recognise her, and her Range Rover was good enough to blend in with anything they had in the street visitor-wise.

As she stared at the huge white house, Elodie couldn't help but compare it with her cottage in Hartsford. The cottage might have fitted into the first two floors of the London house rather neatly and still have had room to spare. Elodie smiled at the memory of the ghostly old man who had drifted around the marital home and hoped that he was keeping Piers and his new girlfriend company.

The worst part of sharing with the old man had been the fact that he used to move things around. Which wasn't so bad for her – sometimes she saw him do it – but for Piers it would be terrifying and, she imagined, it would have been the same for whichever girl had moved in; because one of them would have done. Piers was no good at being alone and the girls he was 'carrying on with', as Margaret said, would have been desperate to live there. So Elodie sent a little thought message to the old man, wishing him well and telling him to keep up the good work. Then she smiled and thought again of her cottage at Hartsford. Suffolk really was home, despite Cori's misgivings.

She quashed the little part of her that felt like the idea of home might have something to do with Alex – after all, Cori had relocated to London from Northumbria and was happy to make her home there now. But she had found Simon, hadn't she?

Putting the Range Rover into gear, Elodie pulled away, just as she began to wonder if it really *was* Alex she was drawn to, or if it was Georgiana's memory of Ben. Because that was the most confusing part.

'There's still a terrible mess in that church, so I hear,' Delilah told Elodie the next day. Elodie was leaning against the counter in the café, lusting over the cakes she had just brought through from the kitchen. There was a spectacular three-layered concoction that had fluffy cream on the top and chocolate sprinkles which was, quite literally, making her drool.

Delilah saw her looking at it and moved it out of her covetous reach. 'Cappuccino cake. Chocolate and coffee and something special in the bottom layer.' She winked and Elodie knew the something special probably involved alcohol. 'And it's to serve twelve people, all right? Not *one* Elodie. Twelve *customers*. Twelve *paying* customers,' she continued as Elodie opened her mouth to protest that for four days a week she was, technically, a customer, rather than an employee.

Elodie shut her mouth again and moved around to the coffee machine. She gave the milk nozzle a desultory wipe with the cloth and Delilah looked at her and raised her eyebrows.

'You want to tell me what's wrong?' she asked. 'Because you've been moping around all morning.'

'I'm not moping! I'm thinking. I'm thinking about what you said and the fact the church is a mess.'

It was a lie of course, and Delilah picked her up on it straight away. 'I only mentioned the church a few minutes ago. Try again.'

By now, of course, the story of the missing body had flown around the village and Delilah had even had some tourists come in that morning and ask where the place was that the vampire had escaped from. Goodness only knew who was spreading that sort of tale and Elodie had a feeling Alex wouldn't be very happy about it. Maybe if it was nearer Halloween, he could have capitalised on the story – but the middle of the summer didn't do a great deal for the undead trade.

Elodie sighed. 'Well it's not just the church. There were a few things we found in that tomb and we have no idea what relevance they have to Georgiana. There's a locket with two lots of hair in and one of the locks might be Georgiana's, but I'm struggling to see how it all fits together.'

'Well maybe someone put them there so they would be found later on. Maybe somebody knew something nobody else did.' Delilah straightened out the jam pots on the shelf. She made all her own jam.

'Do you think that's likely?'

'Do you really think the body disappeared or do you think it was never there in the first place?' Elodie couldn't answer that one, and Delilah continued. 'Was there anybody else who might have had access to it all? I've seen the picture of Georgiana's father and I don't think he looks like a pleasant man, whatever number Earl he was.'

Elodie smiled, ready to tell Delilah the Earl's full title, when the bell rang above the door and they both looked up. Her heart did a little lurch as Alex came through and paused before he stepped fully inside. Today, he was wearing a white tee-shirt that was very close-fitting and stretched across his chest in a way that did funny things to Elodie's insides. He stood there, filling the doorway and looking straight at her, his gorgeous hair dishevelled as usual and those intensely blue eyes mesmerising her.

For one horrible moment, she thought he had discovered the painting was missing and he was coming here to accuse her of stealing it. Then she saw the dark shadows under his eyes, hidden a little by his tan, and the way he stared at her like he wanted to ask her something but didn't know how to, and she couldn't help herself; she stepped out into the tea room and walked up to him.

'Is everything okay?'

He stared at her for a moment and his arms came across his ribcage as he hugged himself. 'No. I really think we need to talk. Don't you?'

Then he moved his hand and drew a locket out of his pocket. It was of course the one from the tomb and her heart lurched again. She made a noise somewhere between a cough and the sound "hrmph" and then she couldn't say any more.

'I think we need to compare some information. Because I have a feeling this means more than we first thought.'

Chapter Eleven

Elodie was standing there, looking pale and twisting a pink cloth between her fingers.

After a moment or two, she said: 'It might be a good idea. But—'

'I'm sure I can spare you for a little while.' Delilah lifted the jug from beneath the coffee percolator and filled up two mugs. She pushed them across the counter and smiled. 'Milk and sugar over there. Elodie knows where they are.'

'Black is fine.' Alex didn't take his eyes away from Elodie.

'Fine for me too.' Elodie turned around, collected the mugs and handed one to Alex. 'Tea garden?'

'Sounds good.'

Elodie nodded and led the way.

Once they were outside, Elodie chose a table over in the far corner. It was in the shade of a weeping willow tree and had trellis after trellis nearby, covered in dainty pink roses and creamy golden honeysuckle. With the scents of the flowers and the lazy buzzing of the bees as they flitted from lavender bush to lavender bush, it was hard to imagine two days ago such a horrendous storm had hit the village.

Elodie laid the pink cloth out neatly in front of her and began to fold it up into tinier and tinier squares – anything, it seemed, to avoid looking at Alex. He reached out and put his hand on top of hers. She jumped a little, but stopped twitching with the cloth.

Her hand was cool and soft and Alex didn't want to move his away from it.

But he did and cradled the mug instead and decided that the best thing to do was just cut to the chase. 'So are you going to tell me what you saw the other day, or do you want me to go first?'

Her head bobbed up. 'In the kitchen? With the locket? You saw it too?'

'Yes.'

'Oh.' Her rosy lips formed a perfect little circle. For a moment, he was rather distracted by those lips. He couldn't shake the memory of them on his, all those years ago. But he blinked and forced himself to look over her shoulder instead.

He could see the church from here with its tumbled-down roof and it gave him the incentive to continue. 'I think we both remembered something odd that evening.'

'Was there a red ribbon in what you saw?'

'Yes.'

Her eyes flickered and she stared into the coffee. 'It's not the first time I've seen – them. Us. Like that.' She raised her eyes and for the first time he saw fear in the clear blue depths. 'It started in the church with the storm. I saw – things – happening. To do with the pistol and with the locket and sort of remembered things that I had no idea about.' She shook her head. 'I know some people think I'm odd because of what I see, but I can handle the *usual* stuff – the children in the nursery and the man in my old house and that old woman that toddles along the high street, just outside here. But I've never seen anything like that. I've never felt like I was *part* of it before. Never felt like it had all happened to me. And it's terrifying, to be honest. I haven't quite figured it out yet.' She shoved the mug to one side and the black liquid sloshed onto the wooden table top and began to drip down between the slats. She sat back in the seat and looked at him as if he could offer an explanation. He couldn't.

He tried to put the idea of an old woman wandering unseen along Hartsford High Street out of his head and concentrate on the Georgiana stuff instead. 'Okay. So you saw pictures or whatever it was about the locket.' He looked at her and raised his eyebrows, a silent plea that she should be honest with him. 'And you saw a love-knot being made.'

'With that red ribbon,' she confirmed quietly. 'And your hair – or his hair – was dark and mine – or hers – was blonde and we plaited it together.'

'And then they halved what was left,' he said. 'Yes?'

'Yes.' She took a deep breath. 'And another time, they were ...' Her voice trailed off and she dropped her head again, poking at a knot hole in the wood as the colour rose in her cheeks.

Alex nodded, his stomach churning. He knew he'd have to press buttons that had long since been unpressed. 'What else did you see in that snapshot we both experienced?'

'It started to get ... intense,' she admitted. Then her head came back up, her chin lifting a little. 'And that's why I had to leave. I hope you understand why now.'

Alex nodded. 'I didn't want you to go. But I was pleased you did.' He frowned. 'I don't think that came out right. I'm sorry.'

'No, it's fine. I wanted to stay with you. But I couldn't. You know?' She looked down again and her cheeks flushed to match her cloth. She splayed her hands out on the table and seemed to find her fingernails very interesting to study. 'If I'd stayed, I didn't know what we would do. Us, I mean. Me and you. God. I'm making a mess of this, aren't I?'

'No. No, you're not. It was like watching – us – you know – back when ...' There. It was out and he couldn't take it back.

Elodie blanched. 'Exactly. That's the first time I saw – *it* – happen though. Lucy interrupted them another time, or it might have got to that point sooner.'

'Lucy? Little Lucy under the stone angel?'

'Yes. She found them in the attic together.'

Alex shook his head. 'Why now? Why are we seeing these things? Remembering these things? Lucy! Good grief.'

Elodie looked as if she was about to say something else, then changed her mind. However, he, for one, was pleased things were out in the open. It seemed as if Elodie was relieved too; she leaned across the table and rested her chin in her hands and fixed her eyes on him. For a moment he was swimming in their bright blue depths – and not for the first time. But despite what they were feeling now, all that had to remain buried in the past, that long ago summer. He couldn't take the chance of it all going pear-shaped again.

'I've been thinking about it all,' Elodie said, bringing his thoughts back to today. 'I've been thinking a lot. Sometimes it happens when we're in the exact same position or the exact same place as Georgiana and Ben were. That's his name, by the way – Ben. It's like it's all a recording, and we're the projectors. We're reliving their memories – they must have saturated this place with their emotions. The storm and all that electrical charge boiled it over. Sometimes it's just like a flashback, just at that moment where you sort of zone out and daydream. When I was in your bath, I relaxed and half fell asleep, and I saw them meet. Georgiana and Ben – the first time they'd met properly on the Faerie Bridge and it was like I was her. I could feel everything she felt, see everything she saw. It was so real.'

'How strange.'

'Yes, and I think you're involved because you are part of the Hall's history and linked to Georgiana; and I'm involved because – well, I'm just like that.' She pulled a face. 'Some things you don't like to share too much, but Hartsford is *me*. You know? Much more than London ever was.' She lowered her eyes. 'Even with whatever went on before I ran away down there, my heart never left here.'

Alex nodded, leaning towards her and putting his own chin

in his hands. 'That sort of makes sense. And you admit now you did run away? It wasn't just an offer too good to miss?'

'Oh, I ran all right. But you know that I had my reasons.' She looked up at him and their eyes drilled into one another, until she looked away first. 'I didn't tell you about any of the other times I saw Georgiana and Ben. When we were in the church and I touched the locket; it was like a flashback to the first night they ever came across each other. Do you know, the impression I got was that he was a highwayman and it was uncanny – it was as if their souls were bonded together. I mean, does that even *happen* in real life?' She looked at him as if he could offer an explanation.

With you it did, he wanted to say.

But instead he shrugged. 'Maybe.'

'I saw them in the attics as well.' It seemed as if now she had started, she couldn't stop telling him. 'But Cassie came in, just like Lucy did, and we were in the same places as they would have been. And when it happened with the love-knot, it was because we were both concentrating on it. And it meant a lot to both of them. But other times, it's just Georgiana's memories, like I'm flitting in and out of her life. Oh God, just to know that you *understand* it all! It feels so much better.'

'I do understand.' Alex reached across to take her hands in his, properly. She didn't resist, and he squeezed them. 'If we can talk it through, it might help us make some sense of this whole damn business.'

'I just want to find out where Georgiana is, and if this is what I've got to do, I've got to do it. You know I asked you about Jasper?'

Alex thought how right her hands felt in his, then nodded. 'I do recall that, yes. But then you had an incident in the mud.'

'Well forget about me and my mud-wrestling. I saw

Jasper too. He was in the coach with Georgiana, and then something Ben said made me think about the way he died. Jasper's got that big fancy monument in the churchyard and the other family members have huge memorials; pointy ones and the like.'

The 'pointy monuments' Elodie meant looked a little like draped urns sitting on top of miniature Cleopatra's needles. Georgiana's parents had one, but Georgiana had her marble monument in the church itself, and Lucy had her little angel. But: 'I don't see the relevance?'

'Jasper disgraced himself and the family by being an idiot, didn't he?'

'According to legend, yes.'

'But he got a massive monument and an advert in the paper to hide whatever he was supposed to be guilty of. And Georgiana was given a huge white marble thingy, even though she's not inside it and it seems she was having a love affair with a highwayman.' She looked at him. 'That behaviour wouldn't have endeared her to many people in that era, especially not her family. So, I'm wondering if perhaps they wanted her to be seen as an absolute angel. When every piece of evidence pointed to the fact she wasn't anything of the sort.'

'Maybe.'

'In that day and age, she'd have been deemed a trollop for even sleeping with a man once. And who's to say that Ben was really going to be able to come back for her, despite how they apparently felt about one another? Maybe he just knew what to say to a girl?' She raised her eyes and they sparked. 'You know. To get a quick tumble with a wench?'

Alex's eyes flared back. 'Ben might have been a decent guy, just trying to do what was right. You never know.'

Elodie laughed shortly and removed her hands from his. She pushed her fringe out of her eyes. 'Regardless.

Naughty Jasper gets an article in the paper and an elaborate monument. Naughty Georgiana gets a nice marble tomb – it's like their memorials are inversely proportionate to the misdeed.'

'The greater the disgrace, the greater the "top show" as Margaret says.' Alex understood. 'And Lucy was only a kid, so she got a nice little angel and died before she could cause any scandal of her own.'

A frown touched Elodie's face, as if she was perhaps thinking of Lucy and any potential disgrace that may have manifested in a life cut too short. 'Indeed. Well, that's my theory anyway.' She shrugged her shoulders. 'It doesn't help us to know where to find Georgiana, but it might be a reason for her not being in the tomb.'

'It's better than grave-robbers, anyway.' Alex smiled.

'Much better.'

She pulled the pink cloth towards her and moved the mug back as well, then peered into the mug and pulled a face. 'Dead fly,' she said. 'I'm not drinking that.'

'Don't blame you. But if you promise to come to the Hall after you've finished up for the day, I'll make you a fresh one.'

'It's a deal.' Then her face shadowed a little. 'If I run out on you again, though, it's nothing personal this time. You know?'

'I know,' he said softly.

But part of him wished the same sort of vision would happen again and Cassie wouldn't be around and Elodie wouldn't run away from it.

'Maybe we should just glue ourselves to each other's hips for a few days?' Elodie suggested light-heartedly. 'Then we might randomly have a few more visions.' She shrugged again. 'It's just a suggestion.' She blushed and looked away, then busied herself with collecting the mugs.

It was a suggestion Alex kind of liked. But he didn't dare tell her that.

It felt so much better, having it "out there". At least Alex knew Elodie hadn't acted weirdly for no reason. It was odd, though, that he'd only felt it the once.

She put it down to the fact that, as Alex's psychic abilities were negligible at the very best, whatever emotional pattern had struck Ben that day had been strong enough to get through even to Alex.

She had only been half joking about the gluing themselves together idea. There was nothing she would like more than to try that and see what happened. And the idea of Alex in Ben's outfit was still foremost in her mind. She felt her cheeks burn even as she walked back into the café and put the two mugs on the counter.

'Well, at least you look a bit better now,' remarked Delilah. Elodie noticed, with regret, that most of the cappuccino cake had been devoured. Delilah suddenly grinned and pushed a box towards her. 'Here you go. Two slices for you. Thought you and Alex might fancy some later.'

Elodie stared at her. 'How did you know I'm seeing him later?'

'I wasn't sure,' Delilah said, 'but you've just confirmed it.'

'Oh.' Elodie had fallen into that trap neatly enough. Delilah laughed and went back into the kitchen, and Elodie violently rubbed the milk nozzle of the coffee machine again. The pink cloth was starting to smell a bit, so she wrinkled her nose and dropped it into the basket to wash later.

She wondered what would happen when she and Alex were back at the Hall and she flushed again at the memories it stirred up – Georgiana's memories, she reminded herself. That led her naturally enough onto the items they'd found in the tomb and why they might have been placed there.

Elodie knew she didn't like that duelling pistol much, and instead she tried to concentrate on the Bible and the key. She couldn't understand why anyone would have put a Bible in an empty tomb, and she wiped the benches with another cloth, trying to think of a reason. She thought all the way through serving three more sets of customers, and she thought again whilst having a cup of tea in her break.

The only thing she could come up with was that Bibles gave people comfort – almost like how the Ancient Egyptians had taken all sorts with them into the afterlife; perhaps the Bible was supposed to help speed Georgiana to her own afterlife.

But the family was a church-going family. They had their own church, for a start. And yet somebody believed that Georgiana needed that little bit of help.

You should go to Hell for what you have done.

The words were crystal clear and Elodie jumped, her cup paused halfway to her mouth. She looked around, but there was nobody near enough to have spoken so loudly. It had been a woman's voice, and it was now swiftly followed by another, hysterical, woman's voice.

To Hell? Then I look forward to it.

Her hands shaking, she put the cup down and stared at it, trying to steady her breathing.

The only thing to do was to try and find out whether Georgiana's memories were linked to that Bible at all.

And it seemed like the place she needed to be to understand that was the church itself.

She had changed from her café uniform of a black skirt and white blouse, topped with a gingham apron, and put on her jeans and a bluebell-coloured short sleeved top. She was standing at Alex's door, clutching Delilah's plastic box and waiting for him to let her in.

Cassie's motorcycle wasn't on the driveway, tucked away beside their wing, so Elodie assumed she was either out for a little while or she had gone back to university. Her question was answered when Alex appeared at the door looking a lot more relaxed than he had done earlier.

'Hey Eldorado.' He used the childhood nickname he'd made up for her. 'Cassie's gone back. She sends her apologies.'

'That's not a problem.' She stepped into the house as he moved to one side to let her get by. 'I think she was more interested in the locket than anything else and she got that open for us.'

'She did.' Alex ushered her into the kitchen where there was an aroma of fresh coffee. 'Told you I'd make a coffee, didn't I? Almost as good as Delilah's.'

She sat down at the breakfast bar and watched him work. 'We'll need forks too. I have cake. And at least I don't have to clean the nozzle here.'

'You can clean it if you want,' he said, nodding towards the kettle. 'But it's the old-fashioned type. I'll even let you put on your waitress outfit if you like. I've always liked you in gingham.'

'I'm fine. I thought you preferred the French Maid look anyway.'

'None of our staff will let me introduce that here. Unless you want to be the first? Be a trendsetter? Tell them the Look comes fresh from London. Perhaps we should try to recreate that wonderful marketing leaflet – only with you wearing a French Maid outfit. The customers would go wild.'

"That leaflet" was one advertising Hartsford Hall, and featuring Elodie, dressed as a milkmaid, holding up a plate of Delilah's cream scones and leering out at the potential customers. The scones were level with her chest area, so it looked, at a quick glance, as if she had two massive, round, inviting scones as boobs. Elodie thought she looked like a harlot, but everyone else, especially Alex, seemed to like it. He'd told her so with that same twinkle in his eyes, and she had almost crumbled.

But no.

She hadn't wanted to go there. Not again. And yet now, her feelings had changed …

Despite that, Elodie's stomach lurched a tiny bit at that comment – did he know she'd been to London recently? And, more importantly, what her purpose had been? The image of the girl on the old, flaking portrait came into her mind, along with the damaged marble tomb. She was so close to knowing what Georgiana looked like, yet so far. It was odd to think that Alex probably knew already. But if he knew—

'Alex, what did Georgiana look like to you? You must have seen her.'

She watched him as he paused and then brought the mugs and cutlery over to the breakfast bar. He sat opposite her and studied her. His gaze made her feel slightly hot and very exposed.

For want of anything better to do, she pushed the cappuccino cake over to him, and took a slice for herself. 'What? What is it?'

'If you want my honest opinion, she looks like you. That's why it was so weird – kissing – you know. It made me remember …' He trailed off and looked down at his mug.

She stared at him, although it shouldn't have been surprising, really. She lowered her own eyes and poked at her cake with the fork. 'Ben looked like you. I know what you mean.'

'Interesting.'

'So do you think they did look like us, or we're just imagining it? Even if it is their memories. Are we just putting each other in there?'

'Perhaps it's a bit of wishful thinking to complete the scene.' Alex half-smiled and took a sip of coffee.

'Perhaps.' Elodie felt a little uncomfortable with the psychology behind that one; she decided now was a good time to change tack. 'Can we take the Bible we found back to the church? I don't think we're going to get anything at the house about it. You see, I've been thinking about it and I only seem to remember things Georgiana did. And I doubt she put it in her own tomb, so perhaps – by some long shot – Ben did. And if he didn't. Well.'

'Well indeed. If neither Ben nor Georgiana placed the Bible there, there won't be any burning memories.'

'Exactly. Then it would be safe to assume it was put there to help her on her way. Whatever emotional moments occurred relating to that Bible, I would suggest the strongest grid would be by the tomb. The big question would be who *did* put it there. Because somebody clearly thought she was heading to Hell in a handcart.'

'Or somebody had overheard her being told that,' said Alex.

He had finished his cake. Elodie pushed the remainder of her slice towards him, defeated.

'Are you sure?' Alex looked at the cake. Elodie nodded. 'Okay. Give me a minute, then we'll head up to the church.'

'Sounds good to me.' And as Elodie watched him finish off every last crumb, she sent a little thought message out to Georgiana.

Please, Georgiana, if you're anywhere around us when we get to the church, it would be great if you could let us know.

The rest, she supposed, was up to Georgiana.

Chapter Twelve

The Hall was, thankfully, closed to visitors by the time they left the kitchen with the Bible wrapped in one of the big, clean towels Elodie recognised from the bathroom, and a torch in Alex's back pocket. Polly's altar cloth had been folded up and left in the lounge, ready to clean up and put back on display.

Alex had managed to get some scaffolders over, the day Elodie had been in London, and the church was as safe as he could make it, but not safe enough for the general public yet, he'd told her. They didn't want to run the risk of anyone following them and asking awkward questions.

'Oh, did you get anyone to cut up the tree?' Elodie asked, remembering how that had been Alex's plan originally. 'Because I haven't seen anyone up there today.'

'No. I can't get anybody to come until the end of the week, so I suppose we just have to live with it until then.'

'A lot of trees must have come down with the storm. All the tree people will be busy.'

'There's a queue, that's for sure, but I hope our name rises to the top of the list pretty soon.'

'You really don't like that tree, do you?' She laughed. 'You're very weird.'

'Not as weird as you,' he countered, with a twinkle in his eye that promised more if she dared to believe it, 'seeing your ghosts and your shadows and everything.'

Thankfully, they had reached the church and she didn't have to look at his twinkling eyes any more. Or imagine that martial-arts toned body in black trousers and black boots and very little else ... *Stop it, Elodie!* 'I can't deny I'm weird, but I can try to explain it,' she offered, crushing those images. 'It's not all the time. It's just sometimes.'

'Do they choose to be seen?' asked Alex. 'I mean, the *normal* ghosts. Not the things that have been happening to you lately.'

'Not all of them have the capacity to choose. Some are just recordings, doing what they always did. They haven't got any consciousness and they are the ones I see most of the time. The other ones who want to talk to you are few and far between.'

'And the ones like Georgiana and Ben?'

'That is something I've never experienced before. They're more like memories. You know. You've seen it too. So maybe you're weird as well?' She flicked a teasing glance up at him, and he laughed.

'Perhaps I am. But you never seem scared.'

'I'm not. I'd just like to know why it's suddenly happening like that.'

'Do you think they had a hand in the storm and the way it hit the church?' Alex asked as they looked up at it, surrounded by scaffolding. It was like an old drunkard being propped up by several pairs of helpful hands and escorted home from a cosy pub. Although perhaps that was a somewhat sacrilegious comparison.

'Poor old church,' Elodie said with a sigh, trying to focus on that instead of Alex and his midnight blue eyes. 'Who knows? It's definitely stirred *them* up, so it worked for them if so. Oh, well, let's give this a go.' She took the bundle from Alex and he opened the door to the church.

'It just seems awfully strange,' he commented, 'that a body can disappear, or was never buried and nobody has any record of it. I wonder if she even died here, on the estate. Or if it was elsewhere.' He shrugged and stepped into the church. His voice echoed back to Elodie. 'I just hope she sees fit to tell you where she is, if nothing else.'

'Me too,' Elodie murmured and followed him in.

* * *

The church was dark and dreary and cold. It also smelled quite bad and Alex wrinkled his nose. 'So this is what real damp smells like.'

'Apparently so. Ugh.'

'Maybe it's just as well we rescued Polly's altar cloth. I don't think the old girl would appreciate it staying in this environment.' Alex wound his way through the debris and went over to Georgiana's tomb.

He touched her cheek and tried to see the resemblance to Elodie that he had witnessed in the vision; there was certainly a little. 'She definitely looked like you.'

'Ben had your smile and your eyes. And your colouring. Dark hair.'

'Georgiana had your eyes and fair hair.' Elodie's eyes had always been the thing he'd found most attractive about her. It was her eyes, blue as the sky and hazy with cider, that had made him decide to whisk her away on Prom Night; but look how *that* had ended.

Even now, after all that had happened since then, and since he'd had a chance to know her as an adult, there was a hell of a lot he still found attractive about Elodie; but it had always been her eyes that drew him the most.

Elodie made a half-hearted attempt at a smile. 'Unless Georgiana and Ben had a child who is, somehow, related to one of us, I'm not sure how we look so much like them.'

'At this point, nothing would surprise me, but it's a theory. As far as we know, the Hartsford direct line died out with those three siblings.' Alex walked away from the shattered tomb and over to the pews where Elodie was busy unwrapping the bundle.

The Bible lay in the middle of the towel and they both looked at it as if it would jump up and growl.

'I just don't think Ben would have had a hand in leaving it

here. It was more than likely put in to save her eternal soul as you say.' Alex was curiously reluctant to touch it.

Elodie picked up the Bible and walked over to the tomb. She paused by Georgiana for a second, then put the old tome on top of the effigy. 'Oh, this is silly. I just don't think her body was here – ever. And I've dragged you here thinking we'll get a memory popping up – I'm sorry.' She looked around the church. 'But I can feel her watching us. If it's not her, it's someone very like her.'

'Can't you just ask her?'

'It doesn't work like that. They don't always communicate. I can just *feel* her. Over there.' She pointed to, of course, the darkest and dankest part of the church. She looked at Alex, her eyes burning into him. 'Can't you feel her too?'

'No.' He looked where she was pointing and shook his head. He turned away from the area. 'There's nothing. Nothing and nobody.'

Elodie looked back at the shadows, and her next words made Alex's skin prickle. 'Oh, my!' Her eyes widened. 'There's a *light* in there now. Alex! Look. It's a candle!'

And it was. Right at the back of the darkest part of the church, over near the altar, a single, orange flame flickered and danced.

'Come on!'

'Elodie, it's not safe through there!' Alex shouted after her, his voice echoing in the big, empty building. 'It's where the beam fell in.'

'But perhaps it's Georgiana and she's trying to tell us something.' She started to climb over the beam, despite his protests.

Elodie had been very single-minded when they were younger, and Alex had learned the hard way it was no use arguing with her. 'Elodie!' He began to follow her. 'Seriously?'

'Have you got your torch, please?' She held her hand out

behind her. He passed it across to her and watched her go further into the darkness towards the candle.

'Here we are.' Her figure dipped as she bent over and the torch beam swung around the area, lighting up the white plastered walls and flashing off the brass memorial plates. 'No sign of anyone living.'

'Nobody *living*?' Alex repeated.

'Nope. I'd like to think someone just paid us a visit.' She flashed the torch light around again and then settled it on the candle. The light wavered just a little and she made a funny little noise that seemed like a mixture of excitement and disbelief.

'What is it?'

'I wouldn't like to swear to it, but I think she's given us a clue.' Her voice was softer now. 'Look. What do you think?'

She stepped to one side and Alex reluctantly went towards her. The candle was, after all, still lit. What if the ghost was still there too? He just hoped he didn't come face to face with an eighteenth-century girl in there – that would be a very different kind of interesting addition to Alex's world.

'What do you see?' Her voice wasn't much more than a whisper. 'Just here.'

He stared at the area she was holding the torch over. She had it directed onto what had been a highly polished wooden surface. Now, the surface of the altar was covered in dirt and puddles of water.

Apart from that, there was a big dribble of wax next to the flickering candle.

'Can you see what it looks like?'

Alex looked at the dribble for a moment and then peered at it more closely. 'It looks like a letter. An old-fashioned letter. Cursive handwriting.'

'And can you see what letter it might be?' Elodie's body

was very warm next to his, her breath close to his neck as her hair tickled his cheek.

He tried to ignore the sensations her proximity set off around his body and peered at the wax. 'It looks like an *L*.'

'*L* for *Lucy*,' replied Elodie. He sensed her turn towards him and he swivelled his face to hers. 'Georgiana is telling us Lucy put the Bible there. I'm quite sure of it.'

'Elodie …' he began.

Then a bitterly cold whirlwind ripped through the church, swirled past them and blew the candle out in its wake.

Elodie gasped and caught her breath, and the inside of the church wavered and tumbled into disarray. Memories flooded into her consciousness – long-buried, mixed-up memories that were bubbling to the surface like lava. Lucy was there – Lucy was trying to talk – Lucy was tumbling into the chasm, forcing her thoughts into the gaps between.

'When you were happy, you were nice to me.'
'When Ben was here you were happy.'
'You're going to Hell.'
'I have to stop you going to Hell.'
'I love you.'

Lucy had a little basket on her arm. She was staring into the marble tomb; into the gaping void. Her father had said her sister was locked away in the crypt in her coffin and she wouldn't come up, into her beautiful stone sarcophagus, until it was a very quiet night and they could do it carefully with nobody watching. Lucy wouldn't even be allowed to see it. Nobody would. She didn't know why, but Father had to be obeyed. Always.

'These are for you,' Lucy muttered to Georgiana, to the lovely statue of her pretty sister on the top of it. 'I found some things in the woods and I think they're yours, but the

Bible isn't. The Bible is from me.' Her voice sounded odd and stilted. It had been so long since she had spoken to anyone that she had quite forgotten she possessed a voice and had to think very, very carefully about her words. She laid the Bible down. 'No. Not Hell. Not for you. Now you will be safe. And I am safe too, I think. And nobody must see these things. When the man comes to put you in here and you're all closed up inside, I can still look at you on the top. And you will be in the attic in your picture as well, and I will still see you.'

Lucy laid her hand on the white marble and closed her eyes briefly, then her restless gaze flitted around the church until she saw a candle dripping wax onto the altar. She walked over to it, picked it up and stared at the flame. Carefully turning the candle sideways, she drew a loopy "L" on the altar with the wax. She dripped wax on her fingers and pressed them into the "L". She thought it might be burning but she was numb everywhere and it didn't hurt, not really. Not much.

The candle wax was ridged and smudged with her fingerprints. 'There. Now God will know I was here and he will protect us both.'

She left the church with lighter steps and thought it would be all right now.

Chapter Thirteen

'Was that her?' Alex's voice was almost a whisper, his eyes wide and bright in the torchlight.

'I think it was Lucy.' Elodie felt that her expression must mirror Alex's. She was thoroughly shaken; the little girl's emotions had flooded her senses and she felt disorientated and scattered to the four winds herself.

'*Lucy*?'

'Yes, she left the Bible here. There was a whole jumble of memories that came through with that little whirlwind, and they all seemed to come from her. She had some other things too, but I couldn't see. The locket perhaps? And there was a coin ...'

'A coin? Like the one from the dressing up box?'

'Yes. It reminded me of one of Georgiana's memories. Ben told Lucy to go and find a magical horseshoe that would change into a coin in daylight. I think he left it deliberately for her. She was only ten, it was easy to buy her silence, I suppose.'

'Most ten-year-olds would take the money then blackmail you for more.'

'Perhaps.' Alex was joking but Elodie didn't want to discuss that. Now was not the time to mention the nasty little handwritten note she'd found under the floorboards.

'That's the Hartsfords for you,' said Alex wryly, 'above contempt in any way. Of *course* little Lucy wouldn't blackmail anyone.'

Elodie had to change the subject and quickly. 'She was sweet enough to give her sister a Bible to help her, though.'

'She was, yes. But I'm willing to bet Daddy was involved somehow with Georgiana's disappearance. He did his best to cover up Jasper's death.' He pulled a face. 'Hey, when I die, will you put me in a nice respectable hole or build a mausoleum to me? Or does that all depend on my sins?'

She tried to make light of it. 'You'll be in a mausoleum, definitely. But it won't be my job to put you in there. Your wife and children will have to sort that one out.' The words were in the air before she could stop them and didn't sound half so teasing when they were spoken out loud.

There was the briefest of pauses as Alex tucked the bundle under one arm. 'Thanks for reminding me I'm supposed to repopulate this place,' he said lightly. 'And to continue the line so I have kids to tidy up *my* messes for *me*. No pressure.'

'Oh, God, I'm sorry. I didn't mean it like that.' Elodie felt a bit sick; Cassie's conversation about Alex giving up everything to return to Hartsford came back to her. 'You don't need to do it very quickly. You can wait a bit. Can't you?'

'Seems like I'll have to,' he said. 'And it seems like it's up to me to continue sorting my family's messes out, both ancient and modern, as prescribed by my birth right. I can't even manage my own, so God help me with anything else. Never mind.' He turned to her and switched on a smile, all the more fake for its brilliance. 'Shall we?' He indicated the door and Elodie took a few steps towards it. Then she turned and retraced them back to Alex.

'I'm sorry.' Standing on tiptoe, she kissed him on his cheek. She was gratified to feel his arm come around her and hold her for a minute.

'So am I,' he said softly.

She knew she was, on the face of it, apologising for what she'd just implied and was sympathising with the position that Alex was in, through no fault of his own. But beneath that, for both of them, there were so many undercurrents that she thought she might drown if she gave way to them.

* * *

They walked back towards the Hall in silence, but somewhere along the path Alex's arm had come to rest about her shoulders and she hadn't shrugged it off.

She stopped, reluctantly, at the fork that led off to her cottage. 'Thanks for coming to the church with me to see about my silly idea with the Bible.'

'It wasn't that silly. It sort of worked. And at least you got your candlelight. That was quite special if it really was a message.' He looked at her, almost searching her face for answers to some unspecified question. 'I don't suppose you fancy coming back to the Hall, do you? We can finish that Post Office wine.'

'Oh, Alex! Normally I'd love to! But I really have to be getting home. I need to call Cori – I promised I'd search out some contacts to help her with her latest web commission and then talk her through a few things.' It was only half a lie. She had promised to do all of that, and she was *going* to do it; but she knew Cori would also be talking to her about the portrait and she couldn't risk Alex overhearing anything about that just yet.

'Oh. Okay then.' His face fell and his arm slipped off her shoulders. It was very cold without it there. Then, suddenly, his head snapped around to her, dawning horror in his eyes. 'Hang on – Cori? You're not going back to London, are you?'

'God, no!' she replied quickly. 'No. Not at all.'

'That's good.'

She chanced a glance up at him and was mesmerised by the fact he was staring right back at her, his sometimes teasing, sometimes unfathomable deep blue eyes framed beautifully by his long, dark eyelashes. She'd never really taken much notice of his eyelashes before. She'd known, on some level, that they were dark, like his hair. But she hadn't realised quite *how* dark ...

'No. No, I'm not going back.'

'That's *very* good.' He slanted another glance at her. 'Ever?'

'Forever is a long time. "Not for the foreseeable future" is all I can offer at the moment.'

'That's better than nothing.' The arm came back over her shoulders and he started steering her towards the cottage. 'I'd best take you home then. Do you want Georgiana's keepsakes, or do you want me to take them?'

They were on safer ground now. 'I think they'll be fine with me for the night. If that's okay with you?'

'It is.' His arm squeezed her a bit tighter.

She didn't protest.

'Simon says he would love to restore the painting for you.' Cori's voice was warm and, as always, Elodie noticed her rolling Northumbrian accent. She loved it, although she sometimes wondered how the Londoners understood Cori, but Cori never seemed to have a problem.

'Seriously?' Elodie was delighted. She sat down on her sofa and curled her legs underneath her. She watched the little ghost cat that scampered across her lounge every so often in pursuit of a long-dead mouse and smiled. The cocoa-coloured cat was one of Elodie's residuals. He obviously ran that way a lot in his lifetime, and he was quite a welcome companion. Quiet and no fuss. Even less fuss than a normal cat. And she had no vet's bills and no litter trays to clean out. Result.

She turned her attention back to the phone and cradled it more securely against her ear. 'Did he say how long it would take? And how much it would cost?'

Cori's voice came clucking down the receiver like a mother hen. 'Don't be ridiculous, Elodie. We aren't going to charge you a penny. And Simon says it will take …' She turned away from the telephone and Elodie could hear her conversing with Simon. His rich, cultured voice echoed in the background and then there was a clatter as Cori was back. '... about twelve to sixteen weeks.'

'Twelve to sixteen weeks! Bloody Hell Fire!' How was she going to conceal the fact that the portrait was missing for that length of time?

Cori laughed. 'You may need to 'fess up, my love,' she said, scarily seeming to read Elodie's mind. 'Oh, Kitty wants to say hello.' There was another scuffle at her end as she apparently scooped the baby up and held her to the receiver. 'Say hello to Aunty Elodie.' There was a silence then a lot of coo-ing and babbling – and yes, some apparent dribbling – from the baby. Elodie tried to maintain the conversation but it was rather difficult, then Cori took pity on her and returned to the phone.

Simon's voice came closer as he seemingly relieved Cori of the baby and faded again as he took Kitty elsewhere in that huge lounge. Elodie felt a pang of something that may have been broodiness, then dismissed the thought and moved onto other, safer subjects – such as web-design, the information Elodie had promised to find for Cori and gossip about their mutual friends.

Before she knew it, half an hour had elapsed. She came off the telephone with the golden glow that always came from talking to Cori, peppered with the niggling doubt that twelve to sixteen weeks was an awfully long time for Alex to remain unaware of the portrait's current residence. Elodie hadn't really considered much beyond that – how, for example, she would return the painting to the attic. She could always claim the ghost had left it at her cottage, she supposed. But she didn't think that even Alex would be convinced that a ghost had the power of fine art restoration.

Her eyes drifted to the bundle of items on the coffee table, still wrapped up in the towel, and she suppressed a little shudder as a nagging voice in her head reminded her that

that had all been in a grave. The voice of reason said it wasn't a grave as there was no actual body in there, so there was no contamination from decomposing whatever-ness; she stood up and moved over to the objects.

Elodie unfolded the towel and mentally checked the items off. Bible: check. They had reasoned that Lucy might have put it there to speed her sister to the afterlife. Locket: check. They knew what *that* contained. It still occupied her thoughts more than was probably healthy, and she couldn't resist picking it up and opening it again. And there was the key: check. What about the key? That was something they had to think about. And the duelling pistol. That was there as well, of course. Elodie refused to even touch that properly. She tweaked a piece of the towel so the pistol rolled to the side of it. And there, beneath it, was the silver coin that—

'Hang on!' She dropped the corner of the towel and her stomach somersaulted. The silver coin that she had last seen on the window sill in the attic. Tentatively, she picked it up and weighed it in her hands. It definitely looked and felt like the one from the attic.

'I'm pretty sure I didn't put *that* in there,' she said to the empty cottage, 'so I'm guessing *you* did.' She listened carefully. There was a whisper in the trees outside her window, which might or might not have been a giggle, but there was nothing else.

Alex felt like he was getting absolutely nowhere with the tree surgeons he'd engaged to deal with that oak tree.

'Can you at least give me an idea of when you'll be able to come? Yes, I realise you need to catch up on your backlog first. Yes, I appreciate a lot of trees came down. All I'm saying is … Okay. Fine. I'll wait to hear from you then.'

He pressed the end call button harder than was probably necessary and cursed the fact that, in this day and age, you didn't have the satisfaction of physically slamming a phone down on someone. How else could you let them know how displeased you were? At the minute, the bloody thing was blocking half the paths in the wood, and the younger trees it had caught on its way looked increasingly likely to come down as well. Alex wanted to open the estate properly again, and it didn't seem like it was going to happen any time soon.

He sighed and ran his eyes down the to-do list on his desk. There was a huge circle and a question mark against the issue of the church. He was still waiting for a call back from the insurance company about it. They too had been inundated and would get back to him "as soon as possible". He had started to feel like Hartsford Hall was way down on everybody's priority list except his own. He raised his eyes and stared out of the big windows at the estate. This first floor room had been his father's study, and Alex had adopted it as his office. It seemed right, somehow – but it was awfully tempting to watch the world go by at times. He'd never expected to be sitting here thinking about his home being a tourist attraction and what the general public would prefer in the way of estate walks or playgrounds.

Today, he could see the tourists passing by with their picnic bags and ice-creams and he could also see the odd one or two stopping at the roped-off entrance to the church and pointing at it.

It was rather an impressive ruin at the moment, but it deserved so much more than being allowed to fall into disrepair. Then he let his gaze wander over towards Elodie's cottage; she was working at Delilah's today and he missed her being around the Hall. He sighed again and looked back at the paperwork on his desk.

There was a sharp knock at the office door and he shouted, 'Come in!' suppressing the urge to just ignore it. He hoped it was something he could deal with quickly.

'Lunch break!' said a welcome voice, preceded by the most divine, mouth-watering smell. Alex jumped up and out of his seat before the owner of the words had much of a chance to step inside the office.

'Eldorado! You come bearing gifts? Please. Tell me you do.'

'I do. Delilah's lentil and tomato soup and a ham roll. Or a chicken one. You can have either. The other one's mine. Don't look at me like that, the soup is in takeaway cups. I haven't had to carry bowls here.'

'How come you've escaped?' He knew he was smiling. 'I've missed you today. I was just thinking about you.'

'Sure you were. And in answer to your question, I always get a lunch break. It's mine to do with as I please. So today it pleased me to come here. I felt bad about leaving you to drink the wine on your own last night. I have an hour then I have to go back.' She dipped her head and started unloading the food onto the filing cabinet, too late to hide the little pink blush that coloured her cheeks. That made Alex smile some more, and he cleared a space on his desk.

'We can sit here. Unless you want to go elsewhere?'

'I think it's a good idea to get out of the office personally, although I'm happy to do whatever. But I mean ...' She looked at the long window that he'd just been staring out of. '... you do have a balcony, don't you? With a table and chairs on it. Can we go out there?'

'We can indeed.' Alex got up and opened the doors, surprised at the warmth that flooded through the opening, mingling with the smells of the gardens and the woodland. Then he went back across to Elodie, placed his hands firmly on her shoulders, just to have an excuse to touch her, and steered her outside. 'You sit there, I'll bring the food. You've been serving people all morning.'

'Very true. Oh, this is so *nice*.' Alex followed her out,

balancing the cups and sandwiches expertly, and placed them on the table. 'I wonder why I don't do this more often.'

'You're welcome to.' He took the place opposite her. Delilah had even provided cutlery for them and it was very pleasant indeed, sitting there with lunch all cooked and Elodie's long, tanned legs stretched out in front of her, very close to Alex's. It didn't take them that long to demolish the whole meal. In the end, they decided to halve the sandwiches.

'It would be so easy to lose track of time and stay here all afternoon.' Elodie stared at the crumbs and the cups which they had plopped one inside of the other. 'I wouldn't dare do this regularly. Delilah would fire me for being too lax about my timekeeping. Anyway, part of the reason I came over today was because I had to return something to you. Look.'

She delved into the pocket of her black skirt and produced a small, silver disc. 'It's the coin from the attic. It appeared in the cottage with the rest of Georgiana's belongings, although I've no idea how. I certainly didn't take it away with me.' She blushed again and put the coin on the table. 'You might know a little more than me about it, but I think it's genuine enough.'

'I must admit, I didn't really look at it properly when I was up there. Let me see.' Alex reached over and picked it up. He turned it around in his hands, the sunlight catching off it and sending little flashes of light across the wrought iron table. 'George III and the date is about right. Yes. It *does* look pretty genuine.'

'Just imagine then – if that's the coin we think it is, Ben touched it. It was likely stolen from someone and left for Lucy to find under the guise of a magical horseshoe.'

'Amazing.' Alex turned the coin around again. 'I wish these things could talk. Then maybe we would know what happened to Georgiana.'

'These things *do* talk, but we can only hear them if the circumstances are right.'

'Well it's certainly not talking to me right now. I suppose I should be glad in some ways.' He dropped the coin onto the table.

'Isn't it frustrating?' Elodie threw her hands into the air helplessly and let them fall onto her lap. 'Lucy found the coin by the river and Ben must have left it there for her. It's a small part of the story but it seems like it should be so much more. Oh, well. We still have the key and the pistol. But then,' she said, laughing self-consciously, 'we still don't have Georgiana.'

'Not yet we don't. I do honestly think if the time is ever right, we'll find her.'

'That's a bit philosophical. Too philosophical for a lunch break. Speaking of which ...' Elodie looked at her watch. 'It's almost time to go.'

She stood up and Alex followed suit. He moved around to her side of the table and handed the coin back to her. As Elodie took it from him, her face started to go all fuzzy and the blackness swept in from all sides.

It was dark, a deep, velvety evening in late summer and the warmth of the day was still with them. They had managed to keep their liaison secret for nigh on seven months now, but it was becoming more difficult every day and the threat of exposure was a constant shadow hanging over them.

'Lucy showed me this coin,' Georgiana told him, 'and said it was true about your horse.' She laughed and placed it in the little purse she had dangling from her wrist. 'I don't know how you managed to fool her so, but I'm thankful it worked.'

'I have to be careful who I can trust. She's a shrewd young woman.'

'Too shrewd. She's camped out in the attic tonight, apparently hoping to meet you again. I discovered her in

there asleep and I took the opportunity to borrow the coin.' She shook her head. 'When she found me there the first time and showed it to me, I thought it was very fortunate she had not encountered me moments beforehand. Still, it's a lesson to me and I must learn to be more cautious and lock doors behind me. There are some things I'd never wish her to find.'

'It's always best to lock doors.' He reached over to her and pulled her closer. 'It doesn't do to be disturbed. Which is why being outside, making use of this wonderful balcony, is awfully convenient.'

'Nobody will disturb us out here. I've most certainly locked the door into the room. It's rarely used, but one can never tell. It's supposed to be Mama's sitting room, but she prefers to hide in her bedroom instead.'

'I'm grateful for your foresight. One cannot take too many chances.'

Something flitted past them and Georgiana ducked her head. 'Oh, these dreadful bats! I do wish they would stop attacking me!'

'The bats have as much right to be here as we do. Perhaps they have more right than I. I doubt they're attacking you, though. I've never yet seen one do that personally and I've met many of them during my endeavours. They're an interesting creature and perhaps one of the most exciting things to encounter during my work.'

'Oh, so you hold the bats in a higher regard than you hold me?' teased Georgiana. 'I'm most upset.'

'You, my love, were quite the most exciting creature I ever had the pleasure to meet. It won't be much longer, then we can get married and I can take you away with me. I've almost made enough money to look after you properly. It'll be soon – sooner if I can make it so!'

'I'm very glad to hear that.' Her lips found his in the moonlight. 'I don't know if my father will ever forgive me, but I don't care. He still hasn't forgiven me for the night I first met you. Jasper told him that for me to dance with you, as you'd asked, was our only option or we would have been penniless; perhaps even dead. Father, however, doesn't think my actions were befitting a lady of virtue at all.'

'I would like it noted that I did not steal your virtue that night. I'm severely insulted,' he said between kisses. 'I stole an Allemande. Like this. Remember?' He bowed to her and took her in his arms. They began to trace the steps out on the balcony. 'Dance with me one more time before I leave you for tonight.'

'Is there not a better way to say farewell to you? Come, let me show you.'

And she drew closer into the circle of his arms and placed her hands either side of his face. She drew his head down to hers and he didn't resist...

And this time, when the world shifted again, Alex was standing with Elodie on the balcony outside his office with their lips pressed close together and their arms around each other.

Chapter Fourteen

Elodie didn't pull away. Her eyes were squeezed shut and she wasn't too sure for a moment whether she was Elodie or Georgiana. And either Alex or Ben was an exceptionally good kisser. Which she already knew.

As her senses started to realign, she gradually opened her eyes to a bright, sunny afternoon and Alex inches away from her face.

'Alex!' she sort of croaked. 'I'm so sorry.' She let go of him and stepped away. Thank God there was a stone balustrade running along the edge of the balcony or she would have pitched right over the edge. She held tight to it, just in case.

'I guess they must have been up here too then!' He looked at the wall and she followed his gaze. For the first time, she noticed the decorative stepping up the side of the building. An athletic young highwayman would have no trouble clambering up there and shimmying along to the attic windows.

'So that's how he got into the attics,' she whispered. 'But because of Lucy hiding up there, Georgiana met him here instead.'

'Look, I'm sorry too.' Alex looked a little startled and she noticed with a pang of regret that he had stepped backwards as well. 'I dread to think what I might do if we're ever together and something more happens. I didn't stop myself that time.'

Elodie reached over briefly and dropped the coin on the table; she didn't want to stray too far from the balustrade. The coin certainly didn't seem so innocuous now. However, she was pleased he had said "didn't" rather than "couldn't". It was a small thing, but, like the coin, she felt it was significant. She just shrugged her shoulders, not quite sure what to say.

He *didn't* stop himself from kissing her. He therefore *wanted* to kiss her.

And that way danger lay.

'I think it's a good thing that it happened ...' *Hell, yes, it had been a good thing!* '... because it proves we can feel the same memories.' She hung on tighter to the balustrade in case she flung herself at him again. 'And you're a very good dancer. Where did you learn that? Oxford?'

'I've honestly never danced an Allemande before,' said Alex. 'I suspect Ben did everything.'

She nodded. 'It's just like a recording, isn't it? Their thoughts, their memories. Their actions.' She burned up from inside again, remembering his kiss and his embrace. 'That's what I'm telling myself anyway. I've had almost thirty years of seeing ghosts, and I've never ever felt threatened by them. Honestly, Alex.' But she couldn't help herself. She reached out and touched his arm. 'You, of all people, know what I've experienced over the years. You're the only one I ever talked to about it properly. It's the past. It's all shadows.'

'That kiss felt very much in the present.' His sapphire blue eyes smouldered into hers.

'And I didn't feel threatened.'

And she hadn't. She'd loved it. She'd loved coming to and being wrapped in his arms and with his lips on hers. But this was *Alex*, part of her said. She thought she'd stopped having a crush on him *years* ago. She'd stopped one warm night in July, in the Hartsford stables while the moon shone into the room and her world crumbled around her in a mess of sea-green taffeta ...

They were lying on the straw, the comforting, warm smell of hay and Hughie and the other horses surrounding them. They had taken it slowly. It had been Elodie's first time – she didn't want to ask Alex if he'd ever done it with anyone else, but the way his hands found all her secret places and the way his mouth tasted every inch of her made her suspect it wasn't.

'Oh, Alex,' she breathed, feeling like a Victorian maiden, her petticoats hitched up all around her, her knees bent up and him crushing the taffeta of her skirts with his body.

He had been as leggy and lithe as a young colt back then – and he'd made her gasp with pleasure as little fireworks shot around her body, and she'd clung onto him, shuddering into a climax that made stars and rainbows pop around her mind.

Afterwards, they had lain, their arms around each other, staring into each other's eyes, and kissed some more. His fingers had traced their way across her bare skin and she tingled everywhere he touched.

Then there had been a creak as the stable door opened and Elodie heard a giggle, then a lower-pitched laugh and some whispered murmurings. Somebody else had found the stables and they seemed to have the same idea.

She froze, unable to untangle her arms from his body or even curl up into a ball and hide like a tortoise within a taffeta shell.

'Who's that?' Alex had asked sharply. The voices stopped, and there was another, suppressed giggle.

'I could ask you the same thing,' replied a male voice, amused. The giggle came again and Elodie wanted to die, right there and then, right on the spot.

'You know who I am,' said Alex, raising up on his elbow. 'I reckon I've got more of a right to be in here than you have.'

'Reckon you have, Squire,' said the boy again. Elodie didn't miss the sarcasm in his voice and she closed her eyes in despair. It was Grant – one of the popular, sporty crowd. The giggle, then, belonged to Shona, his long-term girlfriend. Well, they'd lasted for two terms which was something of a record for both of them.

'Alex,' hissed Elodie, 'just get rid of them!'

'Hang on!' That was the girl – definitely Shona. She had a horrid, whiny voice and it was emphasised by the wooden stalls and cavernous spaces of the stables. 'Viscount Wotsit's got someone in here with him. Who is it?'

'There's nobody here!' snapped Alex. 'Will you two just do me the honour of pissing off?'

'Liar! It's Elodie Bright, isn't it? Gave it up to you at last did she? Little Miss Princess couldn't keep her legs together, eh? We always knew she was after you.' That was Shona.

Elodie, shocked to her core, sat up and stared at Alex. She was willing him to say something to defend her honour, like a proper Victorian Miss would expect.

Instead, he pressed his fingers to her lips and shook his head. 'God no, it's not Elodie,' he said over his shoulder into the darkness. 'I'd never do it with her. Now, piss off. It's nobody you know.'

Grant had whooped triumphantly. 'Sorry to disturb you then, Little Lord Fauntleroy. Enjoy, enjoy your tumble in the hayloft with your slag.'

Shona collapsed into giggles. 'Bet you don't dare tell the little jumped-up bitch that one!' she said. The sound of their laughter faded as they left the stable and clashed the door shut behind them.

'Well,' said Alex, breathing out a sigh of relief. 'That got rid of them.' Elodie saw his teeth glint in the moonlight that came through the window as he smiled down at her. 'Now, where were we?'

'Just fuck. Right. Off,' she said and slapped him hard across his face.

Elodie studied him as his eyes slipped away from her, a slight crease between his brows. She watched him while he ran his fingers through his hair and stared out at the estate, his eyes sliding past the fallen oak tree and towards the church.

And it was when he looked back at her that she realised she hadn't suddenly begun to feel this way about him again. She'd felt like that about him forever. She hadn't buried any of her feelings at all, not even after that fight in the stables. Not even when she was married.

'Alex—'

'Elodie—' He spoke at the same time. 'I'm so sorry about Prom Night – I've hated myself ever since. God, I've wanted to tell you so many times. I was an utter idiot. Absolutely stupid.'

'I hated you too. But why? Why did you say it?'

'Because I didn't want them calling you names. I wanted to protect you. I thought if they knew it was you in there, they'd never let up from the bullying. I thought I was cutting you some slack.'

'You weren't. You just made me feel like a second-rate slut. I thought you loved me. You said you loved me, and then we did it, and then you were telling them you'd never do it with me! You were my first, Alex. I wanted you to be my last.' Her voice suddenly caught on a sob, remembering that eighteen-year-old who thought her world had ended. How could she still love him so much after that? But she did. She did and she always had and there was no getting away from it.

'Oh, God. Elodie. Elodie, I'm so sorry. I hated it when you went off to London, but I didn't know how I could try and stop you. You wouldn't even speak to me!'

'I wasn't going to stay here and have them laugh at me, and you act like it was no big deal. I knew you'd had girlfriends before, but I'd never had anyone serious and I thought you were it.' She shook her head. 'I suppose I should be grateful. I got on that course down there and got into the theatre and had a good couple of years before – well – before I got involved with Piers. And when you and I fell out, I hated you with a passion! I really did.'

'I deserved it. But you know what I'm like – far too stubborn to admit my faults.' He shook his head. 'I'm admitting them now though.'

'Me too. I know I'm not perfect, and I need you to understand that some of it is a hangover from London.' Elodie dipped her head, feeling the heat rush to her cheeks. She knew she had come back to Hartsford a very different person and lost herself along the way. She didn't like it much. She'd loved London to start with, and she could probably have coped with Piers if he was the only issue, but one thing just fed into another and the enforced rest after the hospital stay had given her too much time to think. And, more precisely, too much time to think about Alex.

Now was as good a time to admit some of that as there ever would be. 'What happened is that London finally crippled me, what with Piers messing about, and my stupid asthma and all the corresponding rubbish that went with it. I had to be harder down there, but it wore me out. If I'd let myself stop for a second, or been kinder to myself, I think I would have cracked sooner. It's taking me a while, but I'm fighting back. Some of it'll be with me forever and I hate the fact I can't do anything about it. All I can do is make the best of what's left of me and try to put the bits back together.' There. She'd said it. She missed the old Elodie, the eighteen-year-old Elodie, but she had to begin to accept she'd never be the same person again. Too much had happened and she'd been broken into pieces because of it.

Alex reached out and took hold of her chin, tilting it up towards him. He smiled down at her slowly, his eyes warm. 'For what it's worth, I like you either way. I liked you before you went down there and I still like you, so that's good, isn't it? I changed too when I was away – and I wasn't in a good place when I came back; so I know exactly what you mean.'

'Thank you. I know you've had to deal with things I never

saw, and it can't have been easy for you either. I'm sorry.' A frown shadowed her face. 'I'm so pleased we talked; but I guess I really should go back to work now. I don't want to, but Delilah will be sending out a search party.'

Alex nodded and took his fingertips away. 'Tell her the lunch was very welcome.'

'I will. See you?'

'See you,' he confirmed.

It was progress.

Elodie almost floated back to the café. It felt so wonderful to have finally admitted all that to Alex, and she knew they had turned a corner.

'Enjoy your lunch, my dear?' Delilah asked, taking the plates and the cutlery from her and dumping them in the dishwasher.

'Very much so.'

'Did Alex enjoy his?'

'I think so, yes.'

'Good. Any more news on the church then? Someone was saying it's all roped off.'

'It is. Alex is having difficulty with the insurers, but I'm sure things will work themselves out. The tree surgeons seem to be missing in action as well. Alex is more bothered about getting rid of the oak I think.' She leant on the counter and put her chin in her hands. 'He really hates that tree.'

'It's very old. I think it's maybe a good thing it's come down now. If it was weak enough to fall down anyway, we should be grateful nobody was underneath it when it happened. A good gust of wind and – well – let's not go there.'

Elodie shuddered. 'You're right. It was lucky nobody was injured. It's a big estate and there are usually people everywhere. The river's gone back to normal, but there's a heck of a mess on the banks.'

'And that'll be another big job, I guess,' mused Delilah.

'But I think if Alex needs some help to clear that lot, he'll find volunteers in the village. There's a legend about buried treasure in that river you know.'

Elodie laughed. 'Yes, the legend about the Faerie Bridge. And I think I know how that started as well.'

'Really?' Delilah looked at Elodie, her eyes full of interest. 'What's your theory on that then?'

'I think it goes back to Alex's great-great something relation, Lucy.'

'Georgiana's sister,' said Delilah with a nod. 'You've met her, have you?'

She said it so matter-of-factly. Delilah knew about Elodie's gift anyway, so it was pointless trying to skirt the issue.

'Let's just say I've encountered her. Lucy found a silver coin by the bridge in the late 1700's. I think it had been hidden on purpose by someone to kind of buy her silence over something. She was very young at the time and she believed it was all to do with the faeries. I suspect she never found a giant pile of them like some would believe – it was hardly the Brantham Hoard.' Elodie referred to a Saxon treasure trove of ninety silver pennies someone had found in that Suffolk village in 2003. 'But it's surprising how tales evolve over the years.'

'It is. Well now. One silver penny. God bless her.' Delilah dropped her voice and leaned in to Elodie confidentially. 'This isn't common knowledge, but some say she was a little disturbed after her sister and brother died, you know.' She tapped the side of her head and pulled a face. 'Poor child. Her story tends to get forgotten whereas everyone knows about Georgiana and Jasper. She just gets remembered for dying young and being the end of the Kerridge line. It was some cousin that took over the Hartsford title after that. The lawyers found him in Paris, I think.'

'Lucy was disturbed?' Elodie couldn't remember anybody

else telling her that about Lucy, but she recalled Alex's tale about the French cousin. Trust Delilah to know about it anyway. Her family had worked at the Hall for generations. Some of the recipes she used in Coffee, Cream, Cupcake had been handed down for centuries. 'How come?'

'They said it had always been in her to some extent. Lucy had never been quite as rational as a normal child and it caused quite a bit of upset in the family at times, but it came out properly after Georgiana died. The child was distraught. Used to sit in front of the tomb for hours on end and talk to it.'

Elodie shivered. 'I used to do that too. And I'm not disturbed. I just wanted to hide from the bullies in there. I don't see how they can base the theory on her sitting by the tomb. She probably just missed her sister.' And, Elodie wanted to add, she seemed to have had a lot to do with trying to protect the contents of the tomb.

'The child used to see things in the woods as well. Around about that old tree you just talked about. I wonder if that's why Alex doesn't like it. What's it called? Genetic memory?'

'Yes. Perhaps. Interesting.' It was *very* interesting, now that Elodie knew Alex was experiencing Ben's memories. Looking at it from that perspective ... it was more than simply interesting.

Delilah wiped the bench down and continued. 'Lucy used to say there was a horseman there. They told her it wasn't possible. Then, the tale goes, she rambled a bit about highwaymen as the fever took her away, and that's how the legend of the horseman in the woods stuck. I've seen Alex on that black horse of his. He's the very image of a dashing highwayman, don't you think?' Delilah's eyes twinkled merrily. 'Cassie always loved the story of the highwayman when she was a babe. Asked for it all the time.'

Elodie knew that after Alex and Cassie's parents divorced,

and the former Countess went off to live in France, Delilah and Margaret – and her own mother – had more or less become surrogate mothers to the children. They'd loved them as if they were their own, and still did. Delilah smiled fondly at the memory now. 'Alex wasn't interested in the family stories. He was more for running about and climbing trees with little Miss Elodie, as I recall. Getting into mischief. Messing about at the stables with real horses. And asking when his mum was coming home.' She sniffed in disgust. 'They had enough to contend with in dear old Mama. We all did our best for those little 'uns.'

Alex's mother was but a distant memory to everyone, including her children. He was lucky he'd had other people around when he was growing up. They'd all swooped in and saved the family. 'You've been very good to Alex and Cassie, Delilah. I think you and Margaret and my mum did a great job between you. It's lucky we lived on the estate – Alex never had to come far to find us if he needed anything. He was always hungry – but then, we both were. My poor mum was forever making us sandwiches so we could take them out exploring! Then we'd pitch back up and expect dinner cooked for us too.' She smiled at the memory. Her mother still sent the odd food parcel from France for them – only it now included grown-up things like wine.

'Well, I never had any children of my own,' said Delilah, 'so they made up for it. And there's Margaret with five – so what difference did another couple make to her brood? And your mum just had you, and you and Alex are the same age and were inseparable from the minute you could walk. Cassie was just a natural addition.'

'I suppose so. You know, at first I loved London and the lifestyle down there – well, until Piers and everything else finished it off for me – but I know for sure that my heart is here. Definitely.'

'Definitely,' Delilah agreed. And as she turned away, Elodie wondered if that little smile she had on her face meant that Delilah thought Elodie's words were just a teeny tiny bit loaded.

Chapter Fifteen

Alex stood at the doorway to Elodie's cottage, flipping the silver coin over and over. She'd left it on the table at lunchtime and he'd pocketed it.

'I hope you don't mind me turning up?' he asked, and smiled down at her.

I just wanted to see you. But he didn't say that out loud.

'Not at all.' She stepped aside to let him into the cottage.

'I've got a proposition for you.'

Elodie raised her eyebrows and folded her arms. 'Oh, really?' she asked, leaning back against the door frame, a smile twitching around her lips.

'Really. It's a beautiful evening. D'you fancy a walk along to the Faerie Bridge? This coin got me thinking and I wondered if we could find anything else out if we went along to the bridge.'

'I don't mind at all. That would be lovely. Why don't you wait in the lounge? I'll just get some shoes on and I'll be with you in a second.'

'Okay. I'll not go very far.' He didn't want to leave her at all.

'I can't lose you in here.' Her voice came from the kitchen, combined with an odd clattering as she obviously knocked something over to get to her shoes. 'Bugger.'

Alex grinned and turned away, looking at the room; the shelves in the alcoves either side of the fireplace were full of books on history and costumes and vintage clothing. He pulled one down and flicked through it, looking at some fabulous gowns by Worth and imagining, unbidden, a picture of Elodie floating towards him in a gossamer white dress. In her hands was a bouquet of flowers and serenading her was Margaret on the organ and—

'Shut *up*, Alex,' he muttered, trying to close the pictures off. It was the image he'd had of Elodie that day she got married to Piers. He had tried to block it out, because in his head she wasn't walking towards Piers, she was walking towards him, Alex.

But the reality of the situation was, of course, that she had breezed past him, leaving nothing but a lingering scent of freesias and lilies and roses. He didn't know if the scent came from her perfume or from her bouquet, but he'd never been able to smell any of those flowers since in any sort of combination without having a little knife twist somewhere in his chest – around about where his heart was, funnily enough.

'It's not Elodie. I'd never do it with her.'

What an idiot – why had he even said that? And then he'd had to suffer the consequences for years. Had to watch her marry someone else.

He didn't think she'd even noticed him sitting at the back, that day.

And the London creep was standing all suave and smarmy by the altar, smirking at everyone as if to say, 'look what I'm getting, you bunch of country bumpkin losers.'

Of course, it was the guy's wedding day and he was entitled to be smirking. But Alex thought he was simply a tosser.

Alex had gone back to the Hall and got very, very drunk that night. It hadn't helped much at all.

He had hated his eighteen-year-old self with a passion.

'Ready.' Elodie walked into the room and jolted him out of his memories. Her eyes flicked to the floor as if there was an animal or something there that he was about to tread on and he looked down, following her gaze, but there was nothing to see. A little breeze whooshed past his ankle.

'He won't hurt you,' she said – but Alex wasn't sure if she was talking to him or the floor, so he held up the tome in his hand.

146

'Great book. Is this where you get all your inspiration from?'

'Oh, it's one of the places. It's a lovely book, that's for sure – this one's nice too.' She leaned across him to reach for a hardback, and she was so close that he could feel the heat of her body. He closed his eyes briefly.

'I got the inspiration for—' Then she stopped and shrugged, the book still in her hand. 'Yeah. You don't want to know that really. Wedding dress.' She wrinkled her nose. 'It's a pity. It was a lovely dress.'

'It was. Shame your husband was a tosser though.'

'Yes. A waste of a good dress.'

'So you're over him, then? No regrets at walking away?' It seemed that, once the floodgates of tosser-ness had opened, he couldn't stop himself. They'd more or less established that she was over him earlier, when they'd had that conversation on the balcony, but the devil inside him needed to hear her say it again.

'Well over him. And no regrets. But I didn't walk away. I drove at high speed. Picked up a speeding ticket on the motorway.' She frowned. 'If I never see him again it'll be too soon. Why, last time I was down, I just knew there was a different woman there and—' She stopped again and blushed. 'Yeah. I just wanted to look at the old house. Needed closure, that's all. Visited Cori. You know. Come on then. Let's go.'

'Okay,' he said. 'You don't need to explain yourself to me. If you go down there, you go down there.' And the floodgates opened a tiny bit more. 'But I'm kind of used to you being here again.'

'I'm used to you too.' She looked up at him and smiled as she pulled the door closed behind her, and they set off up the path. 'I won't be going back to the old house any more. It's definitely not my home. It hasn't been that for a while. Cori said she couldn't imagine me calling Suffolk home after being down in London, but I disagreed. Hey, maybe some nice country estate will provide me with a little cottage and some Living History work to cling onto – just to keep my hand in. You never know.'

Alex stopped dead in the middle of the path and this time one of his demons decided to speak for him. 'I can do as many Living History weekends as you want. Just tell me how many you can cope with.'

'Oh! I'm just teasing! You don't have to work it around me, you know. You can do craft fairs, or local farmers' markets. They're quite popular and good for bringing the visitors in.'

'What else can *you* do?' The demon had its talons in, for sure. And he knew his eyes were boring into hers, silently begging her to get the point of the conversation – quite literally.

'Me? Well, I can organise art exhibitions. Or photography exhibitions. Costume displays. I have contacts that could help.'

'I like those ideas. What else can you do? Tell me more.'

Anything to keep you at Hartsford.

Elodie looked a bit stunned. 'Okay. Because I didn't want to suggest anything in case you thought I was trying to take over, but I was thinking it would be nice if ...'

And she was off, the ideas flowing like the River Hartsford: open air theatre, country fairgrounds, well-dressing, scarecrow weekends, working more closely with the Folk Museum ... Cassie had already suggested a Country House Weekend, based on the lavish parties the bright young things of the family had enjoyed between the wars, and she'd mentioned dragging out that old marquee from the squash courts for it, so that was something to consider, wasn't it?

By using strategically placed murmurs of agreement, Alex encouraged her to continue talking as they wound their way down towards the river and the lake. At the very least it encouraged him to believe that she was intending to stay here for a little longer and she was indeed over Smarmy-Boy.

Alex was nodding at her suggestions and even making the odd agreeable noise, so Elodie thought he was pretty on board with some of the things she was suggesting. Suddenly, she was enthused about her future. And her future seemed to be inextricably linked to Hartsford.

If anything was ever to progress properly with Alex and herself, she'd never want to go anywhere else anyway. But was that what he wanted? She wasn't sure. Her ideas filled in the time it took for them to reach the Faerie Bridge, and she stood on the sandy bank looking up at the pretty little arch, trying to imagine what it had been like back in 1796 or whenever little Lucy had found the silver penny there.

Elodie found that if she stood quietly and tuned out the present-day intrusions – like the faint hum of traffic, the airplane leaving a cloud of vapour behind it, the distant chatter of the last straggling tourists in the pleasure grounds beyond the bridge – she could almost sense what it had been like then. And in fact, it was surprisingly easy to get a picture of Lucy that day. Her energy was still there, as if she had simply come and gone within the last few minutes.

In her mind's eye, Elodie saw a little girl run down from the Hall. Her reddish-blonde curls were bouncing around and she was holding up the skirts of a white dress, the ribbons from her red sash flapping out behind her. She pulled up in front of Elodie, and looked around, scouring the ground for a silver penny or a magical horseshoe.

'I think Lucy stood about … here.' Elodie moved to one side, feeling as if she was obstructing the little girl. 'And I think it was early evening.' Closing her eyes, she tried to attune herself more to the earth and the energy around her.

This wasn't called the Faerie Bridge for nothing – it could be quite an eerie place at twilight. 'She'd been agitated all day, trying to get away from everyone. And Georgiana lost her temper with her. Georgiana told her if she was going to go looking for trinkets, she should go and stop bothering her. Lucy said she would simply refuse to share *any* trinkets she found and that was *that*.'

Elodie opened her eyes and found Alex watching her, faintly amused. 'She sounds like Cassie was at that age. In fact, she sounds like Cassie *still* is if she puts her mind to it.'

'Lucy's energy is so strong. I can sense her. It's that sort of place. That sort of evening. What? What is it?'

His eyes kept sliding away across Elodie's shoulder and focusing on a corner of the bridge. 'Nothing.' Suddenly, he began patting his pockets down and swore. 'Damn it! I've lost the penny. I must have dropped it on the way down. For God's sake!'

He flicked his eyes back along the way they'd come, as if he would see it sparkling on the pathway, and then Elodie remembered the experiences she'd had with that very same coin. 'Oh! I wonder—'

'What? I – ouch!' He stumbled as if someone had shoved him from behind. 'What the hell?' He turned around and glared at the empty space.

'That probably answers my question. Which direction did she aim you in? Let her do it again.'

'Elodie! Ouch! *Hey*!' Once again, Alex stumbled forwards – further this time – and Elodie could see he was heading towards the corner of the bridge he'd been focusing on moments earlier. 'God, it's like tiny little bony hands in the small of my back!'

'Okay. The bridge it is, then.' Elodie linked his arm with hers and pulled him across to the ancient brickwork.

And there, on a ridge between two old stones that were balanced on top of each other, was a silver coin.

The Faerie Bridge was packed tightly together by some skilful dry-stone work, which probably explained why it had never needed to be cemented into place.

It had odd little steps going up the side and was really the most incredible arched bridge Elodie had ever come across. The closest thing she could liken it to was a packhorse bridge – those wonderful pieces of bucolic architecture that are usually covered with cobbles and look far too steep for anything but a packhorse or a 4×4 vehicle to cross. The steepest one she had ever seen was at Carrbridge in Scotland. That one, however, was almost washed away by floods, and much as the Carrbridge one sort of resembled the one at Hartsford, the Faerie Bridge had survived quite a few spates of the River Hartsford.

But on one of those little steps up the side was Alex's silver coin.

'It's there. Look!' she told him. Alex was still patting his pockets down, looking a little bit angry and a little bit confused. He was gorgeous, standing there with the evening sun making highlights of black diamonds in his hair, and Elodie's heart flip-flopped as she watched him.

'But—' he started.

She touched him on the arm, so she could feel he was solid and real and right next to her, then let go of him. 'Let's see if she's showing you anything else. Come on.'

Elodie leaned over and looked at the coin. It certainly appeared to be the same one that had been following her around the estate for the past few days.

She picked it up and Alex growled in protest. 'Leave it! If that's the one from my pocket it's bloody haunted!' His eyes drifted across to the bridge again and Elodie followed his gaze. 'Is it just me,' he asked sharply, 'or is that bit there odd-looking?'

He was homing in on the same spot time after time, and Elodie nodded. 'Yes! That's it, then. We'll look there.'

It was the ridge to the left of the stone the coin had appeared on, a ridge that kind of went around the bridge structure and into the interior of the arch. Again, Elodie felt that gust of wind rush past her. The hairs stood up on her arms and she took a deep breath. 'Okay. Let's see what we have here.' She walked towards the bridge and peered underneath it. 'Any ideas?' she asked as Alex poked his head underneath as well.

Elodie turned to look at him. His face was inches from hers and their eyes met.

For a moment it seemed as if her heart stopped beating and she definitely stopped breathing. '*Oh.*' The word was little more than a whisper.

A spark flared in his eyes then died. 'Right there, d'you think?' He took hold of her hand and gently directed it to a hole in the stonework. Those little fireworks zinged up her arm again and she worried that she'd fall at his feet in a horribly messy heap – her legs were definitely threatening to give way if she wasn't careful.

Elodie calmed herself down and, assessing where she was on the sandy bank, put one foot on a rock in the river, and the other on a tree stump.

Alex released her hand and took hold of her waist. 'Is this okay? I don't want you falling in.'

'Yes.' Her chest constricted and she caught her breath, but she knew it owed nothing to the asthma this time. Trying to ignore the tingling warmth of his hands through her thin, cotton shirt, she poked her fingers into the crevice and felt around until she located a cold, rough object.

She gasped. 'I think we have something!'

The "something" had sharp, square edges and didn't feel at all like a brick or a stone. Checking her hand, she saw a smattering of mud on her fingertips, but no rust.

Elodie leaned in and worked whatever it was free. She slid it out of the crevice and there was a sort of scraping sound, and once she had it in daylight, she realised she was holding a small, dull-silvery coloured box with an overlay of mossy green and mud.

She jumped down onto the ground and gave the box a little rub with her fingernail, dragging a channel through the green. 'Pewter. Doesn't rust.' She shook it and there was no sound of rattling, just a sort of *kerchunk* as something inside lifted and dropped.

'They used pewter a lot in the Georgian period,' said Alex quietly, his hands in his pockets now.

Elodie looked at him and held it out. 'Do you want it?'

He shrugged. 'I doubt it's Ben's. It's more likely to be Georgiana's.'

Turning the box around carefully, Elodie saw a little hole, just big enough for a small key to fit into. 'I don't have any of Georgiana's memories coming in, and if it was important, I would think that she would – oh! *Lucy*! Of course! Lucy hid it down here. I suspect our little key would fit right in there.'

'That would explain those bony little hands.' Alex shuddered at the memory. 'Back to the cottage then?

Elodie nodded, thinking of the items they'd found in the tomb. This box might solve the mystery about the key. But they still had the pistol to contend with.

Chapter Sixteen

Elodie's cottage was warm and bright, with the evening sun coming through the windows and making the place all mellow and welcoming.

They both had bare feet and were in her tiny lounge once again, sitting cross legged in front of one another with the box between them. It seemed like neither of them particularly wanted to open the box. Elodie had already cleaned it over and over with a soft, soapy cloth and then spent a good deal of time polishing it up with a Tate Gallery tea towel and some metal polish. 'It's come up nice and shiny,' she said, rather inanely.

'Yep.'

They both sat and stared at the small, pewter container for another few minutes. Elodie gave it another little rub for good measure and folded the tea towel up neatly. She laid the folded cloth on the floor beside her and clasped her hands together in the space between her knees.

'Cori's Simon gave that tea towel to me. Remember? He works at the Tate.'

'That must be a great place to work.'

'Oh, yes.' She nodded. 'He doesn't like the modern stuff much. His doctorate is in the Pre-Raphaelites.'

'Interesting.'

They stared at the box again.

'Why don't we want to open it?' Elodie suddenly asked. 'It's not going to bite us.'

'I think we're scared about what we might find.'

'This is personal. This was hidden away for a reason, wasn't it? Oh!' She looked towards Alex, but seemed to be looking through him, rather than focusing on his face.

'What is it?' He swivelled around as best he could. 'What's behind me?'

'Nothing. I'm just thinking about the attic. There was a loose floorboard in the attic and Georgiana didn't want Lucy to find whatever was in it. She stepped backwards. And there was a tiny creaking sound. Lucy must have realised what it meant and went back to search for it.'

'So you think this box was hidden there?'

'I don't know.' She stood up and walked over to the window, looking across the gardens to the house as if she was thinking of something. She wrapped her arms around her body. 'To be honest, I'm a bit worried about opening it. I don't think it holds anything that's going to put either of those girls in a good light.'

Alex stood up and took a couple of steps forward.

He joined her at the window and stared outside as well. 'How about we leave the box and do something completely different? Get away from the cottage and everything and maybe go to the pub? If you're worried about it, the box can wait until you're ready for it.'

He looked down and Elodie nodded. He'd forgotten how tiny she was in her bare feet. He remembered her on Prom Night. She'd had high heels on and the top of her head had been level with his nose and they'd laughed about the fact she was the tallest she'd ever been that night. They'd had a good time, until it all went horribly wrong. He shuddered, regretting it all over again.

'The pub sounds good,' Elodie replied. 'The box can definitely wait. I don't think I want to deal with it all right now.'

'Great. Come on then. The Green Dragon? They do the best food.' It was the oldest pub in the village. There was also a wine bar at the very edge of Hartsford, and many of the younger people went there. It was nice, all chrome and glass and coloured bottles, but the food was served in poncey little portions and always left Alex feeling cheated.

'The Green Dragon,' Elodie agreed and moved away from him, sliding her feet into some wedge-heeled sandals that were tossed in the corner by a pile of interior design magazines. She grew about two inches in a matter of seconds. 'Just let me get changed first, then I have to do one thing before we go.'

She headed out of the room and was back a few minutes later in a long, floaty white dress to complement the sandals.

Then she reached into the book shelves and brought out something that looked like a thick, tightly bound sausage of green vegetation. 'Sage. I'm going to purify this place before we go. I need to get rid of any negative energy that might be hanging around the box. After all, we know nothing about it and neither of us wants to open it.' She looked at the pewter container and frowned. 'Yes. I'm going to smudge it all, I think.'

'Smudging?'

'Smudging. Just bear with me. It's one of my oddities.'

Elodie found a box of matches, struck one, and lit the end of the sausage. A lovely, herbal smell came out of the vegetation, along with a wisp of greyish smoke. Elodie moved around the room, waving the sausage around and murmuring what sounded like incantations.

Alex briefly wondered where she'd learned about sage, but it was most peculiar; even he could feel the atmosphere of the place lifting. And at the end, when she blew out the few flames on the end of the sage bundle and laid it carefully in a little dish on the windowsill, the room felt so different.

'That's it. I'm done.' She coughed and wheezed a little, and glowered at the sage. 'I have to get out before I choke myself to death on the smoke though. Let's go and enjoy our drinks in peace.' She smiled and led the way out of the lounge. 'I'm going to leave the front door open, it'll be good to freshen the place up.'

'Whatever you say,' Alex replied. 'You seem to know what you're doing.'

'Only sometimes.' She flicked a gaze upwards. 'Sometimes, I get it horribly wrong.'

'Me too,' responded Alex. 'Horribly wrong.'

'Nobody's perfect!' said Elodie with a laugh as she went outside and waited for him to catch her up.

You are. You're perfect.

But he just smiled and said nothing and fell into step with her.

Alex was at the bar, waiting for Bob the barman to serve him. That was the only thing about the Green Dragon: you couldn't be in a hurry.

Alex lowered his head and smiled at the thought. He wasn't in any hurry. The only thing waiting for him away from here was the pewter box, and that wasn't going to run away. It was much more preferable to be here with Elodie. He looked up and cast a glance over at her. She was looking right back at him and she gave him a little wave and a smile. He grinned and waved back. She was still nursing the free glass of wine Bob had given them as a "thank you" for stocking some of his micro-brewery ales in the Hall gift shop.

Bob was deep in conversation with someone about horses, usually something Alex would be interested in listening to, but instead he perched on the edge of a bar stool and found himself drifting off. The modern-day world seemed to slip away until he realised he was sitting at a much older sort of bar ...

There was rowdiness, singing and bawdy jokes all around him, the smell of fetid, sweaty bodies and ale, and the feel of dirt and sawdust beneath his feet. He became aware of rising voices nearby and turned slightly to see what the commotion was. His pistol was comfortably at his waist, his hat pulled low-down over his face as he waited for his associate. He feared nobody in the gambling den, nobody at all, but he sat up a little straighter when he realised what was happening close by.

One of the men in the group was in his early twenties. His face was handsome, with that aristocratic look that might be taken for arrogance. He was dressed in a dark coat, a white shirt and tight, pale-coloured breeches. A white cravat was knotted around his neck and his hair was fair and curled, carefully styled with long sideburns and falling to just below his collar. He was a young Dandy, and, more than that, was the young man he'd last seen tied, by his own hands, to a coach wheel.

The young man –Viscount Somersby, no less, Georgiana's brother Jasper – was sitting at a table, several empty bottles of wine near him and a glass half full at his elbow. He was dealing cards, then there was some sort of altercation. Jasper stood up and thumped the table with his fist. He knocked over the glass and the men opposite him stood up.

'My sister is not a whore! How dare you tarnish her name as such?'

'It's true, little Viscount. The bitch can't keep off her back long enough to stand upright.'

'You lying piece of filth! Take that back at once!'

'You take me back to that nice Hall of yours and let me have my pleasure with the whore myself. She's givin' it away to any man that asks!'

'How dare you—'

'I dare very well. I could take payment for your debts by using the dirty little slut's body – that suits me very well, Sir. Very well.'

'You—'

Ben was just about to intervene and himself defend Georgiana's honour – he couldn't stand by and hear her insulted like that – but he never got a chance. Before he had time to even stand up, Jasper had reached for his pistol, but out of the shadows one of the thug's henchmen grabbed Jasper's arm and slammed it hard into the table top. His pistol fell onto the floor and the man bent his arm around his back; there was a sickening snapping sound and Jasper howled in pain. Another man came over and seized a handful of Jasper's hair, pulling his head backwards.

Ben was halfway out of his seat, his hand on his own pistol, when there was a glint and a flash of metal. Jasper's shouts stopped abruptly and there was blood dripping onto the floor and soaking into the grime. The men laughed and shouted and dragged Jasper out of the inn, his feet leaving a path in the sawdust. Jasper's handsome face was grey, drained of blood. In contrast, there was a huge, dark patch of the stuff staining the front of his shirt.

Ben was frozen to the spot. He had seen men die before, but never like that – and never someone he felt he had known, even slightly. He was sickened and horrified, and he wished he'd shot the bastards first. He looked at the door and the people spilling out of it, the crowds clamouring for more entertainment, but he knew the lad was gone. His thoughts now fled to Georgiana and his heart screamed in pain. The lad had died defending his sister's honour and it seemed likely it was because of him.

He would carry that guilt to his grave and he cursed under his breath, swearing that someday he would avenge Jasper's death and show him for the hero he was. He watched as the customers began to shout and point, then, unnoticed, he moved swiftly to the table where Jasper had been. He picked up his pistol and slid it into his waistband. There was no need

for anyone to find that and sell it. The least he could do was
try to give it back to Georgiana.

'Sorry about that, lad. Terrible business.' Bob was shaking his head. 'Dairy herd trampled the tents again at the campsite. Fence broke. Nobody hurt, but the fence was destroyed between the horses' field too, and they ended up in the barns eating the hay. What can I get you?'

Alex stared at him. The man he'd been discussing the horses with was walking across to his table with two drinks and Bob was ready to serve him.

'Oh. Sorry. I was miles away.' He smiled weakly. 'Yes, terrible business. Bottle of red please. A lasagne and a penne *arrabiata* as well. If you don't mind.'

Bob looked curiously at him. 'Why would I mind?'

'Yeah. Good point. Sorry.' He raked his fingers through his hair. 'It's been a long day.'

'At the end of a long day, it's good to sit in the pub and enjoy a meal,' said Bob with a nod.

'It is.' Alex looked over his shoulder at Elodie. She had picked up the menu and was skimming through it, unaware of the tragedy that had just played out.

One thing was for sure, though. Jasper had been a hero after all and he'd died protecting his sister. Alex had always thought he was one of the most fascinating relatives he had and at that moment he felt closer to him than he ever had done before. He looked back again at Elodie. He knew he had to tell her. She was the only one who it would make sense to.

He carried the bottle over to her.

She saw him coming over and drained the glass she had, before smiling and putting it on the table next to his empty one. 'I bet that bottle wasn't free,' she said.

'It wasn't. I needed a refill, though. Do you know what the

biggest legend of this old pub is?' He filled up the glasses and pushed Elodie's towards her.

'The Green Dragon? Isn't this the place where Jasper was supposed to have died?' Every villager had heard that tale.

'Yes. And I just found out that he did.' Alex sat down and put his elbows on the table, staring at Elodie.

She mirrored his pose. 'Really? How come?'

'Ben saw it happen. It was an honourable death in the end; his father should have been immensely proud of him.' The words were sarcastic and Elodie looked shocked.

'You saw it, you mean? Just now?' Her eyes travelled over to the bar, then came to rest back on Alex. He felt that little jolt, so familiar and so damned painful now, as the bright blue depths stared into his.

'Yes. Ben remembered it and let me know about it. The pistol we found – it's Jasper's for sure.'

'But why didn't he protect himself? He was supposed to be a brilliant duellist. Isn't that the term for it?'

Alex nodded, distracted. 'Yes. Duellist.' He pushed his hair away from his forehead and looked towards the door. 'But that's not much use when you're not dealing with honourable men. He never had a chance to draw. He was drunk and they grabbed his arm and kind of twisted it back.'

'Ouch!'

'More than that, I think they broke it.'

Elodie clamped her hands over her mouth. 'Oh, no!'

'It gets worse. They held him down and stuck a knife straight into his heart. Poor guy. And do you know what he was doing?' Elodie's hands were still covering her mouth and she shook her head, eyes wide and troubled over the top of her fingers. Alex took a drink of his own wine, then spoke: 'Jasper was defending Georgiana's honour.'

'Oh, God.' Elodie removed her hands and grasped the stem of her glass. She tipped it up and took a big gulp. 'Her honour! That's awful. Oh, no – what a messed up ... *mess* it all is.' Tears sprang into her eyes. 'Poor Jasper.'

'Completely. So yes, it might have been a brawl he died in, but he died to protect his sister's reputation. Ben knew it, as well. He took Jasper's pistol from the floor and hid it. That must be how it ended up back with Georgiana.'

'I have no words.' Elodie shook her head.

'You know,' said Alex stonily, 'I'm thinking their father was a tyrant and their mother was mentally unstable. Who the hell would let their kids be treated like that? What is so bad that you have to make your daughter an angel to hide whatever she did and go so far as to take an advert out to spin lies about your son's death? Although who am I to talk? Our mother's denied us for years. Maybe it's a thing with the Hartsford families.'

'You'd *never* be like that with your children. But I'm equally sure Cassie would never, ever be classed as an angel.' Elodie tried to smile and put her hand on top of his briefly. It was warm and it didn't stay there long enough. 'I'm sorry your mother is an old soak. I really am.'

Apparently Alex's mother was very partial to a drink or two. Or three. It was one of the few things the old Earl had told his children about her, commenting that her choice of a wine merchant as her second husband was probably for a reason. Elodie had always thought that a particularly harsh thing to say, but Alex had tried to joke about it instead, coming up with the nickname 'the old soak' about his mother. It seemed a bit cruel, but who could blame him?

'Me too. I'm quite glad she's in France.'

'Anyway. Should we talk of nicer things? Cassie did a great job on the locket, didn't she?'

'She did. And you know something?' He leaned back as Bob's wife appeared with the food and put it in front of them. 'Thanks, Sue.' He waited a moment until Sue had disappeared out of earshot. 'We've still got the box to investigate, not to mention the pistol, and maybe they'll help us fathom it all out.'

Elodie paused and poked at her pasta with the fork. 'Would you come back with me tonight Alex? After we've finished here? I've decided I want to look at the box and get it over with. We owe it to Jasper as well as Georgiana and Ben. Will you stay a little while with me at the cottage, and we can sort it out? Please?'

Alex paused. If only the reason she wanted him back was nothing to do with the pewter box and everything to do with the fact she wanted *him* to go back. End of. But no. He'd blown it too long ago. Forget it.

He raised his eyes to hers and smiled. 'Of course.'

'Thank you.' She hid her face as she ploughed into her pasta sauce. Her cheeks were tinged with pink, but he wasn't sure if it was the heat or the wine or the spicy pasta.

'My pleasure,' he replied. It seemed inadequate, somehow.

Chapter Seventeen

If she was completely truthful, it was more the fact she wasn't really ready for him to go home at all. It was too nice being with him and she had loved that brief touch of their hands. She had pulled away before she took hold of him properly and scared him off.

Although, with how it all panned out in the end, she was awfully pleased that, in the twilight of a long, summer's day, Alex escorted her back to the cottage. It was, after all, Alex who saw the smoke curling out of her partially open front window. 'Hey, look at that!' he cried. 'Smoke!'

'My cottage!' Elodie started running towards it, until Alex grabbed her and pulled her back towards him as easily as if she was on a bungee rope.

She sort of *boing*-ed back to him; he thrust her behind him and then he began hurtling towards the cottage. 'You stay back!' he yelled.

Elodie faltered, but she fell back. It was impossible to keep up with him anyway. All she could do was shout after him: 'Be careful!'

When Alex pulled up in front of the cottage, he stopped and sniffed. 'It's that stuff you used to smudge the place with. The sage,' he called over his shoulder. He ran over to the lounge window, then banged his fists on the glass. 'Bloody hell, Elodie, it's set the pewter box on fire!'

'Impossible!' She hurried over next to him and waved some smoke away. Coughing, she peered through the neat little panes; sure enough, the smoke was coming out of the box and filling her lounge, then drifting out of the window. Nothing else was on fire; nothing at all.

She could have sworn that she didn't leave the box on the windowsill.

And she knew for a fact that the box was still closed when they left to go to the Dragon, but the key was sitting in the lock, almost defiantly.

'Who did that?' she asked, tears springing to her eyes. She didn't know if it was worse that someone had gone into her little house uninvited or that someone had set the precious box alight. Without thinking, she walked over to the door and pulled it fully open. The smell of sage was incredibly strong and that, combined with the smoke, made her choke. Her house looked like a Victorian opium den and her airways were constricting. What a horrible end to the evening! 'Bloody *hell*!'

She felt a hand on her shoulder and then she was gently pulled away from the door.

'You're not staying here tonight,' said Alex. 'It'll kill you. I haven't forgotten finding you in the squash courts last year. Let me check what's going on.'

'Can I at least come in and get my inhaler?'

'No. I'll get it – where is it?'

'Upstairs. In the bathroom.'

'Okay. Stay there.' Alex disappeared into the smog and came back with it. It was just as well, because the more agitated she was becoming about the fire, the more she started to lose the capacity to breathe, and the more her chest tightened.

'There you go.'

He handed it to her and she grabbed it gratefully. 'Thank you.' She took a big puff of it and sat on the grass outside the house, taking a few gulps of fresh air before going to the window pane again. She peered inside, knocking pathetically on the glass like the ghost of *Wuthering Heights*' Catherine Earnshaw. Alex had opened the window wider and managed to douse the smouldering contents of the box with a vase full of water, and the beautiful roses from Margaret's garden which had filled the vase were lying on the floor.

Alex looked up, seeming to register the fact Elodie was at the window, and came over to see her. 'Are you okay? Blue lips don't suit you.'

'I'm fine. What's going on?'

'Exactly what it looks like. Someone opened the box and set fire to the contents. I'm coming out now, but just tell me where I can grab you some overnight things first. You're coming to the Hall tonight.'

'The Hall?'

'The Hall.'

'Oh!' Then she remembered the weekend case she still had packed from her last trip to her parents' place in the South of France. She'd washed everything there and just repacked the case. Sure, it had flimsy stuff in it, in the hope of nice warm weather, but she never really wore any of her holiday clothes in Suffolk – so what was the point in taking it all out again at home, just to repack for her next visit? 'You could try the top of my wardrobe in the main bedroom. There's a pink overnight case. I've got enough in there for tonight.'

'Great. I won't be a minute.'

He found the bag exactly where she said it would be and lifted it down easily. It was quite light, but he assumed it must have everything she needed in it. He was glad she had already taken her inhaler and crushed the horrible image of her having some kind of attack and dropping dead at his feet that night.

She hadn't looked particularly well when she was peering in at the window before. One more thing to blame Piers for. She'd told him her ex had taken to smoking cigars and that had made the whole condition worse. She'd been hospitalised for it once, apparently. But he felt he had no right to comment on it and had cursed Piers long and hard for that one.

And secondary to his worries about Elodie, were those

about how the sage had just happened to light up and how the box had just happened to open up.

He pushed the thought out of his head. The most important thing was to get Elodie back to the Hall and sort out a bed for the night. It was almost ten o'clock and it was getting quite dark.

Elodie was hovering about outside the cottage and she looked like a restless spirit herself. She reached out to try and take the bag from him and he held it up, out of her way.

'No. I'll carry it.'

'But you've got the box and stuff,' she said and reached out again.

'And I'm happy to carry them all. Come on. I'd pick you up and carry you too if I could, but it's not very practical right now.' He began to walk towards the Hall.

'But Alex—' She suddenly stopped and doubled over, fighting to inhale. 'Wait … a second … please.' She took another puff of her inhaler and stood up again.

'Look at you. That's just with walking up here.' Alex slowed down and continued, trying not to show how worried he was about her. 'I've opened all the windows. The place will be quite safe tonight and we'll see how it is tomorrow. Why didn't you tell me how bad it is?'

'How bad what is?' she asked, breathlessly.

'The asthma.'

'Because it's too embarrassing to admit it! It's because of London and …' Her voice trailed off helplessly and Alex felt the anger boil up again. Bloody Piers!

'But what if you had an attack at the cottage? What if nobody was around to help you?'

'I'm fine,' she insisted. 'It hasn't been like this for a couple of weeks—'

'A couple of weeks,' he interrupted. 'Well that says it all, really. Weeks.' He felt his face close up. She was impossible.

She could have died. 'Have you even told your parents? I bet you haven't. I feel like ringing them up myself!'

'I wouldn't want them to worry, and anyway, I don't often have a houseful of smoke.'

'Regardless. I just want to …' It was his turn to trail off. *I just want to look after you. I just want to be there for you.*

Fortunately, they were almost at the Hall and it was easy to change the subject. A red and black motorbike was parked diagonally across the drive and that meant only one thing. 'Look! Cassie's back. That was a short trip. D'you think she's had a falling out with the latest boyfriend?'

'Is she still with Tom?' asked Elodie.

'Kate's brother? No. That was doomed to failure. Even Kate warned her that he's a serial boyfriend. I think the latest one is called Sam.'

'Oh, I can't keep up.'

'Me neither, usually. Let's see what she says.'

Alex led the way into the Hall and shouted through the open door. 'Cassie! We're here!'

'Who's we?' Cassie popped her head out of the lounge. 'Elodie! Hello!' She looked freshly scrubbed and smelt of bergamot shower gel – in contrast to Elodie, who thought she must look like something the cat dragged in.

'Hey Cassie. Sorry to spoil your evening. There was a slight incident at my cottage. I can't sleep there tonight.'

'You're not spoiling it. Fire, flood or pestilence?'

'Fire. Sort of. It's been a weird old night.'

She was, she realised, dog-tired. The wine, the walk, the box, the fire and the asthma attack had drained her. The world started to go a little woozy and she wobbled her way into the lounge where she collapsed into a big, squashy armchair and, closing her eyes, rested her head against the back and tried to concentrate on breathing.

Alex's voice floated above her as he squeezed her shoulder. 'I'll make some coffee. You sit there, don't worry. Cassie, can you take this upstairs please?'

'Sure!' Cassie's voice was cheerful, but Elodie didn't have the energy to even smile in response. There was a sort of breeze and the smell of sun tan lotion and fabric conditioner that she associated with her overnight bag, and she assumed Alex had passed it over her head to his sister. Cassie's footsteps trotted out of the room, followed by Alex's, and she felt herself falling asleep. It wouldn't do. It wouldn't do at all, if she napped now. Would it?

She woke up about half an hour later. That was quite lucky – she could quite easily have napped the night away in the chair and she wondered, sleepily, what Alex would have done in that case. She shifted in the cosy armchair and opened her eyes.

Alex was sitting on the sofa and had the box on his knee. There was a pile of black sogginess to one side of him – the sofa looked none too respectable with that there – and he was holding a piece of charred paper in his hand, examining it with a magnifying glass.

'Welcome back,' he said. 'I was going to give you another half hour then carry you upstairs. Do you want to have a look at this?' Finally, he looked up at her and her heart broke just a little. He appeared worn out and confused. 'There's not much to see, but you might be interested in what there is.'

'Hmmmph.' She made a non-committal sort of sound and hauled herself out of the chair. Her chest still felt a little tight, but she was breathing more normally. The sleep must have helped. She went over to the sofa and sat near Alex, the pile of wet, mushy charred paper between them.

'These are the contents of the box. Or what's left of them anyway. The top ones are ruined – that's the pile down there.'

He nodded to the blackened rubbish. 'But this one was on the bottom. I don't think the fire got to it properly and the water didn't soak all the way through to it.'

'It's just as well the fire stayed in the box.' She shuddered to think of what might have happened to the cottage – and also, there was a chance that she might have been in the cottage at the same time as the fire. If it had spread and if she'd been in her bedroom asleep ... It didn't bear thinking about.

'Indeed,' replied Alex. 'And this piece of paper I'm looking at has something written on it. I wonder if they were Georgiana's letters?'

'I think we can safely assume it *was* Georgiana's box and Georgiana's letters, even if Lucy hid it away. The key was in the tomb after all.'

'That's what I think. Do you want to have a look?'

'Yes, please!'

'Here. Be careful, it's fragile.'

He passed the piece of paper over to her, along with the magnifying glass. She bent over it and squinted through the glass.

She could just make out some spidery, brownish coloured ink which may have, at one time, been black. The edges of the sheet were charred and breaking away in her hands, but there was something written in the centre that looked like *ill, orry, ho he is.*

'Oh,' said Elodie, 'I wonder what it all said originally?'

Deep down, though, she knew exactly what it said. The writing was horribly similar to that poisonous little note she'd found under the floorboard in the attic.

You will be sorry. I know who he is.

Elodie put the letter on her knee, heedless of the ash and cinders that were dropping from the old paper. 'And the rest have been destroyed. Am I correct?'

'Sadly, yes.' Alex reached over and took her hand. 'They

didn't want us to read them. Something too private to share, perhaps?'

'Maybe they were love letters,' she said weakly. She would hazard a guess there were a few blackmail letters in there too, if that fragment was anything to go by. The letter she had found in the attic must have been pushed under the floorboard in a hurry to be stashed away later – either by Lucy or Georgiana. She no longer knew. Nasty notes saved from one sister to another – for whatever payback each one of them could take. The rash, silly decisions of argumentative siblings. It was dreadfully sad.

Elodie stared at the paper and at Alex's hand on top of hers. If they were love letters, they would have given them both tender memories. It would have been the ideal time for them to slip back into the Georgian era – Ben holding Georgiana's hand whilst they exchanged letters – but nothing. It was like a barrier had been put up. It had to be Lucy.

Please don't tell.

The little voice that whispered in her ear was desperate.

Please don't.

Elodie loosened her hand from Alex's and rubbed her temples. 'We were never meant to read these. We have to respect her privacy.'

She didn't say whose privacy.

Elodie looked back at the sheet – and watched, helpless, as it curled in on itself from the edges and disintegrated completely, the pieces fluttering to the floor like tiny black snowflakes. And it was gone. Just like that.

She closed her eyes briefly and imagined a little girl with reddish blonde curls pushing the box into the crevice under the bridge. She imagined her dropping the key into a little purse and hurrying away back to the Hall, dreadfully sorry for what she'd done, blaming herself for what had happened.

Poor little thing. She was only ten.

'I think it was Georgiana's box of treasures,' Elodie said flatly, 'and I think we already guessed too much of what she was hiding. I don't think there's anything we need to pursue in here.'

Elodie stood up and brushed the ash off her knees. It hardly seemed wrong to do so, as the floor was covered with the flurry of black stuff anyway and it had added to the mess on the sofa. 'I think I'm ready for bed now. It's been too much today. I need some rest.' She yawned. 'Which room am I in?'

Thank you. Thank you!

Elodie was careful not to let Alex see any reaction at all. Whatever was in that box was not meant to be discovered. And she would destroy the note she had found, just as soon as it was practical.

I loved her. I did. I tried to help. I'm sorry.

'How can you be so matter-of-fact?' Alex asked, looking at the ash. 'That paper just self-destructed!'

'It happens.' Elodie couldn't deal with questions as well as a blackmailing eighteenth century pre-teen. 'Now, where am I sleeping?' She just wanted to be pointed towards her room and left alone. She remembered the lovely bathroom and the fresh scent of Cassie's bergamot shower gel and for a millisecond wondered if she had time for a bath. Then she decided that falling asleep in the tub and being rescued from near-drowning by Alex was not really a good way of spending what little was left of the day. Although the idea of being in his arms was very pleasant indeed, and half-drowning didn't seem too bad if that was the case. She shivered, remembering the squash courts last year. It had been terrifying, until he burst in the door and ran over to her. She still didn't know how he'd known where to find her.

'The pink room.' Alex dragged his gaze away from the ash. 'The spare one. It's small, but it's nice.'

'Great.' Elodie yawned again. The lounge was vaguely

imploding around the edges of her vision and she knew she had approximately ten minutes left in her before she collapsed in a heap where she stood.

'I'll take you up.' Alex stood up and captured her hand.

She gave it to him willingly. 'Alex, can I ask you a question?'

'Of course.'

'How did you find me in the squash courts – that time?'

He paused and looked at her, then shook his head. 'You know, I'm not really sure.' He began leading her through one of the corridors, up the stairs and along to a door tucked into the corner of the wall. 'I just somehow remembered something vital I needed out of the storage. And I started to run up there, like I had to break the world record. And then I found you. We were lucky.' He squeezed her hand, as if he understood how it might have panned out. 'Anyway, I'm pleased it happened that way. Look. You're in here.' He pushed the door open. Almost immediately, Elodie's nose was filled with the smell of rose pot pourri ... and cardboard. Lots and lots of cardboard.

'What the—?' Alex snapped the light on and Elodie winced as the brightness attacked her retinas. She squinted past him and saw boxes and boxes of stuff piled up on the bed, on the floor, and all around the room. There was one little channel through the middle of it all, but no way she or anyone else could sleep on that bed.

Alex ripped open the nearest box and pulled some bubble wrap out. 'Bottles of wine!' The next box contained books. The next, dozens and dozens of quirky bits of stationery. 'It's all stock for the gift shop. I am going to kill Cassie. Seriously, I am going to murder her. Good Lord, when she said she'd directed people in with deliveries, it might have been nice if she'd told me where she'd directed them to! Ah, *no* – she said the spare room, didn't she? She did – she did tell me.' Alex swore roundly and stared at the mess in the room.

'So where do you think my overnight case is?' Elodie shuffled a couple of boxes of pocket money toys around, as if the case would magically reappear beneath some windmills and bouncy balls.

'I told her to take it to the bedroom. There's only her room and mine left to sleep in. I mean, she— Oh, no. She can't have ...' Alex stared at her. 'Elodie, I'm so sorry.'

'What about?'

'Let's just say it won't be in her room.' He turned and took her by the shoulders. 'I didn't engineer this, I swear it.'

'Ah, I see.' Elodie smiled. Cassie was incorrigible.

'Yes, I think we'd best check my room. I'm guessing there's a pink overnight bag in there.' He turned her around and pushed her gently out of the room. Along the corridor, past the bathroom and to another door – his room. There, on top of the very comfortable looking king size bed was Elodie's overnight case.

'Oh, thank goodness!' She headed into the room like a homing pigeon. Five minutes and counting before she collapsed in a heap.

'I'll be downstairs if you need me,' said Alex, starting to leave the room. 'On the sofa.'

'No, you won't!' Elodie turned to him. 'You're in here, Alex Aldrich. Right here. With me.'

'Elodie!'

'You can't sleep on the sofa, it's covered in crap. Please. Sleep here.'

And with that, she flung the case on the floor, heard it burst open and dropped onto the bed, on top of the duvet.

And Alex swore later that within a minute, she was fast asleep.

Chapter Eighteen

So what was he supposed to do? The most beautiful girl in the world was fast asleep on his bed; her hair was spread out on the pillow and her cheeks were flushed against the snow-white cases.

Alex looked at Elodie for a couple of minutes and scratched his head. The gentlemanly part of him said that he should leave her be; just walk out of the room, close the door and head downstairs to sleep on the sofa.

But the other part of him realised that she didn't look very comfortable, so he pulled the duvet out from beneath her and up over her feet, in case they got cold. Because she had told him, last winter, that she loved her fluffy bed socks and her feet were usually like ice.

He stroked her hair back from her face and his heart twisted because she was truly the only person he'd ever really wanted and he couldn't quite believe that she was actually here, even though, he acknowledged, it should have been under better circumstances.

He knew what she said before about the lounge being full of ash and the sofa being covered in the stuff was true. And it didn't count as taking advantage of her, because she had already told him to stay in that room, with her, that night.

But it didn't feel right stripping off, so instead, he lay down, fully clothed, next to her and made sure there was a decent gap between them – and, probably because he was bone tired himself, he fell asleep pretty quickly.

And it felt so right having her next to him, that when, sometime in the night, he half woke and she was snuggling up next to him and the moonlight was coming through the window, his heart felt like it was going to burst with joy and it was the most natural thing ever to pull her closer to him and go back to sleep holding her.

It was a little chilly when Elodie woke up. She wriggled her feet a bit further under the duvet and snuggled up closer to the warm body beside her. In her half-asleep state, she knew that the body smelled too good to be Piers (who was a man that, latterly, stank of cigar smoke, strong whisky and a horrible expensive cologne that made her itch). The person next to her smelled of the outdoors and wood smoke and citrus. And sage. Yes, there was a definite hint of sage there, which meant ...

Elodie forced her eyes open and saw, in profile, Alex's face, all angular and bathed in moonlight. And he was smiling, just a little. Her arm was flung over his chest and, although he was still wearing a shirt, she could feel the hard muscles underneath the fabric and the slow, regular breathing that told her he was dead to the world. It was a million miles away from their Prom Night debacle on the hay bales.

Her heart did a little flip-flop and for a moment, she tensed and wondered if she should leave her arm where it was or move it. She willed herself to take some deep breaths and relax, and then decided it would, indeed, be easier to leave her arm there – because her head was resting on Alex's arm, which was curled around her, and his fingers were lying lightly on her shoulder.

She had the oddest image of a jigsaw – one of those that boasts 'seamless click technology' – where every piece is smoothly fitted into the next, so there could never be any doubt in the mind that the two pieces attached to one another were meant to be together.

She had never felt that about Piers and herself.

But Alex and her, well, they felt great together. And they fitted perfectly.

She butted her head further into the gap between his neck and his shoulder and closed her eyes again. This was fine, this was innocent. This was not the Prom Night. They were—

'Hey there.' His voice was sleepy and a little husky. It did funny things to her insides.

'I thought you were asleep!' she whispered. 'Sorry.' She felt herself blush and tried to move a little further away, embarrassed that he had caught her snuggling into him like that.

'Are your feet warm enough?' he asked, quite seriously.

She couldn't help it, but she giggled. 'Yes thanks. I can't remember pulling the duvet up at all.'

'I did it. I remembered about the socks.'

Elodie smiled into the silvery night. 'Well done.'

'My pleasure.'

The bed creaked again as he turned over on his side to fully face her. 'Are you okay? Is it all right for me to be here?' He pulled his arm away from her neck and she felt a little bereft.

'It's fine,' she said. 'It's fine.'

Hold me again, Alex. Please. I liked it.

'Sure?'

'I'm sure.'

Please. She was desperate for him to put his arm back and to pull her closer again.

'That's good then.'

He turned over again, and the cold night air washed over her.

'Alex—'

'Yes?'

'Nothing. Sorry.'

She turned away as well and stared at the window.

'You absolutely sure?' His voice was low, and it seemed to have those undercurrents again.

'No. I'm not sure.'

Alex lay with his back to Elodie and stared at the door, wide awake now. His heart was pounding and he had a sense that everything that had happened so far had been inexorably leading to this moment. It would be so easy to just turn over and take her in his arms properly. So easy to tell her exactly what he was thinking and exactly what he was feeling. So easy to—

There was a sound like a door banging shut from downstairs.

'Oh, for goodness' sake.' Alex cursed under his breath, then sat bolt upright and slid himself off the bed.

'What is it?' Elodie sat up too.

'The front door. It's open. It mustn't have caught properly on the latch. It does this sometimes. I won't be a minute.'

He ran out of the room and she heard his feet pounding down the staircase.

'Okay,' Elodie said into the empty room. But there was a little prickle of unease crawling up between her shoulder blades.

She glanced at the window again and watched the shadows move across the glass, then clambered out of bed and stood up. She walked over to the window, almost positive there was something out there – something unearthly. Her sixth sense was kicking in and she had long ago learned to trust it. Perhaps it was the ghostly horseman – or perhaps it wasn't.

Elodie struggled a little with the latches – they were those old-fashioned ones that don't make it easy for a person to open – and eventually managed to throw the window open. She leaned out, her hands on the sill, and tried to see outside, her eyes straining to look into the far distance of a world where the sun was just beginning to rise. Just on their side of the lake she saw a figure moving erratically through the estate and towards the Faerie Bridge.

Elodie's first thought was that it was a poacher, but when she squinted even more, the person didn't look like your usual poacher type – it was a woman, for a start. Elodie could tell by the way she walked and the fact she had long, straight hair. It was a relatively tall, slim woman, who seemed to be wearing little more than shortie pyjamas and possibly carrying something with her, dragging it along behind her. Elodie's heart jumped – she wondered if it was a rifle, but to be honest it looked more like a spade.

It was as if a lightning bolt struck her. '*Cassie*!' She turned to the doorway and ran out after Alex.

'Alex! Alex! Wait!'

He was just pushing the door shut and leaning rather heavily on it to make the latch catch, when Elodie came tearing down the stairs, her filmy white dress making her look like a spirit.

'Wow!' he said as she floated towards him. If one can float at the speed of light, because that did indeed appear to be the rate at which she approached. 'Careful on the stairs!' he warned as she stumbled down the last couple and he caught her just before she fell, then set her straight on her feet again.

'Cassie's out there. I've just seen her by the lake. I think she's got a *spade*. She's heading to the woods.'

He laughed. 'Cassie? With a spade? What do you think she's going to do? Batter a deer and drag it in for a venison breakfast?'

'It's not funny. Look, why is she wandering around at—' She cast a look around, apparently for a clock, because she settled her gaze on the grandfather clock in the corner. '—three in the morning?'

'Battering livestock for breakfast?'

But Elodie was in no mood for a joke. 'Alex!' She shook his arm from her and hurried past him. 'I'm going after her.'

'It won't be Cassie. She'll be tucked up in bed now.'

'She's not, I swear!' Elodie pulled open the door and ran outside.

Alex was horrified. She couldn't head out there in the middle of the night on her own. He knew she wouldn't get very far for a start.

'Elodie!' he called after her and started to run.

She was out of breath before she'd even reached the ha-ha.

Damn her lungs. She hadn't had a bad attack for several weeks, but tonight all the excitement and the smoke had brought yet another one on. So it wasn't long before Alex caught up with her, then gently overtook her.

'Alex!' It was a pathetic little attempt at speech, more like a breathy gasp. She gave up running and steadied to a hurried walk, which was much better on the lungs but not very effective at keeping pace with Alex. She also wished she'd brought along that inhaler.

Just as Alex reached the lake, he stopped and looked across towards the oak tree that still lay there waiting to be chopped up for firewood.

'Good God, Elodie, you're right,' he called over his shoulder. He pointed at the person on the other side of the lake. 'That's Cass, all right.'

Cassie was walking in a straight line. She didn't look erratic anymore and she was heading directly for the oak tree, heedless of anything in her way.

'It's the ley line!' Elodie said, incredulously. 'Look! It's like it's *pulling* her.'

In fact, Cassie marched like a sleepwalker; tall and straight, her head facing forward and her arms out to the side. She dragged the spade as if it was a kite on a piece of string. If she'd been wearing a long white nightgown instead of her shorts, she would have doubled as the lady in Millais' *Somnambulist* painting. Elodie had seen the portrait in the Bonham's auction when Bolton Council sold it – and Delaware Art Museum was a little too far to travel to see it again. But when they had Cassie doing *that* in the garden, why did she even need a portrait?

'Where the hell is she going?' asked Alex. 'She doesn't look natural.'

'We need to catch up with her.' Elodie looked down the river at the Faerie Bridge. 'You'll have to run and get over the bridge, Alex. I can't. I'm sorry.'

She leaned forward and tried to steady her breathing, and could have cried. Even after she had been diagnosed and ultimately hospitalised, Piers had flatly refused to give up the cigars. He said he had an image to maintain and that her terrible lungs were her fault for not going to the gym every day and keeping healthy like Sophia in marketing did. His cigars had made her condition ten times worse and she'd never really recovered.

'What on earth are you sorry for? You're not to blame.' Suddenly, Alex put his hands around her waist and pulled her towards him; then he leaned down and kissed her, which kind of left her reeling a bit. If the kiss and the feel of his warm hands through the thin muslin hadn't actually made her gasp out her last breath, it almost felt like it did.

'But you know what?' he said and stared out over the lake. 'I don't think even *I* can run fast enough.'

And with that, he let go of her waist and dived into the lake.

* * *

Colin Firth looked absolutely splendid swimming across that lake at Pemberley. But, to Elodie, Alex looked even *better*.

He crossed the water with a strong front-crawl and she just stood on the shore, in that half-light between moonset and sunrise, gaping at him. The man had technique, no doubt about it. And then when he emerged on the other side, he strode out onto the bank and his shirt – white, of course – was all un-tucked and glorious and Mr Darcy-like. He'd been in the rowing team at Oxford, she knew, so he was probably well-used to hurling himself into rivers.

'My goodness.' Elodie's chest constricted again. But that time, it was definitely lust, not asthma. Alex had bare feet, just like her. Neither one of them had had time to put any shoes on before haring down here. She stood for a moment longer, staring at him as he picked up speed again and ran after Cassie; then she shook herself and headed towards the bridge. She would have to cross the water the old-fashioned way. Alex would reach Cassie first and she trusted he would find out what she was doing before Elodie got there.

But the man was like a dripping wet, white-clad, dark-haired magnet and she needed to get to him as soon as humanly possible.

It was lucky that the sky was clear and it was almost dawn. He would have lost Cassie in the woods had it been any darker.

As it was, the moon was giving him some light as well, enough to see glimpses of his sister through the trees at any rate. She was dragging a spade alongside her and he had no idea what she was doing, whether she was sleepwalking or whether it was something more sinister.

'Cassie!' His voice sounded loud in the night air and, despite the warmth of the evening, he shivered a little. The damp fabric of his shirt clung to him and the forest floor beneath his bare feet was soft where yesterday's sun hadn't quite managed to bake it hard through the canopy of leaves. Here and there, little scurrying noises and startled flaps came out of the undergrowth and he forced himself to keep his eyes on the path ahead. He didn't want to lose sight of her. He swore as he stumbled over a branch and something sharp dug into the sole of his foot.

'Cassie!' He tried again, grimacing as he stubbed his toe on a stone that seemingly had been lying in wait for him. But Cassie, in contrast, was simply floating along, tall and straight, her head never changing direction. It was exactly as Elodie had said – as if the ley line itself was pulling her along it.

He knew that Cassie would soon break out into the clearing and she would be right next to the fallen oak tree. He wanted to reach her before she did that. The oak tree was right across the path – and if she was genuinely sleepwalking, who was to say she would divert and go around the thing? He sensed more than simply a stubbed toe if she kept at it.

'*Cassandra*!'

She paused for a moment and tilted her head a little, as if she had heard him. He ran faster; but then she was off again. She disappeared into a thicker part of the woods and he crashed through it, gaining on her.

He saw her in the clearing by the oak tree. His heart lurched as she approached the fallen giant.

Then she stopped, right beside it.

She looked at a spot in front of the tree, took hold of the spade and struck the ground.

Alex hurried over to her. 'Cass! What the hell are you doing?' he shouted.

Cassie looked towards him and he swore. She seemed completely different. Her eyes were blank – totally and utterly blank, glinting hazel in the moonlight instead of their usual chocolate brown.

Then, without speaking a word, without changing focus or acknowledging his presence in any other way, Alex's baby sister raised the spade and aimed it straight at the side of his head.

'I have it on good authority that he's out there! A highwayman, a murderous, treacherous bastard. Ben. They say the villain is called Ben, but the devil alone knows his surname. He attacked my daughter, forced himself upon her. Broke into my property. He murdered my son. The dog must die! Hang him – hang him from the highest branch on the oak tree. Let them all see him! Let everyone who travels on the drovers' roads be warned!'

Lucy huddled in the shadows, sitting at the bottom of the staircase, ramming her fist in her mouth. It was her fault, all her fault. She had told Papa in a moment of spite about Ben – about kind, dark-eyed Ben who had left silver pennies for her by the Faerie Bridge and who loved her sister.

'I have seen them together!' she had yelled, the day her sister had found her rummaging in her jewellery case, looking for the pretty locket. Georgiana had been angry, so very angry. More furious than Lucy had ever seen her before. Georgiana had grabbed Lucy's arm and thrown her out into the corridor, screaming at her for being an awful child and a nuisance and a blackmailer and how she wished the faeries would come and take her away.

Lucy had run downstairs and burst into her father's study. 'Georgiana is in love with a highwayman! He's called Ben and he lied to me about the silver pennies. But I knew, I knew he was a liar and he was kissing Georgiana and I found them and she hit me. She hit me Papa, and I did nothing wrong.' She had stood in front of him shouting all sorts of things about Ben and Georgiana, spilling out everything she knew and making up things she didn't.

'And she has a locket and she won't let me see it!' Her voice had risen to a crescendo at that point, furious that Georgiana would never, ever let her look at it. 'And all I wanted to do was see it! And she won't let me!'

To Lucy, that was the worst, the absolute worst of it. It was such a pretty trinket, and all she wanted to do was look at it and maybe wear it for a party. Her Papa hadn't thought that though. He had thought it was much, much worse that Georgiana was kissing Ben. It was as if the locket wasn't important at all and it was the most important thing ever.

Lucy had stood before her Papa, her fingers digging into her palms so they made little crescent moon shapes, and her head had begun to pound with anger and all he could do was start shouting about Ben and how they had to kill him.

Lucy, huddled on the stairs now, caught a little sob in her throat and rammed her fist further into her mouth. She bit down hard and she tasted blood. She didn't want kind, dark-eyed Ben to hang from a tree until he was dead. That's what they did to bad people and he wasn't a bad person. She was worse, much, much worse. He was good and happy and kind and he made Georgiana happy.

Lucy was a horrible person.

'It's all my fault,' she whispered around her fist. 'It's all my fault.'

She squeezed her eyes shut and clung to the newel post as the study door slammed open and she heard her father and a dozen other men thunder out and demand their horses be brought around immediately.

'It's all my fault. I'm sorry. I'm sorry. I love you.'

Chapter Nineteen

Once Elodie was on the other side of the Faerie Bridge, she paused, trying to get a handle on where everyone would be. She could almost feel the energy of that ley line pulsing away and, like Horace the spaniel scenting a rabbit, she lifted her face to the wind and peered through the pre-dawn woods.

She started walking as quickly as she dared towards the fallen oak tree. The energy was leading her to the clearing, tugging her along in Cassie's wake and she only wished she could go faster.

When she finally made it there, with her breath rasping in her chest, Cassie was digging industriously away at a hole in the ground and Alex was lying sprawled out beside her.

'Alex!' Elodie yelled, only it came out more like the noise of a deflating accordion. Dropping down beside him, she turned his head towards her. There was a graze just above his brow and a trail of blood, warm and sticky, running down his face and staining his white collar. He grumbled softly as she touched him and his eyes opened and focussed on her.

'Oh, my God!' She turned a furious gaze towards the dark-haired girl and demanded an answer. 'Cassandra Aldrich! What's *happened*?' But Cassie was apparently completely oblivious to her presence.

'Elodie?' Alex's voice sounded faint, but he was sitting up. 'You look like a ghost in that dress.' He laughed weakly. 'Glad it's you.' He dropped his head briefly into his hands and then looked back up at her.

'Yes, of course it's me. Are you okay? Can you see me? Just one of me?'

She waved her hand in front of his face and was gratified

when he drew back a little from her flailing fingers. 'Yes, I can. Just one of you. Please stop it.'

'What happened?'

'Cassie hit me.' He raised his hand and touched his temple. 'Ouch. Ouch, ouch, ouch.' He stared at his fingers as if he couldn't quite believe all that blood was his. 'She caught me a glancing blow as they say. I ducked. Thank God for martial arts training.'

'Why did she do that?' Elodie said heatedly. '*Cassie!*'

Cassie didn't pause. She didn't even blink. She just kept digging.

Elodie couldn't bear it. Alex was sitting on the ground in his damp clothes with blood running down his face and Cassie was completely ignoring him. What the hell was wrong with the woman?

Furious, she scrambled to her feet and raised her hand. She drew her arm back as far as she could and slapped Cassie *hard* across the face. Just about as hard as she had slapped Alex on Prom Night.

Cassie faltered in her digging, but she didn't even look around. She kept staring at the hole in the ground and mechanically throwing shovelfuls of earth to one side.

Elodie swore then, very loudly and very roundly. The wheezy bit at the end of the word and the consumptive cough kind of diluted the impact, but at least she felt better for doing it.

Thud; thud; thud.

No response; only the steady drop of earth on the ever-increasing pile Cassie was creating.

'This is ridiculous.' Elodie swore again. Instead of hitting the girl and knocking her to the ground like a skittle, which was what she really wanted to do, she tried to catch the shovel as it came up towards her. Cassie, however, shouldered her out of the way and Elodie ended up wobbling and sitting

187

down hard near Alex again. This time, as her bottom hit the ground and she exhaled suddenly, she sounded more like a bagpipe tuning up.

Thud; thud; thud.

'Well at least she didn't hit you. You don't sound very healthy, Elodie.'

'You don't *look* very healthy.' She peered at him and took his face in her hands, running her thumb over the cut and wiping the blood on her dress. Alex flinched but didn't stop her. 'It's not as bad as it looks,' she said. 'I think it's mainly just a nasty graze. As you said, thank God for martial arts. She might have killed you.'

They both stared at Cassie frowning.

'It's not *her*,' said Alex. 'She'd never attack either of us.'

Cassie made them jump by suddenly throwing the spade down with a clatter and kneeling down, peering into the hole she had been working on.

It was eerily silent. Elodie couldn't hear anything but her own heart thumping and she started to shake.

Alex's arm crept around her shoulder and, slightly damp though it was, she was grateful for its warmth.

Cassie turned around, ever so slowly, and finally focused on them. Her face was deathly white and her eyes were swimmy and scared. Elodie had seen many, many creepy things before, but this had to be one of the creepiest.

'Oh, thank goodness. There you are!' The voice that came out of Cassie was nothing like her own. It was a soft, sad little voice with extremely clear enunciation. 'It's all my fault. I'm sorry. I love you.'

It sounded exactly like Lucy's voice had done, when the little girl gleefully brought Ben's silver penny to Georgiana in the attic, so many years ago. Delilah's words drifted into Elodie's mind again: *Lucy had never been quite as rational as a normal child …*

Then Cassie closed her eyes, pulled her knees up, wrapped her arms around them and dropped her chin into her chest. Her shoulders started to shake and she began to sob.

There followed one of those moments where one doesn't quite know what to do. Alex wanted, more than anything, to stay with Elodie and continue sitting with his arm around her.

He wanted to pull her closer and protect her. She sounded terrible and didn't look that much better. God knew, his own head was pounding and his temple was throbbing and it was only now, despite what he'd told Elodie, that he'd stopped really seeing two of everything.

But then there was his sister, all hunched up and crying. And yes, it hadn't been much fun ducking out of the way of a rogue shovel, but was it any different to when he'd pushed her off the Faerie Bridge years ago? He'd been in a temper and she'd landed awkwardly in the water and broken her arm. And it didn't look as if Cassie had done this deliberately – it didn't look like that at all. She'd even apologised, sort of. Hadn't she?

Elodie made the decision for them. She slipped out from under his arm and stood up, walked over to Cassie, and knelt down beside her. Then she pulled his sister towards her, so Cassie's face was buried in Elodie's shoulder, and she smoothed Cassie's hair down and held her closely.

'Shhh, it's okay.'

And Alex knew that his job was to look into that damned hole and discover whatever was in there. He stood up very carefully and let the world stop spinning for a moment; then he lurched over to the hole and knelt down beside it.

Even as he prepared to look down, he hoped it would be some sort of buried treasure – the un-inventoried family jewels or a swag-bag of goodies left by a gentleman thief who rode the woods by moonlight.

But of course, it was neither.

His heart thumped when he saw it. The fact that the oak tree roots were apparently buried in Hell came quite close to reality at that moment.

He sensed Elodie watching him and he turned, walking away from the hole to join her. He sat down quietly, and his hand found hers. They entwined fingers silently. He didn't really know what to do. Hartsford had thrown yet another massive curve ball at him, and this was perhaps worse than finding the empty tomb. Although not, perhaps, entirely unexpected.

Still, at least the only thing that was there to witness his indecision was the fleshless, white skull in the hole.

Elodie looked across at the abandoned shovel and felt the reassuring pressure of Alex's fingers on hers. Part of her wanted to stay well away from the hole, but another part seemed to be impelling her towards it.

'I suspect I need to call the police.' Alex's voice was flat and broke into her thoughts. 'I'm sure that's what you're supposed to do when you find a body, no matter what state it's in. However old it is.'

Elodie felt sick, but she found herself agreeing with him. 'Yes. I think you're right. Can I just – if it's okay – go and have a look?'

Alex nodded and smiled wryly. 'You didn't want to see her in the church.'

'I know. I'm not entirely sure I *do* want to look at her. But I'll see if I can do it.' She eased her fingers out of his and stood up shakily. She took a couple of steps towards the hole, then stopped and looked over her shoulder.

Deep in the woods, she heard something – a desperate whinny, as if a horse was in distress. Hughie had never sounded like that, at all, even when he had been almost laughing at her in the past; and she was fairly sure it wasn't Hughie now. The sound came again and she spun around to see if Alex had registered it. Had there been any inkling of a horse in trouble, she knew he would have been up on his feet trying to locate it; but he hadn't flickered, hadn't moved. He only shuffled closer to Cassie, and put his arm around her.

The sound came again, and she knew, somehow, the whinny was another shadow, another emotion intertwined with the story they were being told. Another memory.

Elodie turned away from the grave and hurried a little towards the noise, until she had left the clearing completely. There was a thud, something like a hoof pawing the ground, then silence crept in around her and Georgiana's memories flooded her mind ...

'I'd like to make a gift of this to you,' said Ben. Dark stubble was dusted across his cheeks and his chin and he seemed on edge. 'I painted it from memory. I hope you find it acceptable.'

'Acceptable? It's beautiful! But I've never looked like that.' Georgiana held the portrait, angling it into the puddle of lamplight, and stared into her own eyes – or at least the eyes that Ben had seen in her.

'Yes, you have. You've always looked like that to me.' He reached over and touched the red ribbon in the portrait-girl's hair, then, surprisingly, moved his hand to the lantern and doused the light. Georgiana gasped slightly and blinked to accustom her eyes to the moonlight. 'Always. From the very moment I met you. I even painted your ribbon. I still have the other half. Right here.' He moved his hand to the back of his neck and she followed the movement. 'And I have the rest of you here.' He curled his hand into a fist and touched his chest, right where his heart was beating, strong and sure beneath the white shirt and the dark coat. 'I don't know how much longer we have left together, but it isn't long enough.'

A look, which might have been fear, crossed his face and suddenly her own heart was seized with a crushing dread.

Her stomach lurched. 'I don't understand,' she whispered. 'Where are you going? Why are you leaving me? I thought you said you'd soon have enough money to…' Her voice rose in panic and she clutched the painting to her own chest. 'Where are you going?'

'I don't want to leave you, but it's not my choice. If I go now, we might have a chance.' He shot a glance behind him and she strained her eyes towards the shadows in the woods. She could hear the regular hoof beats of a harras of horses, the shouts of men carrying through the night – her father's the loudest voice among them. She understood with a sickening jolt why Ben had plunged them into darkness.

'Where is he? The villain! The thief! Murderer!'

'Murderer?' Georgiana looked at Ben. 'What does he mean?'

'He's trying to blame me for Jasper's death …'

'Jasper? But it was a brawl. A brawl over a hand of cards in an inn, with a stranger! I saw his body! He was beaten and stabbed!'

'I know. But the Earl has nothing else he can accuse me of. Except my loving you.' The pain in his eyes was indescribable. 'Please, take this too. Use it if you have to. It's my turn to try and protect you. And I'm no angel, so my kisses are sadly lacking in Godly protection.'

He produced a pistol – Georgiana recognised it as Jasper's duelling pistol; the one that had been missing from his body when she found him on the steps that awful, awful morning. 'Ben! Where did you get this? You were there!'

'I don't deny it. I was in the Green Dragon the night he died. He was defending your honour, my love. I saw it all. I took this afterwards. Nobody else was entitled to it and believe me, those men have now paid the ultimate price for what they did to him. I made sure of it.' His handsome face hardened for a second. 'I know your brother would want you to have it and want you to use it if you have to. Do not hesitate to protect yourself. Do you understand?'

He looked so earnest that all Georgiana could do was nod. 'I will – but I still don't see why—'

She stared at the pistol as he wrapped her fingers around it and pressed them to his lips. 'I have to go, because if I don't and they find me here ...' He didn't need to continue. She understood perfectly.

Hurriedly, she pushed the rolled-up portrait into the cleft of two branches of a nearby shrub and closed the gap between her and Ben. She wrapped her arms around him to give him a quick embrace. 'Go now, Ben. Go!' She pulled back and looked up at him. She couldn't stop her tears and he kissed them away. 'Send for me,' she told him, her words tumbling out. 'I'll have some things packed and I'll come and find you. You never have to come here again.'

'Georgiana.' He pulled her back in towards him. 'I'll come back for you if I can – I promise.' He threw another quick glance over his shoulder. The shadows were moving towards them, a seething mass of blackness and shouting and steaming breath. 'Until we meet again.' He pressed his lips against hers, hard and passionate, the things he didn't have time to tell her clear in the kiss. 'I love you Georgiana. Wait for me.'

'I promise. I'll wait for you by moonlight, as always.'

He ran towards his horse. Blaze was whinnying and rearing, trying to tell him they had to leave. One swift movement saw him in the saddle and with a sharp dig of his heels into the horse's flank, he disappeared into the night.

The group of men, led by Georgiana's father, filled the horizon, cresting the little hill. They yelled something and, as one, steered the animals to the left, following Ben.

Georgiana ran towards them all screaming, then she stopped short and turned away, running back towards the Hall, her fingers pressing against her mouth – the mouth he had so recently kissed, the mouth that was still bruised from his. She clutched the pistol in her hand, not liking the feel of it, but knowing why he had given her it. She had to do some packing so she was ready, just in case ...

Elodie stood in the dawn-lit woods and realised it was silent apart from the birds waking up and the leaves rustling in the trees. There was no horse, no Blaze – and definitely no Hughie. She wrapped her arms around herself and turned a full circle. She was pleased she knew who had painted the portrait of Georgiana, but the romance of that was secondary to the danger Ben had been in that day.

She realised she was facing the clearing – and suddenly desperately wanted to go back to Alex and make sure he was safe. It was a silly notion, perhaps; but she rushed back to him as fast as she dared.

She decided she wouldn't look at the skeleton after all.

Office hours couldn't come quickly enough that morning. They sat in the kitchen at the Hall watching the hands on the clock move slowly forwards and held cups of coffee that went cold before they managed to drink them.

Elodie had glossed over the most recent memories, whispering the story to Alex well away from Cassie, and Alex had nodded, understanding, then turned his attention to the discovery in the woods; she knew he was trying not to speculate on what had put the skeleton there. They both knew how much danger Ben and Georgiana had been in that night, and neither Alex nor Elodie wanted to take the story to its potential conclusion.

Alex had closed the Hall to tourists for the day. They

didn't want visitors around; it was nothing that anyone else should witness. All the volunteers had been told the truth of course, just in case they worried when they saw the police vans and forensics people turn up.

The Home Office Pathologist didn't take long to come, and once he was there the investigation team worked diligently to get all the evidence they could. They eventually called at the house and asked if anybody would like to join them at the oak tree to discuss the initial findings. They were satisfied it was an old burial and thus didn't think they would be interfering with a new murder investigation.

'I'll go.' The graze on Alex's temple was still looking a bit raw, and there were some nasty bruises down the side of his face too, where Cassie must have caught him as he ducked out of the way. Elodie wanted him to go and get it checked out at the hospital, but he refused, saying that so long as he was walking, talking and making sense he thought he'd pretty much be okay. There was, though, an open packet of painkillers next to his coffee cup and his mobile phone was lined up next to them, in case the forensic people called from the woods and needed anything urgently.

And, of course, every time Cassie saw him, she burst out crying and kept trying to apologise.

'Call it quits for the broken arm,' he had told her. Which just made her cry all the more.

Cassie had said straight away that she didn't want to go and look at the grave. If the skeleton was Georgiana, she wanted to remember her as the girl sculpted in marble; the girl who might be in that painting from the attic. The girl who Elodie quietly knew was indeed in that painting from the attic.

Alex stood up to leave the room with the Detectives, or whoever they were, and smiled down at Elodie. 'It's okay. You don't have to come either. We'll get it sorted. If it's Georgiana, we'll get her back to where she needs to be.'

He was halfway out of the room when Elodie slid off the high stool at the breakfast bar and went after him. 'I'll come if you want me to. Don't feel you have to deal with this yourself.'

He smiled down at her, then ran his hand through his dark, messy hair. 'No. You stay here. I think Cassie would appreciate the company.'

Elodie looked across at Cassie who was certainly looking pretty miserable, then turned back to speak to Alex; but he had gone, closing the door quietly behind him.

'Well now.' Elodie didn't really expect Cassie to answer, but she did look at her, Cassie's eyes puddling with fresh tears.

'I honestly don't know what made me do it,' Cassie said. 'One minute I was in my room, and the next I wake up and I'm sitting by the oak tree. And Alex's got blood on his face and you're looking like death warmed up.'

'Remind me to never wear this dress again,' Elodie said ruefully, looking down at it. 'Alex said I looked like a ghost. You think I looked like death warmed up. It's better with a suntan, I promise. And maybe with no bloodstains on it.'

'It's not just that dress.' Cassie laid her forehead on the table and banged it gently once, twice, three times off the surface. The coffee cups wobbled a little. 'I'm an idiot. I'm sorry.'

'What for? For saying I look pale and recently deceased?'

'No!' she said, talking into the table. 'Sorry. I didn't mean it like that. What I really meant was, I'm sorry because I found the grave. If I hadn't started digging, then I wouldn't have hit Alex and you wouldn't have been forced to come after me. In your dress.'

'It's not your fault, Cass. Look.' Elodie bent forward and rested her own forehead on the table next to Cassie's, then turned a little so she was facing her. Slowly, Cassie mirrored her movement and stared at Elodie. 'It wasn't you out there. It didn't sound like you when you spoke and it certainly didn't look like you. Nobody blames you.'

Cassie nodded miserably. It must have been awkward to nod with one's head on the table, but she managed it, somehow.

'I know you'll understand me when I say this. Not everyone would. But you – you'll understand.' Cassie took a deep breath and sat up. It was Elodie's turn to mirror her and she sat up with her. 'I think someone took me there. I don't sleepwalk and I just felt – different. I know this place is haunted. I've seen the children in the nursery and I've seen – other stuff – myself. Not so much now, but when I was younger. I just think it was one of them.' She frowned. 'Sorry. I'm stupid.'

'No! No, I don't think you are. This place hangs onto all sorts of energy. If it's any consolation, I think the same.' Elodie looked down at her hands. 'Someone was determined that you would find that grave and they led you to it.'

'Am I susceptible then?' asked Cassie. 'Do you think that's why they chose me?'

'Maybe. If you've seen the ghosts, they'd know they had a way in. Not everyone can see the children in the nursery, you know. Maybe you just need to know how to control it a little more; how to fight them off if they *do* try to push you too far.'

Cassie smiled. 'I knew you'd understand. I'm so pleased that you don't think I'm a horrible person. I don't tell anyone about what I see or hear – sometimes it's just odd words I pick up from nowhere. Or I see a flash of a dead person.' She shivered and fell silent for a moment or two. Then she nodded at Elodie. 'It's the same for you, isn't it? But this time it was weird, it was all strange memories, flashes of sitting in the hallway. I was terrified and guilty and suddenly I was there, showing you that.'

'I totally get it,' murmured Elodie. 'It comes with living here, I think. You can't really help it.'

'Hartsford talks to you, doesn't it? It likes to show you its secrets.'

Elodie didn't think Cassie expected an answer, but she nodded anyway.

Chapter Twenty

Alex knew he'd always hated that oak tree. The labourer who had spun those yarns had consolidated that view, but maybe the genetic memory theories had something to recommend them after all.

The forensics team had been cleaning the soil away all morning, and the chap who was in charge, Dave, was actually very jolly – he said he thought he had identified the cause of death and if Alex liked, he could go through some basics with him.

Alex didn't know if he 'liked'. It was hardly a Facebook status ('found ancient skeletal body in my garden today – huzzah!') but Dave knew Alex wanted to know anything he could tell him about it, so Alex nodded and agreed. Dave ushered him to the edge of the hole and they both stared in.

'Can you see here, the way the ribcage is shattered?' Dave began. Alex's stomach was churning, but he forced himself to look properly. Georgiana – if this was Georgiana – was tiny. In life, she couldn't have been more than five feet tall. In death, she looked pathetic.

He could see, however, what Dave meant. The rib cage had a big hole in it, just near the breastbone. Fragments of bone were lying inside what would have been her chest cavity and Alex could see a vile-looking nick on her backbone as well. In fact, there was a crack right through the spine and a pile of what might have been destroyed vertebrae. Next to the spine lay a small, round object.

'That's the bullet,' said Dave. 'Sometimes these things go right through. This one didn't. It's shattered the vertebrae and broken the spine. If the gunshot didn't manage to kill her, she wouldn't have been going for many walks in the future.' He laughed, but Alex scowled. It wasn't a laughing matter.

Alex fixed Dave with a glare. 'So you're sure it's a woman.' His voice sounded weirdly distant.

'Certain.' Dave pointed at the lower part of the skeleton. 'No doubt she's a woman. The shape of the pelvis tells us that. Looks like she gave birth at least once and her teeth are awful. Sugary diets and poor dental hygiene were a curse at that time for the wealthy. Wisdom teeth were through, though. She's beyond her twenties. I'd guess early forties? We won't know any more until we get her back to the lab.' He turned and grinned at him. 'We'll do some carbon dating, see if that tells us when she was buried. The boys are onto the forensic geology over there—' Dave nodded across at a group of white-clad people – three of whom Alex was fairly certain were women rather than boys. '—and then we'll be able to tell you more. And see, there's still cloth on some of the bones too. We can date that if it's preserved well enough. I think you've got a bit of history here, lad. Anything we should know to give us a clue?' He looked at Alex, cheerful as a robin with the same little black, all-seeing eyes. 'Any family secrets? Skeletons in the closet? That kind of thing?' Dave laughed at his own joke.

'One or two.' Alex frowned again. The cut on his face reminded him of its presence and he winced, putting his hand up to rub it. He mentally ran through the list of attributes Dave had given the skeleton. Something didn't add up.

'What happened there?' asked Dave, nodding at Alex's temple.

'My sister did it,' Alex replied without thinking. 'Sorry – did you say this woman possibly had children? And she was in her forties?'

Dave laughed. 'You see. Family feud. You might be the one

that ends up in another grave.' He laughed and laughed and Alex thought how funny it was that you could go off some people so quickly. 'But in answer to your questions, yes. I've been in the business too long to get in too much of a pickle with my bodies. In her forties, yes. Children. Yes. Of course, that doesn't mean it was a live birth, but—'

Alex let the words drift over him as he turned back to the skeleton. 'We had a family member go missing in the eighteenth century.' He frowned. 'I was wondering if this was her.'

It wasn't too far off the truth. Georgiana had gone missing – the mere fact they'd only just discovered that didn't mean that it hadn't originally happened in the eighteenth century.

But somebody must have wanted the world to think Georgiana was dead. And if this wasn't her – a nineteen-year-old who hadn't, as far as they knew, had any children – then who was it?

'Well, lad, just so you know,' Dave interrupted Alex's thoughts, 'it'll all take a while to get her sorted. We can't release her until all the tests are done and we know for sure what happened. We don't know if it's murder or suicide. Doesn't seem like natural causes to me though. Not many guns leap up and kill you naturally in my experience.'

There was a clatter nearby and Alex looked up. A group of people were bringing boxes out of the back of a van. They were going to put the skeleton in the boxes and take it away. Alex didn't want to be around to witness that. Not at all. So he took one last look at the sad collection of bones and said a little prayer for whoever it was.

Then he thanked Dave and his team, took the pathologist's card and walked slowly back to the Hall.

'She's going to the lab,' said Alex when he came back. He

looked wrecked as he sat down between Cassie and Elodie. 'But I don't think it's Georgiana.'

'Not Georgiana?' Elodie stared at him. 'How? It makes sense that it *should* be her.'

Alex nodded. 'Dave the Jolly Pathologist thinks it's a woman in her forties. And he says there's evidence of childbirth. It doesn't help.'

'Can they say how she died?' asked Elodie, blindsided.

'Gunshot wound to the chest. Like we didn't already suspect a shooting.'

'The duelling pistol?'

'Seems likely.'

'I think we're going to have to—' Elodie started, when they were interrupted by the front door slamming back against the doorframe, a loud "*Woof!*" and a friendly "*Yoohoo!*" coming down the corridor.

'In here, Margaret!' shouted Alex. 'Come on in, Horace. Good boy!'

Horace bounded in and jumped up at all their feet, wagging his feathery tail like it was super-charged. Then Margaret came in and Cassie jumped out of the chair, evaded Horace and flung herself at Margaret. 'Oh, Margaret, what a *horrid* day it's been!' she wailed.

'Oh, sweetheart!' Margaret patted her on the back and made all the right noises. 'Come on. Let's get this place tidied up a bit and you'll all feel better.' Margaret always believed a cup of tea and a tidy house improved everything. 'Pop the kettle on, Alex. We'll get the tea brewing and I'll make a start upstairs. I bet my baby's room is the worst again.' She hugged Cassie and chuckled, then bustled out of the door, Horace jumping around her ankles and chuffing excitedly.

'Baby's room?' Elodie raised her eyebrows, and hid a smile.

'Mine.' Cassie had the grace to look embarrassed. 'I'm not that good at tidying up.'

'I'd noticed.' Alex chuckled.

'Well shall I just stop coming *home* then?' Cassie snapped and flounced out of the room, slamming the door behind her.

Alex put his head in his hands and groaned. 'I can't deal with that today,' he muttered. 'Cassie in a temper. Well. She can come back when she's calmed down. *Horace* is less bother. And we've still got the pistol to sort out yet. Great.'

'Mmm. And I don't know if *I* can deal with the pistol,' Elodie admitted. 'I just want to end this now. We know the damage pistols can do and you must have seen what happened to the woman under the tree. What if we see it all happening with Georgiana? What if she *did* get shot? Why else would the pistol be buried in the tomb?'

'Exactly. I was hoping finding the skeleton would solve most of it, especially if it was Georgiana. I didn't want to go down the pistol route if we could help it. You think I want to see it happening? I don't want to see her die. God.' Alex stared at Elodie for a moment longer. 'I don't want to see *you* die. Even if technically it's not you, just a memory.'

'We need to find out what happened though. What if Georgiana was murdered too? What if, God forbid, Lucy did it by accident? Or her Papa did it because she was seeing Ben? Or *Ben* did it?'

'You see, *that's* what I'm worried about as well. What if Ben killed Georgiana?' Alex fixed his eyes on her and they were like deep blue-coloured granite. 'To me, it's clear that we need to know more about Ben. And the pistol might be the key. We both know we have to do it. So we might as well get it over with. Georgiana is still missing. This is our last hope of finding out what happened.'

Elodie stood in the Long Gallery, watching Alex unlock the cabinet which held the single duelling pistol. His shoulders were set, his eyes still stormy and she knew he was probably thinking about what might have happened.

On the top of a Tudor wooden unit, next to Alex, was the other pistol; the one from Georgiana's tomb. Elodie was trying not to look at it. It was just horrible – she was, in essence, looking at what was probably a murder weapon.

'The first thing to do is just to check they are definitely part of the same set,' said Alex. 'I meant to do it before but I got distracted and didn't.'

Elodie nodded dumbly. But he was still standing with his back to her, so she suspected he didn't know that she'd agreed.

Alex carried the beautiful wooden box over to a *chaise longue* that was pushed up against the side of the wall, the idea being that tourists could sit on it if they found the walking too much. Then Alex went back to the Tudor unit and brought the pistol from the tomb over to rest beside the box. He proceeded to inspect the two pistols and then lay them side by side. Even Elodie could see that they were a perfect match; apart from the fact, obviously, that one was nice and shiny and the other one was dull and dirty.

'Yep, they're a pair.' Alex nodded at the grubby pistol. 'It's bound to hold some of her memories but it's unlikely they'll be happy ones.'

Elodie frowned as she tried to work it all out. 'The facts all point to the oak tree. A body was buried there, and that person seemed to have been killed by a pistol. Probably the one that was hidden away. This one.' She stared at the weapon. 'Oh, I'm going to regret this, aren't I?' She took a deep breath; then she picked the pistol up from the *chaise longue*.

It was the middle of the starlit night when he had fled, and there was shouting. A lot of shouting. Georgiana quickly hid

Jasper's duelling pistol in the bodice of her gown and started to hurry along the gallery. She had quickly dressed and was planning to take her horse and ride out to the woods to find Ben. She had heeded his warning about protecting herself with Jasper's pistol; but it seemed she was too late.

'We got him!' her father cried. 'We got the bastard. The men are dealing with it. He's finished. I told them he murdered Jasper – that duel story never fails me!' The Earl let out a bellow of laughter. 'Two reprehensible situations dealt with at once. The stupidity of a drunken boy and the inexcusable behaviour of a slut.'

Before Georgiana could react, a door crashed open and her mother fell out of her bedroom, slopping red liquid out of a glass all over the polished floors. Georgiana hadn't seen or heard from her in two days. She could see from the state of the Countess what had caused her absence and Georgiana was disgusted. More than that – ashamed. The woman staggered towards the staircase, trying to push past her daughter before she realised who she was.

Then the Countess stopped and stared at Georgiana and raised one, shaking forefinger. 'There have been rumours. Rumours I cannot allow to circulate about this family. Now, it is finished. But may God help you! The county knows it all – they know you have thrown yourself away and they know who on. You've brought shame to us all!'

The ground shifted beneath Georgiana's feet and the room wavered. She stared at her mother, unable to defend herself, holding onto the windowsill lest she crumple into a sickly heap. They had only loved each other like that a handful of times – but once – once, she had heard the door creak and passed it off as the old wood flexing in the cooling evening. What if someone had seen them? What if they had seen fit to tell tales?

Her mother sobbed – an ugly, messy sound – and raised her hand as if to strike her.

Georgiana managed to croak out a few words, ducking out of the Countess's way. 'I love him! We are to be married.'

'You are a harlot! A whore! You shame me! You shame us all!' The Countess pushed her face up so close to Georgiana's that the girl could see the bloodshot state of her eyes and smell the stench of filth and old liquor on her. 'You brought him to your room and you prostituted yourself. He is a murdering thief. A highway robber. He will have bedded hundreds of women. You are diseased: ruined. No man will take you now. No man. He killed your brother. You should go to Hell for what you have done.'

A veil of red descended over Georgiana's vision and she clenched her fists to prevent herself from punching her mother. 'To Hell? Then I look forward to it. And as for you, you are drunk and delusional. You know that he didn't murder Jasper. Jasper was killed in a brawl. It matters not what my father wishes the world to believe. Jasper died like a dog on the highway. He did not die in a duel or in any way like a gentleman would die. It was a brawl. His body was dumped on the steps of the Hall with his bones shattered and his pistol missing. I found him, for God's sake! I know what happened! Everyone knows what happened! Father has disowned him for his misfortune, and you haven't been sober since. Why, I believe it has driven you half mad! Yet he was only a boy. I loved him. He was my brother. He made one mistake. But all he had seen for years was you drinking yourself into a stupor.'

At that point her mother did strike her. The Countess raised her hand and slapped Georgiana so hard her ears rang and she stumbled over a Tudor cabinet.

'You are selfish and you are a liar. Your brother was worth a thousand of you!' her voice caught on another, more pathetic sob. 'I cannot believe my daughter – my daughter! my own *child! – could be so immoral. How could you throw yourself away on a thief and a murderer? How? Well.' Suddenly, she began to laugh hysterically, which Georgiana found utterly terrifying. 'Now you will never see your beloved murderer again. He's swinging from the oak tree with a rope around his neck. I hope the birds peck his eyes out and you are there to watch it happen.'*

Georgiana put her hand to her mouth to stifle her screams and ran to the window while her mother stumbled down the stairs yelling congratulatory comments to the Earl.

The oak tree. She had to get to the oak tree.

She prayed she would not be too late.

Elodie dropped the pistol as if it were made of molten metal. She stumbled and grabbed the edge of the cabinet, fighting back the tell-tale hitch in her chest and a world that was going far too woozy for comfort.

'We do have to go back to the oak tree,' she managed. 'There's something about Ben there.'

Alex made one, sweeping glance that took in both Elodie and the pistol and swiped the weapon up from the *chaise longue*. He tucked it in his belt and then scooped Elodie up in his arms. 'Let's go now,' he said. 'We'll get there more quickly if I carry you.'

He took a few hurried steps down the corridor, Elodie hanging onto his neck, half unsure how she'd ended up in his arms. Their progress was hindered by Margaret, carrying an armful of clothes.

'That child gets more and more untidy!' The connecting door to the family wing of the Hall was standing wide open. 'Sorry, love. I took a short cut. Hope you don't mind.' Margaret smiled at Alex, one quick look, Elodie noticed, taking in the fact Elodie was in his arms. 'Cassie's got so much junk in that room, it was just easier to come this way and cut the corner off,' Margaret continued, not even looking quizzically at them.

'Do whatever you want,' said Alex, nodding. 'Elodie and I are just heading out anyway. You stay as long as you like. Maybe Cassie would be happier in a sty?'

Margaret laughed. 'I don't know about that. The way these things smell, I guess she could be smoky bacon.' She chuckled. 'If I find she's started sneaking cigarettes in again, I'll not be happy with her. I thought she'd stopped that at fourteen.'

She wafted closer to them and Elodie's nose wrinkled. Sage. Sage smoke. Just like the stuff her cottage had been filled with. Her chest tightened and she clung onto Alex more firmly, her heart hammering. *Not another attack – not again!* Her chest had suddenly decided it didn't like sage smoke anymore, which was possibly going to cause her issues for future smudging sessions.

'They're *Cassie's* clothes?' Alex's nose wrinkled in recognition as well.

'These? Why yes.' Margaret lifted the pile of clothes up and pushed them further towards Alex, which meant, of course, that they were also closer to Elodie.

She choked a little. 'Alex – can you put me down please? Please? Next to the window.' She could feel the rasping as the breath started to catch in her chest. 'Or, can we go? While I can still breathe? Please.'

'Cassie set that fire!' he said, horrified. Elodie felt his arms tighten around her protectively. 'Or someone made her do it!'

'Alex. Please? The window. I need—'

'God. Sorry. Yes. Margaret – we'll see you later. I'll see Cassie later too. Thanks. Thank you.' Alex turned and sprinted down the corridor, Elodie clinging on, squeezing her eyes shut and concentrating on continuing to breathe.

* * *

Once they were outside, Alex paused and looked into Elodie's eyes searchingly. 'Are you all right? Do we need to get you to hospital again?'

Elodie laughed weakly and shook her head. 'I'm fine now we're outside. Thank you. That sage smoke just caught me. Right here.' She tapped her fingers on her chest. Her face was at the same height as his for once and he so desperately wanted to kiss that perfect little mouth, but he didn't; instead, he put her gently back on her feet.

She looked up at him searchingly. 'Alex. I have to tell you something about the oak tree. If you come with me, you might find out the hard way and I don't think it will be pleasant for either of us.'

'It's fine. Whatever is up there, we face it together. It can't be worse than finding a body.'

Her eyes dropped to the pistol in his belt. 'Yes, but we know that lady definitely *isn't* Georgiana. She's still missing, isn't she? But Georgiana's memory in the corridor was so strong – her mother told her what happened at the tree and it might have ended badly for Ben. The Countess took great delight in it, the old witch.'

'The Countess? Jane? Was she as bad as they say?'

'She was awful. Drunk, unhinged, said lots of cruel things.'

'My mother married into the right family then,' Alex said wryly.

'She was worse than your mother, but I think she felt Jasper's death more keenly than anyone realised. She was grieving and grieving badly. She told Georgiana that ...' Her voice trailed off and she gazed out towards the tree; then she took a deep breath, looked at Alex and tried again. 'She told Georgiana that Ben had been hanged over there. Now I don't know if it was true but—'

'I knew I never liked that tree!' Alex's hand strayed to his neck and he rubbed it. 'Hanged. Well, that's just fantastic.

What a way to end a love story!'

Elodie reached up and took hold of his hand; she covered it with her own and stilled his movements. 'Are you sure you really want to come up to the oak tree now?'

Alex took a deep breath. 'Yes. Yes. I still want to go there. It's all shadows. All the past. All memories. Hopefully we won't kill each other.' It was a bad joke and he knew it.

'All shadows.' Elodie wasn't laughing, either. 'I'll tell you what I know on the way up there.'

He looked down at her, standing so prettily and so concernedly in front of him; he noted a few freckles sprinkled across a nose that was pink from the recent summer weather. She looked all of sixteen again and his heart melted a little. 'Are you okay to walk? Or do you need a lift again?'

That was a better joke.

She smiled this time. 'I can walk, thank you.'

Chapter Twenty-One

It took them a good twenty minutes to get to the oak tree. It didn't normally take that long, but they walked slowly as Elodie told Alex about the drunken mother and the accusations.

He was horrified, ashamed that the Kerridges had ever been like that.

'At least I'm descended from the French cousin, the Aldrich line,' he said with feeling. Things were different in those days and people were cruel and children, especially girls, were disposable; but to go to all that trouble to laud your son and sanctify your daughter, just to protect the family name, when all along, you had been the people to poison their lives and cause their downfall? It was horrible.

When they finally reached the tree, they stared at the hulk of useless firewood and he wondered which branch they had used to hang Ben from.

'I'm thinking,' said Elodie, who was now looking a little pale, 'that I should go and stand near where they found the body. If I do that and you give me the pistol, I should be pretty well-situated to see what happened there.'

Alex focussed on one of the bigger, sturdier branches that lay at ninety degrees to the fallen trunk. 'I suspect Ben didn't even touch the tree. If he was hanged, then he would just – dangle?'

Elodie laughed nervously. 'You see it too, do you? That branch there?' She pointed at exactly the same one Alex had noticed. 'That would be a good one.'

'Look, maybe this isn't such a good idea?' Alex said suddenly. 'Let's just forget it. I don't want you—'

'Want me what?' Elodie looked up at him. 'Seeing Ben like that?'

'Yes. Because I wouldn't want to see *you* like that.'

She sidled up to him and wrapped her arms around him. 'But we need to finish it, Alex. It's the last piece of the puzzle!'

For a moment his heart skipped a beat, overwhelmed to be in her arms like that; but before he could stop her, she grabbed the pistol from his belt, scrambled breathlessly over the fallen giant and slid down the other side, stopping right next to the old grave.

'Elodie!' Alex began to scramble after her 'No!'

She was back at the tree, the moon hanging in the sky like a silver penny – but Ben was not there. There were footprints and scuff marks where they had dragged something across the ground, then a whole set of hoof prints leading away through the forest, but it was too dark to see where they went and she had no heart to follow them. The end of what looked like a noose remained in the tree, swinging emptily from the strongest branch, and she felt sick.

She pulled the pistol out of her bodice, trying to choke back the great heaving, helpless sobs, and aimed it at her heart. She closed her eyes and raised her face to the oak tree—

'I knew you'd come here!' The voice startled her. Her finger slipped off the trigger as she spun around. 'I'm glad he's dead. Glad, do you hear? It is no more than he deserves for killing my boy!'

'Mama!'

'What are you going to do? Finish yourself off? Go on then. Go and join your murderous lover.'

The woman could barely walk in a straight line. She came close to Georgiana, taunting her. 'Do it. Make my life easier.'

Georgiana wanted to vomit. 'Leave me alone!' she sobbed. 'You don't know what you're saying!'

The older woman grabbed at the chain around Georgiana's neck and ripped it off, brandishing it before her. 'Is this going with you? Is it a gift from him, bought with blood money from murdering my boy?'

Something inside her snapped and Georgiana shrieked, making a lunge for the locket as the Countess hurled it with all her might as far away as she could.

'You're insane, Mama! Stop it!'

But the Countess was beyond reason. She lurched forward and grabbed the pistol, trying to turn it to face her daughter. 'Will death be more honourable to you than living with the shame of your lover? Everybody knows about you – everybody. Will you kill yourself with your brother's pistol? The pistol his murderer stole and gifted you? Yes! I recognise it – does that surprise you? He was so proud of it. He told me all about it. I loved him, I did. I loved my darling Jasper, my only son!'

She wrestled the gun out of Georgiana's hand and pistol-whipped her daughter, hard, across the face.

Twice.

Just as Alex reached her, Elodie made a frightening, gasping sound like her airwaves had just cut off, clutched at her chest and crumpled to the ground. The pistol tumbled out of her hand and landed next to her.

'Elodie!' Alex dropped to his knees and gathered her up in his arms, calling her name. She didn't seem to be breathing at all and her lips were already starting to go blue. He tried to make her sit up, remembering how he'd researched it last year after the squash court incident, hoping he'd never have to use it: *'Asthma attacks usually don't just go away by themselves'*, that information had said. He had been horrified, reading about *'acute severe asthma'* and a *'silent chest'* and had never wanted to witness Elodie in that situation again.

She wouldn't sit though, she just kept flopping around and he finally laid her on the ground. He would have sold his soul to the devil for an inhaler at that moment, but all he could do was start mouth-to-mouth resuscitation.

The few minutes he spent beside her felt like a lifetime. He repeated the breathing and the praying, interspersed with begging her to come back to him. He went for his mobile, but too late he remembered that it was still on the kitchen table from when they'd all been sitting together and he'd been popping painkillers. It seemed like a year ago.

'Dammit! Look, I can't lose you Elodie! Come on, come back to me. Please.'

There was no response. And, eventually, he gave up. She lay there in that white dress which was, by now, filthy from the leaf mould and dirt the tree and the forensics people had spread everywhere. He traced the smears of blood from last night with his fingertips; then he put his head on her chest, too shocked even to let the tears come.

His own words came back to haunt him: *What a way to end a love story.*

And then he felt it. A little rise against his cheek. A tight little gasp. Then another little gasp. Then her chest rose again.

'Elodie?' He sat up and pulled her into a sitting position to help her. He pushed the hair away from her face and patted her cheeks, willing her to open her eyes. 'Elodie!'

'Alex?' her voice was raw, faint. But it was her voice. Her eyes fluttered open and she blinked, focusing on him. 'Alex? What's … wrong?' She raised her hand and touched his cheek and he grabbed her fingers and pressed them to his mouth.

'I thought you were gone. I thought I'd lost you. You just went *down*. I couldn't stop you, I couldn't help you. I—' He shook his head, pulling himself back together before he lost it completely. He didn't want to let go of her. He didn't want to stop touching her.

'She ... never saw ... Ben. Up there.' She stopped, seeming to find it difficult to talk in proper sentences, the words as jagged as her breathing. 'The pistol. And ...' She put her head in her hands. 'Her mother. Hit her. She went down.' She looked up. 'I didn't see ...'

'Shhh ...' Alex drew her closer as he looked around him. Drover's roads intersected the clearing where the tree had been. It was only a tiny leap of the imagination to envisage a handsome highwayman holding up a coach and stealing the heart of a young girl in the process. A handsome highwayman struggling as they hauled him up, up, up into the branches ...

'You've seen enough. I'm getting you back home.' Alex made the decision. 'Finding out their secrets isn't as important as keeping you safe.' He loved her. Had loved her with every part of his being, his entire life. Seeing her lying there on the ground, not breathing, had made him regret for the thousandth time the wasted years. Nothing could ever or would ever change the way he felt – not even death. He understood how Ben must have felt about Georgiana and what had driven them to burn their precious memories into the earth and into the air and into the very walls of Hartsford Hall.

What he hadn't understood was why they needed to share those memories now.

He stared again at the crossroads and the fallen tree and the mound of flattened, fresh earth beside them, and held Elodie a little tighter and a little closer.

He thought that he might be starting to comprehend.

Alex had insisted on carrying her back to her cottage and she felt too weak to argue, although she had downright refused to go to hospital again. 'I'll just spend my life going back and forth if I give in today – so no,' she'd stated in a manner that she hoped brooked no argument. 'I'm walking, talking and making sense, yes? Anyway, who's to say it's not something to do with what happened to Georgiana, and nothing really to do with my asthma? How could you explain that one to a doctor?' He'd been unable to go against that one.

So it was slow progress as she bounced gently in his arms until they got to the little path that led there.

'Will you come in with me? I want to grab my spare inhaler. I think I can remember where I put it.'

'Of course,' replied Alex and put her on her feet again.

She looked down at the filthy mess her dress had become and shook her head. 'I think I'll get changed as well. This is probably fit for use only as a duster now.'

'It's not that bad.' Alex smiled. 'You look beautiful.'

She smiled back. 'It's scruffy. I'm scruffy. And we both know it. I'll find some jeans.'

'The cottage might still be smoky. Will you be all right?'

Elodie took a deep breath. Then another. 'I feel much better now. I'm sure a few minutes won't hurt me. The windows have been open all night anyway.'

'The way you reacted to Cassie's clothes doesn't exactly inspire me with confidence. And you were all but dead up there after your scramble over that bloody tree.'

'I'm glad you were there.' She shuddered. The facts hadn't escaped her attention for one moment and she knew she was lucky to be alive. 'Can we just see how it goes? Will you wait for me?'

'Of course.' His hand went up to the bruises on his face, as if remembering the passing clout from the shovel. 'I might just see if there's anything that suggests Cassie was in there, if that's okay?'

'Feel free. I'd like to know myself, but I don't think she remembers any of it. Cassie would never hurt either of us on purpose. Lucy is mixed up in it somehow.' *Especially with that box having her blackmail letters in it!* But of course she didn't mention that to Alex.

Her cottage looked a little sorry for itself. The windows were open, which gave the impression that it was about to flap its many wings and take off. Elodie opened the door and braced herself for the smell of smoke and sage, and the disagreeableness of her chest complaining, but she was pleasantly surprised to find that there was only a faint whiff of sage and she found she could breathe almost normally.

She did head straight upstairs to find another inhaler though, just in case.

'It looks fine up here,' she shouted down. 'Not too bad at all. I think we aired it out rather well. I'll not be too long.'

'No problem.' A door opened and closed, and she assumed he had gone into the lounge.

Once upstairs, she peeled the dirty dress off and discarded it onto the floor. It needed washing badly, but it was probably one of those silly hand-wash only things and she couldn't bear to think about that right at the moment.

She rummaged in her wardrobe and came up with a clean pair of pale denim jeans and a black top and hurried into the bathroom.

'I'm just going to have a quick shower!'

'Take your time!'

It reminded her of the day of the storm, when she'd been in his bath; when all of this had started to play out. She shivered. Elodie still didn't feel as if she had closure and wanted to finish the story, but it didn't seem as if it would be as easy as she had thought. There were certainly a lot of barriers being thrown up in front of them.

Staring at herself in the mirror, seeing the huge dark shadows under her eyes, she realised she looked and felt appalling; wrung out and desperately tired didn't even come close. It was a far cry from London, when she had hated stepping out of the house without make-up on and without her hair being styled exactly right, but she couldn't give up now. No matter what the past had to show her, she needed to see it. She had always said that the shadows couldn't hurt her – but maybe she had to change that opinion. Being brutally honest, the incident by the oak had terrified her.

After what seemed like the world's quickest shower, Elodie pulled on the clean clothes, then dragged a brush through her still-damp hair. She spritzed some perfume around in the vain hope that it would make her feel a bit more human.

Alex was moving around downstairs, and she wished that things were different; she wished that he would be there on a more permanent basis. Wished that he would spend some nights over in her cottage and fill her tiny bedroom and share her single sofa in the lounge. But that didn't seem very likely at all. They had talked about the hellish Prom Night and that was maybe all that they'd ever be able to do – accept it, apologise to one another and move on.

She grimaced and took one last look at herself, then headed back downstairs with a determined smile on her face. But when she opened the door and saw him in the lounge, his face was set and there was something dangling from his fingertips.

The storm clouds were back in his eyes, but thankfully they softened and cleared as they fixed on Elodie.

'It looks as if Cassie's been here.' He lifted up his hand and Cassie's beautiful Art Deco bracelet swung into her vision. 'Whether she knew what she was doing or not.'

'Your Grannie's bracelet.' Elodie moved across to him and took it, examining the clasp. 'It's broken! There's a link come off.' She looked around and saw the sofa where Georgiana's treasures and the key to the pewter box had nestled so closely together.

The sofa had a throw on it – one of those scratchy, woollen

ones with numerous loose threads that catch on clothing and tie you up in knots without meaning to. Elodie walked over to it and kneeled down, patting her hand across the fabric; and then she found it.

'The link for the clasp. Look Alex. It must have caught on the throw and been tugged off.' She stared up at him. 'It *was* Cassie. She came here, she got the key and she opened the box ...' She hesitated. 'And I bet she's none the wiser. Poor Cassie! Come on – we have to go and talk to her.'

Cassie was sitting on the terrace when they got back, reading a magazine.

She looked up when she heard them approach and waved. 'Hey guys!' she shouted. 'I wondered where you had gone.'

'We were up at the oak tree,' Elodie replied. 'Just having a look at what they'd done.' Alex knew that she wouldn't want them to go into detail about what had happened up there, and he respected that.

'Is it a mess?' asked Cassie, her face crumpling. 'I'm so sorry.'

'No, the police did a good job tidying it up. I think the tree just needs to be chopped up and it'll all be good to go.'

'Oh – yes, there was a message for you on the machine,' said Cassie, nodding at Alex. 'Something about the fact that they could come tomorrow and make a start on it? They apologised for the delay blah blah blah.' She waved her hand around, and Alex followed its motion in the air.

'Did you lose your bracelet?' He nodded at her wrist. 'We found one a lot like it in Elodie's cottage.'

'Oh! Yes, it'll be mine, I bet. Thank you. I really thought it had gone forever.'

'Cassie.' Alex frowned. He wasn't quite sure how to tell her without sounding downright accusatory. 'Did you lose it in the cottage last night, at all? Because I think you were there before you went walkabout with the shovel.'

Cassie flushed at the shovel memory. 'No, I wasn't. I didn't go to the cottage. You weren't in when I came home, but I intended to go over and find you. I didn't make it, though. I popped upstairs to put my bag in my bedroom and I fell asleep. Then the next thing I knew was that you were coming in and saying there'd been a fire at Elodie's—' As fast as it had coloured before, her face paled and she clapped her hands over her mouth. 'Oh, God! Did I go there? Did I set that fire? Is it like the digging? I honestly didn't know – I swear.' Then she looked up at them both, horrified. 'What happens if I do it again? What happens if I really hurt someone next time? And it's not just Alex?' Tears sprang into her eyes.

Alex didn't know what to say to that one. 'Just Alex'? But he let it go for now.

'I'll get it sorted,' promised Elodie, her own eyes full of sympathy. 'I've an idea who it might be, but I don't quite know how to reach her yet. Let me have a little bit of time to try?'

Cassie was nodding, her face deathly white now. 'But who is it? Is it Georgiana?'

'I don't think so,' Elodie admitted. 'It's more like a child. Little kids don't always know that what they're doing is dangerous. They can be quite single-minded. Reckless. But I doubt they're doing it malevolently.'

Alex noticed her fingers tighten on the inhaler she'd hidden in her palm, but he didn't comment on it.

'Okay,' he said instead. 'I'm pretty sure I'm desperate for a shower, so I'm going to head in for one. Are you two staying out here a little longer?' He thought they might need a little space.

'Yes.' That was Elodie. He was right then. 'I might have a chat with Cassie. She has a right to know who I suspect.' She sighed. 'I might be wrong, but I somehow doubt it.'

Chapter Twenty-Two

Alex disappeared into the Hall and Elodie watched him go with a little pang of sadness. Poor Alex. She'd be willing to bet that this was certainly not the way he'd wanted to spend his time today.

Cassie's voice broke into Elodie's thoughts. 'Did you say you thought it was a child who had made me do – that?'

'Yes. And I think I know exactly which child. Georgiana's little sister, Lucy.'

'*Lucy*?' Cassie looked astonished.

'Yes. She's been hanging around here ever since the storm and she's rather desperate to tell us everything she knows. You can't really blame her – she was just a little girl and you know how they demand attention. Her energy was in the church and all over the attics, and we know she left the Bible in the tomb to help her sister.'

'How? How do you know that?'

Elodie lowered her gaze. 'I just do – her memories bombarded me when we were in there, and that was one of them. You'll think I'm quite certifiable now, I should imagine.' She tried to laugh but it didn't really happen properly.

'If you're certifiable, goodness knows what I am.' Cassie shook her head. 'I didn't even know any of this was possible.'

'If the circumstances are right, it'll happen. What is it they say? A perfect storm?'

'Yes. A rare combination of factors that exacerbate a situation. Am *I* that situation then?' It was Cassie's turn to try and laugh.

'Maybe.' Elodie, deadly serious, stared out across the estate. 'Lucy certainly found a way in with you. The nursery felt odd last time I was there – sort of heavy and unsettled

– I bet that's where she's running to for safety. The thing is, she's not staying in one place long enough to talk to.' Elodie returned her gaze to Cassie and smiled. 'At least we know she's just a little girl. Can't be as bad as a scary criminal type.'

'It's bad enough. I could have really hurt Alex or hurt you.'

'But you didn't.' Elodie suddenly felt exhausted and was aware of the door opening behind her.

'Have you sorted it?'

Alex was stepping outside and Elodie forced a smile. 'Not quite. I've told Cassie my theory – and my theory is Lucy.' She shrugged. 'Too much evidence points that way.' She closed her eyes and rubbed her temples. 'Look, I'm sorry – I'm going to have to go home and lie down. I'm just about finished. Too much excitement for one day.'

Alex, his hair still shower-damp and smelling divine, was at her elbow in an instant. 'I'll take you back.'

Elodie managed a laugh and fought back the urge to touch his cool skin, his too-long hair. 'No. I'm fine. The fresh air will do me good. I need to think, and I'm at work tomorrow. So I need to go. I'll see you tomorrow afternoon. If anything else occurs to me, I'll call you.'

'Promise?'

'Promise.'

'Good. I'm pleased you're back, Elodie Bright.'

'I'm pleased I'm back too. Thank you for – today. You know. The tree. And stuff.'

Alex nodded. She was sure he knew what she meant. 'Thank you too,' he said and smiled at her.

Elodie was surprised she didn't turn into a puddle, right on the floor, as his smile melted away the last of her reserves.

Alex left the terrace and walked up the main staircase into the front entrance. Usually, he enjoyed doing that without having visitors milling around and queuing up behind him, but today the novelty was lost on him.

He was more focussed on the fact that somebody had made Cassie ignite a whole box of papers in a cottage that was made up mainly of wooden beams.

It just wasn't the act of a rational being.

What if Elodie had been inside the cottage at the time?

Although would Cassie have even got past her?

And could Elodie have managed to stop Cassie from doing it?

What if Cassie had done some serious damage to herself along the way?

Alex felt like water going down a plughole, going round and round in ever decreasing circles, until someone managed to put an end to the whole thing.

Ugh.

He jogged up the stairs and wended his way through the connecting doors to his office. He knew he could think about things in there without any other distractions. He walked over to the big window and opened it. He stepped out onto the balcony and leaned on the railings.

He had almost lost her for good today.

What if she hadn't come around when she did? What if he'd panicked and done completely the wrong thing? He'd read somewhere that when you gave mouth-to-mouth to asthma victims you had to give them plenty of time to exhale. What if he'd forgotten all that and, God forbid, made it worse? He should have insisted she went to the hospital.

He knew that he'd already lost ten years – he didn't want to risk wasting any more time. Life was precious, and his life with Elodie even more so. If anything ever happened to her, and he hadn't told her exactly how he felt, he would regret it forever. It was time to take a chance and hope she might feel the same.

He stood up straighter and gazed towards the squash courts, fighting back that image of her he'd carried with him since last year. Twice it had happened now. Perhaps, the third time, he wouldn't be there.

He wanted to do everything he could to love her and protect her and keep her with him forever and, deep down, he knew forever wouldn't be enough. Which made it all the more important that he did something and did it quickly.

He could see Elodie's cottage from here as well, and he saw her letting herself into it.

'Oh, for God's sake!' Balling his hands into fists, he slammed them into the balustrade. 'What the hell am I doing *here*, when she's *there*?'

He spun around and ran out of the office, and he didn't stop running until he was at her cottage and pounding on her door.

Elodie had just opened a bottle of wine. In fact, the lid was in one hand and the bottle was in the other, when she heard someone battering her door down.

'What on earth?' She put the bottle and the lid on the kitchen bench and hurried to the door. The pounding continued as she pulled it open. 'Alex!' He was standing there looking flushed and angry and she quailed. 'What's wrong?'

'I can't do this anymore.'

'Do what?' She was genuinely surprised.

'This.' He gestured around, seeming to take in the Hall and the estate and her cottage. 'It's just madness.'

'Running the Hall?'

'No. Not being ... not being with *you*.'

'With me? But you're usually with me. We work together and I practically live right next door to you. You see me all the time!'

'I *see* you. But I'm not *with* you.' He half-turned and

shook his head, staring out over the estate as if the answer to his outburst lay somewhere out there. 'Look. I'm sorry. I shouldn't have come. It's fine.'

'No. No, it's not fine. I've just opened a bottle of wine. Come in. Please. Come and have a glass.'

He turned back to her and his eyes were darker and stormier than she'd ever seen them. 'I don't know if that's a good idea.'

'Why ever not?'

'Because if I come in, I might have to kiss you, and if I kiss you I won't be able to stop myself from doing more than that.'

'Alex!' She stared up at him, searching his face for the slightly mocking light in his eyes. But there was nothing there. He was deadly serious and her stomach turned over.

'See.' He raked his fingers through his hair, then leaned forward so he had one hand either side of the doorframe and his body and his scent and his Alex-ness filled the gap. His eyes darkened even more. 'See, it's even worse when you stand there and look at me like that, because all I want to do is hold you and get closer to you and it's too hard to resist.'

Elodie shook her head, speechless. Her eyes never left his and she raised her hand and touched his cheek. He grabbed hold of it and turned his face towards her palm, closing his eyes and pressing her hand closer to him. He kissed her fingers, one by one and her heart began to somersault.

'Is this real?' she whispered. 'Is this you, or is it Ben?'

'It's me. And it's real. I can't lose you again.' He shook his head and gently pulled her towards him. She stepped out of the house and was in front of him, her hand captive in his. 'I realised today I've wasted far too much time. I lost you to Piers and I thought my world had ended. But you came back and suddenly I had a second chance, but I did nothing about it. I thought I could make do with just having you at

Hartsford and give you space to let you heal.' He laughed, humourlessly. 'I've done the rebound thing. I did that when you left. And then again when you got married. It's never good. And I didn't just want me to be your rebound. But then, who's to say you would have even looked twice at me after bloody Prom Night?' He captured her other hand and lifted both of them up. He pressed his lips to them again, as if he was unsure what to say next. He'd already seemingly bared quite a bit of his soul. 'But what really did it for me was what happened by the tree.' He shuddered and pulled her closer, enveloping her in his arms. She didn't resist. She didn't want to resist.

'It was even worse today than when I found you in the squash courts. I didn't know if I'd be able to bring you round, and the thought of you not being in the world was unbearable. Elodie, you *are* my world. And you've every right to scream at me or slap me again – I wouldn't blame you.' He spoke into her hair, his warm breath and whispered words sending shivers down her spine. 'But I couldn't let tonight go by without telling you how I feel. I love you and I always have. If this whole story about Georgiana and Ben has shown me anything, it's shown me that life is precious and when you find the love of your life you just have to run with it. You're my love, and I don't know if I'll ever be yours, but there you go.' Eventually, he drew away and looked down at her. He glanced away from her, perhaps wondering if he'd said too much. Reluctantly, it seemed, he released her hands and wrapped his arms around himself. 'There you go,' he repeated. 'Okay. This is the bit where I walk off and get drunk and regret telling you all that, because I'm just an idiot.'

He nodded, as if he thought that was the end of it, and prepared to turn away, but she reached out and took hold of his arms. 'Alex, no. You got it all wrong.'

'No? Yeah. I thought so.' The light went out of his eyes. 'I should have guessed. I'm sorry.'

'No, you're *not* to be sorry. The truth is you *don't* walk off now. The truth is you've *always* been my love. Always, always. Way back to Prom Night, way back beyond that. Right now and forever into the future. Piers was my rebound, because I thought I'd lost *you*.' She looked up at him, hardly believing the moment had come at last. It felt good to let the worlds tumble out. They'd been dammed up far too long.

'Really?' It was his turn to stare at her. 'You *never* lost me. Ever. When I told you I'd blown it with the only girl I'd ever loved, it was you. It's my biggest regret and always will be. I wish I'd stood up in that church and said it out loud when you were walking down the aisle to that ape.'

'I wish you had too,' she admitted. 'It's *you* I love and I have done forever. I came back up here to get married because that was exactly what I wanted you to do.'

Alex shook his head and half-laughed; his eyes were glinting again, that teasing light suddenly back in them. 'It would have made for an interesting ceremony. So – perhaps I should come in for that glass of wine now?'

'No.' She smiled and shook her head. 'You're not coming in for wine.' She took his hand and led him into the cottage, quietly closing the door behind them.

They stood at the bottom of the stairs, and it was simply the only thing she could say: 'Hold me. Please. I liked it when I was sleeping in your arms.'

There was a pause; a heartbeat. 'I liked it too.' He moved his head towards her and his lips found hers. 'Is this all right?' he asked softly, eventually drawing away. 'It's not going to send your asthma into overdrive is it?'

'Not my asthma. I can't answer for anything else though.'

He drew her to him again.

She didn't pull away.

She moved closer.

Then she started to fumble with his shirt.

Then he helped her to take it off.

Then she closed her eyes and gave herself up to him.

Chapter Twenty-Three

Three days later, they were in Alex's study in the late afternoon. He didn't quite know how he had dragged himself away from her and pretended life was continuing just as normal, but he had done. They'd made love as if their lives depended on it that first night – she'd insisted she was completely fine after the scare in the woods – and it was a far cry from the Prom Night debacle. It was as if he had finally come home. He still couldn't quite believe it, but she was there, sitting on his desk, and turning the pistol around in her hands.

'It's the only thing left to do,' she said. 'I don't want to do it again, but I have to.'

He caught one of her hands and kissed it. 'No, you don't. We might not like what we see.'

'But we need to see it.' She sighed and put the pistol down. 'I'll be okay if you're there. I know I will.'

'And do you have an inhaler with you?'

He was deadly serious and she lowered her eyes. 'Yes.'

'Good. It's nothing to be ashamed of.' The day after that awful attack, he'd brooked no arguments himself and driven her to the doctor's. She had started to get a little breathless walking back up to the Hall with him and to be fair, she hadn't offered much resistance; she knew herself it had to be done. He felt as if he'd won a very small victory but he was happier that she'd been seen by a professional. The thought of what could have happened under that tree would haunt him forever. He needed to know he had done the right thing for her that day.

She wrinkled her nose. 'I know, but the asthma is too – *London*. I don't want anything from then to spoil what we have up here and it does. It'll be there forever now.'

'And so will I, so there's no need for either of us to worry, is there? We'll deal with it if we have to.'

Elodie smiled at him. 'Hopefully we won't have to deal with it too frequently.' She hopped off the desk. 'Shall we go now? I think I can walk there today.'

'Are you sure?' Jokingly, he got to his feet and scooped her up, cradling her in his arms.

She pounded on his shoulders with her fists. 'I'm sure! Put me down!'

'As you wish.' He let her slide to her feet. Instead, he held out his hand. 'Come on then. I'll carry the pistol.'

Elodie shuddered. 'You're welcome to do so. But I'll need it when we get there.'

'Fair enough. Shall we head back past the stables? I ground myself by being on my horse, or, failing that, I'm happy to be near the stables – don't look at me like that. Hughie is perfectly sweet and it's a nice afternoon for a walk.'

'It's quiet, isn't it?' Elodie said, as they walked across the Faerie Bridge.

'I decided that we'd only open for a half day – I cited unforeseen circumstances, which is a pretty good catch-all. It was busy earlier, when you were at Delilah's.'

Elodie glanced down. She could see the pistol peeking out of his pocket and she couldn't suppress a shudder. The image of that noose hanging from the tree would haunt her forever. She looked up and saw the woods approaching, rather too fast despite the fact they were on foot.

'We're doing the right thing, aren't we?'

Alex squeezed her hand. 'We are. Look, we're almost there. As you keep telling me, they're all shadows. We'll do this and then do something really nice. How does champagne sound?'

Elodie laughed. 'It sounds divine. Hopefully you can magic some up for us.'

'The Green Dragon do a rather nice Moët & Chandon. You can buy it by the bottle, you know. Perhaps Bob might give us a discount.'

'We were lucky to get the free glass of wine!'

'Hey, don't knock it. It's quite possibly the first one he's given away in years.'

They had reached the clearing and Elodie hesitated.

She moved closer to Alex and he put his arm around her. 'We can leave it, you know. I don't want you passing out again.'

'No. Give me the pistol. Please. I'm feeling much stronger today. I know what I'm doing.'

'If you're sure. The first sign of anything amiss, though, and I'm coming after you to drag you back – no matter where you disappear to.'

Elodie looked at him in some surprise. He seemed quite fierce and it gave her little squiggles in her tummy. She knew, bizarrely, that he would defend her with his life if he had to.

'Oh, Alex,' she murmured. Then she took the pistol he offered her and closed her eyes, secure in the knowledge he was there to catch her if it all went horribly wrong.

They were back at the oak tree, and Ben's noose was dangling. Georgiana was lying on the ground, her mother looming over her, pointing Jasper's pistol at her chest.

'Is this really what you want? Is this the only way to escape your shame?' the Countess slurred. She pulled the trigger and Georgiana cringed into the ground, curling herself up into a protective little ball, wrapping her arms around her body, drawing her knees up to her stomach.

There was a click. Then another click, and the Countess shrieked in anger, tossing the pistol to the ground.

Georgiana sobbed in terror, then uncurled enough to grab

the pistol herself. Trembling, she got to her feet, the world swimming, bile rising in her throat.

'The safety catch,' she managed. 'Jasper always taught me to carry it safely.' She fumbled with it, blinking away rising nausea and dizziness. 'You don't know what you're doing Mama! Please. Stop it!'

The woman shouted something incomprehensible, and launched herself at her daughter like a wildcat, making another lunge for the pistol. Her fingertips connected with it as Georgiana screamed and tried to fend her off.

The nineteen-year-old, however, was stronger than the drunk woman, and she fought with everything she had. After all, she had nothing left to lose. Eventually Georgiana twisted the pistol around, wrenching it out of her mother's grasp. There was more of a tussle, and the woman slapped Georgiana hard across the face, the welts already rising where the barrel had hit her before.

There was a bang and a starburst of light. The women froze for a moment, staring at each other; and then, Jane, Countess of Hartsford, crumpled to the ground, a dark stain spreading across her breast as her daughter looked on in horror.

Georgiana began to shake and, not knowing what else she could possibly do, pointed the weapon towards her own heart. She closed her eyes and pulled.

There it was again; that empty click. And another one. Jasper's amused voice, teaching her the rules of duelling, filtered into her mind: 'My pistols have only one bullet. So if you duel and you miss – you'd better hope the other chap is more drunk than you and he misses as well. You could always claim to have deloped to save face though. I say, perhaps you and Lucy could consider a petticoat duel, instead of screeching at each other like banshees next time you argue. My pistols are always loaded, dear heart. Always available.'

Georgiana screamed in frustration, tears rolling down her face, and threw the pistol, with all her might, in the direction the locket had gone. It glinted in the starlight as it spun and turned gracefully against the backdrop of the moonlit woods and came to rest some distance away.

She groped behind her for the trunk of the oak and backed up to it, then slid down, too shocked to cry out or make any noise at all except for terrible, hitching gasps as she saw the carnage before her. 'Oh, Ben. Ben!' she managed. She looked up and saw the end of the noose swinging above her head.

She was lost.

She simply had nobody. Nothing. She was done for.

'Oh, Ben!'

She raised her knees up and put her head between them as the darkened world began to swim in front of her eyes.

She was roused by a scuffling of hooves coming close to her. She raised her face and opened her eyes, ready to submit to whatever her father and his men would do to her. Anything would be better than the future she saw before her.

There was a soft whinny and a puff of breath that hung in the air for a moment before swirling away. A figure clothed in black sat on the broad back of a horse. The horse dipped its head and nudged her, almost as if it was encouraging her to her feet.

'Damn poachers,' the man said, his voice strong, deep and resonant, as bewitching as it always had been. 'It is shameful how alike we all look in the dark.'

He sat on his horse, his eyes reflected the moonlight and his gaze told her how much he desired her, even after witnessing the scene before him. He moved the horse, thank God, so it blocked Georgiana's mother's body from her sight. The girl struggled to her feet, almost scared to breathe, and reached up.

Her hands shaking, she pulled the scarf from the lower

half of his face and his gloved hand caught hers. He dipped his face to kiss her fingers, each finger in turn. 'We have to go,' was all he said.

'He survived!' Elodie opened her eyes. 'Ben survived. It was a poacher. They hanged a *poacher* by mistake!' She raised her hands to her face and felt her cheeks wet with tears. The metal of the pistol was chilly against her skin and she quickly moved it away from her face. 'He came back for her.'

She looked at the weapon and handed it back to Alex with shaking hands, sure now that it had told her all it needed to. Georgiana's memories had been strong, Ben's face so handsome, his eyes so – blue. So midnight-blue, just like Alex's.

'Did he take her somewhere then?' Alex's own eyes were round with hope and – yes – relief. 'When he came back?'

'I don't know. I didn't see. But he came on his horse for her after she—' Elodie paused and bit her lip, looking towards the grave. 'You should know that Georgiana shot her mother. In self-defence. Accidentally.'

'That was the *Countess*?' Alex seemed horrified. He pointed with the gun, unthinkingly, at the grave. 'That skeleton? Good God.'

'Do you still want to give her a decent burial?' Elodie screwed her face up angrily, debating whether the drunk old harridan deserved a decent burial or not. 'She was absolutely vile to her daughter, although much of it was the drink talking. She was clearly insane – I suppose her only redeeming quality was that she seemed to love Jasper! I hope she's burning in Hell, right now.'

'It all makes sense with the forensics; in her forties, with children. Shot in the chest.' Alex shivered. 'I completely agree with you about burning in Hell. I'd light the flames myself, place my pet demon on 24-7 watch if I could. But at the end of the day, she's a Kerridge. She had three Kerridge children. One of them was Georgiana. I suspect the answer is yes, she'll get a decent burial – eventually.' Alex frowned and tucked the pistol in his waistband again. 'But my God they were an awful pair of parents. Bloody hell. I wonder who the Earl paid to have Jane's name engraved on the pointy gravestone!'

'I don't even want to know.' Elodie shook her head. 'That's one thing that can stay a secret. And I don't think I want to share the circumstances of that shooting with the forensics people.'

'Exactly.' Alex held his hand out to her and puffed out a breath. 'It would be a bit awkward to explain how we knew all of that to people of science. I think we deserve that champagne now. Agreed?'

'Absolutely.'

Elodie held out her hand in response, and he tugged her towards him. 'This way.'

'Oh, I'm so pleased I saw that! They deserved a happy ending, they really did.' She allowed herself to be guided by him, even if it did, ultimately, mean going around by the stables. She was so relieved to have seen Ben come and rescue Georgiana that she felt quite light-headed. There was no way she was going to look back at the Countess's makeshift grave though; that was something altogether different, and Elodie didn't know exactly how long it would be before she came back to this little crossroads.

She shivered and was gratified to feel Alex's arm come around her, and at last she felt safe.

They walked back along the other side of the River Hartsford, until they reached a little waterfall. There was a small wooden bridge over the water and Alex ushered her across it. From there, the path wound its way through the kitchen garden and the ornate iron gates onto the big lawns up by the stables.

'Oh, look! The marquee's up!' Elodie laughed. 'Have you been practising with it for the Country House Weekend? It's not going to be until next year, you know.'

Alex looked at the flapping canvas. 'The poor old thing needed cleaning up a bit. It's been stuffed in the squash courts for ten years. I got some of the staff to help me with it yesterday afternoon.'

'Is it *that* marquee?' Elodie paused. 'Seriously? The one from the Prom? I didn't realise that was the one Cassie meant.'

'The very same. It looks a bit tatty, doesn't it?' Alex started walking towards it, frowning. 'I don't know if it can be used for the Country House event, to be honest. It's dropping to pieces.' He indicated a panel which had come loose from the metal frame. Even from here, Elodie could see the stitching was loose and the twine was flapping just as much as the panels were.

She giggled. 'It's rather dreadful, isn't it?'

'It's better close up,' Alex replied with a grin. 'Come on. Let's go and you can see what I mean. I'll call in on Hughie as well. I might take him for a ride tonight. I'll tell him when I go in and he'll be happy. I can zone out a little when I'm out with him. Avoid thinking of Jane and her grisly end.'

'You might get the reputation for being the ghostly highwayman. Think of that!'

'I don't know if I believe in him.' Alex smiled. 'It's a nice story – probably put about by the villagers when the servants' gossip reached them about Ben. They weren't to know he escaped.'

'I really do hope they escaped! I didn't see beyond her pulling his mask off. I heard Blaze in the woods though, if you remember? Maybe there's a grain of truth in it after all.'

'And maybe the finish of their tale is a story for another

day. It's a *better* way to end a love story though – swept away by a dashing highwayman who'd die for you.' He nodded to the stables. 'Hughie could waddle fast if I asked him to, if you want to recreate that one?'

'Not today, thanks.'

Alex laughed and guided Elodie around to the front of the marquee. The door was open, tied back by what looked like a Christmas garland wound through with twinkling fairy lights.

'Interesting use of festive decorations,' Elodie commented, pointing at them. 'Did you find a box with the marquee?'

'There were two boxes, actually.' Alex pulled her gently in behind him. 'And candles and all sorts. I'm going to use them in the Christmas Room this year. I'm doing lunch for everyone. You're invited.'

'Why, thank you. I shall have to check my diary,' she teased, knowing full well that wild horses wouldn't keep her away from him one minute more than was absolutely necessary.

'Here we go. Oh, look. Champagne. How novel.' He stood to one side and bowed extremely gracefully, sweeping his arm out to the side. 'Please – take a seat. Bob doesn't do a discount, by the way.'

'Alex!' She blinked and gazed around at the interior of the marquee. There was a picnic table in the middle of it, flanked by two canvas chairs. A magnum of champagne stood proud in a bucket on the table and two champagne flutes were placed beside it. There were chunky candles of all sizes around the interior of the marquee, and strings and strings of Christmas lights. 'They're all blue and white! It looks like the inside of a glacier. How beautiful …'

'Yes. There were some red and green ones too, but when I put them all in, they looked like a migraine. And I didn't light the candles as I thought the place might ignite and I wasn't sure how your asthma would cope with it.' He shrugged and put his hands in his pockets. He looked around. 'It doesn't look too bad though, does it?' He glanced at her, shyly. 'I could light the candles if you wanted.'

Elodie nodded. 'Yes. Yes, please. I'm willing to take the chance. I've got my inhaler after all.'

He nodded and headed off to the first set of candles. A cigarette-lighter or something flared as he touched the wicks. The candles were beeswax, honey-scented. He moved onto the next set, and the next, and so on, coming full circle to her side again. She hadn't moved an inch; she had been too absorbed watching him concentrate as he lit them all, the flames flickering and highlighting the shadows on his face. Alex had always had amazing cheekbones and they showed sharp in the candlelight.

'Is that okay?' A frown flitted across his face. 'Tell me if it gets too much.'

Elodie just shook her head, entranced. 'Perfect. It's perfect. Thank you.'

'May I lead you to a chair, my lady? And perhaps offer you a glass of champagne?'

The teasing was there again and Elodie smiled. 'Definitely.' She held her arm out primly and he took her to the canvas chairs and settled her in one.

He took the seat opposite and uncorked the champagne, then poured two glasses. 'Cheers,' he said. 'To Ben and Georgiana and their happy ever after.'

'Cheers.' She raised her glass and took a sip. The champagne was cold and bubbly and very dry – just as she liked it best. 'Thank you. What a lovely surprise. A super end to the day.'

'It's not quite the end.' He frowned and put his glass on the table. 'I've got one more thing to say.' He leaned over the table and caught her by her shoulders. His eyes burned into hers, no storms, no doubts, no nothing – just deep blue honesty. 'Listen. When I let you get married, right in front of me, my whole body wanted to jump out of the pew and shout at you. I wanted to beg you to stay here, with me.'

'Alex …'

Then he loosened his grip and straightened up, slid out of the chair and knelt down in front of her, and took her hands again. 'It's true what I told you the other night, I meant every word of it. And now I want to tell you again that I love you. And more than that, I want to marry you. I've wasted ten years without you by my side and it was too long. I've missed you. So please, will you be my wife?'

She looked down at him, shocked. Then she gently worked his grip free and laid her hands on his shoulders, drawing him towards her. She ran her hands gently down his arms, feeling the muscles beneath his shirt and the warmth of him. She took his hands in hers and raised them to her lips, not taking her eyes off him. He dipped his head down and brought her palms to his face, pressing them to his cheeks.

Elodie closed her eyes and lowered her own face. 'If I'd known any of what you said the other night, I would have come straight back. You need to know that too. I hate the fact we've lost ten years. I absolutely hate it.'

She opened her eyes and he looked up at her; his eyes had that spark in them again – a spark she now recognised as desire and undeniable, unquestionable, unbreakable love. 'So is that a yes?' he asked quietly.

'Yes. It's a yes. I love you, Alex. And I can't think of anything nicer than marrying you.' She leaned down and their faces were at the same level again.

The spark in his eyes flared and they found each other's lips in the gap between them.

'I love you, Elodie Bright,' he murmured as they drew apart.

'I love you too, Alex Aldrich.'

And that was the last thing either one of them said for quite some time.

Chapter Twenty-Four

WINTER

'I'm getting married,' Elodie told Cori. 'Have I mentioned it?'

'Only once or twice.' Cori grinned as she opened the door to the Kensington mews house. 'I have a bridesmaid here you can use, if you're short of any. Thing is, *she's* a bit short.' She indicated Kitty who was balanced on her hip and grinning as well. Kitty had a couple of new teeth and was clearly enjoying showing them off.

Elodie laughed and tickled Kitty under the chin, and the baby stretched out her arms to come to her. Elodie took her from Cori and jiggled her around a bit, which she seemed to like.

'I've never had much to do with babies,' said Elodie. 'I tended to disregard any talk of them when I was with Piers. Odd that, isn't it? Neither of us were bothered.'

'And now?' Cori asked, leading the way into her lovely big kitchen to the right of the hallway and flicking the kettle on. The kitchen smelled of coffee and hot mince pies and Elodie immediately felt welcome. She always did at Cori's house. 'A brood of mini-Aldrichs might be expected of you, you know.' She reached up to the cupboard for two mugs. 'What with you being Lady of the manor and all that.'

'An heir and a spare. That's what they usually suggest. One step at a time I think, though. But I have to say, the idea is growing on me.' Cori's eyes lit up and Elodie knew she would be in touch with Becky up in Whitby and Lissy over in Italy, and all of their other friends as well, and they'd all start speculating about how long it would be before Elodie caved in and went for it. 'Anyway, you are definitely coming up for the wedding, aren't you? Just with it being on Christmas Eve.

Perhaps I didn't think it through properly. It's only a couple of weeks away. I can't quite believe it. It's come around so quickly!'

'I wouldn't miss it for the world,' Cori said with a smile. 'Santa is well-prepared, don't you fret. And shouldn't you be worrying about it all coming together instead of dashing down here in amongst the Christmas shoppers? Anyway, it's not like little lady here will know much different this year. *She's* not going to be worrying about anything, especially not about being tucked up in bed for Santa coming. Becky thinks Grace will be shattered from the journey and she should go straight to sleep. She says you're doing them a favour, really.'

Grace was their friend Becky's five-year-old.

'True.' Elodie settled Kitty into her high chair and watched her pulverise a biscuit before eating it. 'I'm pleased you can all come. The church should look lovely. The repairs are all done, the insurance approved and the ladies are decorating it traditionally, with holly and garlands and candles. It'll be pretty.' She grinned, remembering the marquee. 'And we have blue and white fairy lights strung around too.'

'Won't it be a bit weird having another wedding in the same place as your first?' Cori put a mug in front of her and sat down.

'Maybe.' Elodie shrugged her shoulders and wrapped her hands around the mug. 'But it's different this time.'

'Maybe it's the right man this time.'

'I *know* it's the right man. I was stupid to ignore it for so long. We both were.'

'Good. Simon and I saw old Piers the other week at some dreary Christmas party. He had a brunette on his arm. She was dressed in black. She looked like a stick of liquorice. A strong wind would have snapped her.' Cori wrinkled her pretty nose at, in her opinion, such an abject failure of womanhood. 'And she was *so* hard-faced. She never cracked a smile all night. I think she thought it would make her face look fat.' She sucked in her cheeks experimentally and pouted, then pulled a face again. 'Although I suppose the perma-pout and the false eyelashes might have impeded her facial expression.'

Elodie found herself mirroring Cori's pout and sucked-in-cheeks expression. Then she too frowned. 'That's not his usual type of woman. I doubt it'll last. He goes for silicone mostly.'

'Maybe she was hoping he would pay for the op. Anyway.' Cori nudged Elodie. 'Let's not talk about her. Let's talk about *this* beauty. She's who you came down for, after all.' Cori slid off the seat and scurried away into the boot room across the corridor. Elodie had a momentary panic – as did Kitty – when they realised they were alone with each other, but it didn't last long. And when Cori came back, she was reverently carrying a small rectangle in front of her.

Cori laid it on the table, took one look at Kitty stretching curious, crumby little fingers and moved the package to the other side of Elodie, well out of the child's way. 'Here she is. What do you think?' She carefully opened the bubble wrap.

As the wrapping peeled away, Elodie realised that someone had framed Georgiana's portrait. 'Oh, Cori! Who did this?' The frame was all carved and gilded and Rococo-ed – if that was even a word.

'Don't you like it?' Her face fell. 'Simon thought—'

'Shhh.' Elodie laid a hand on Cori's arm. 'I love it! But the frame – it's practically an exact match to the ones in the Hall. She's got a proper family portrait now!'

'Oh, that's a relief!' Cori hugged Elodie. 'God, how awful if you'd hated it! No, what happened was Simon said he'd come across this style of frame so often for that period that he knew the original would have been like that. He could tell she was Georgian by her clothes and obviously what you said about Georgiana confirmed it – and her name kind of gives it away anyway. Those fancy frames would have been like wall art for the eighteenth century. This one is a replica, of course, but he managed to get it from someone he knows at Camden Market.'

'It's beautiful. And this is Georgiana, finally. My word.' Elodie looked up at Cori. 'I can't thank you two enough. You have to let me pay.'

'We won't hear of it. Don't be so silly. Here.' She pushed the picture closer to Elodie. 'It might not even be her. But Simon enjoyed the project. Any more work like that,' she said, smiling brightly, 'just sling it our way. I enjoyed seeing her come to life as much as he did.'

Elodie nodded and leaned over the picture. 'Alex will know if it's her. I think it is, though. She looks like the statue on the tomb.'

And she looks like the girl in the portrait Ben painted, the one that he gave her when they ran away …

'I think she looks a bit like you,' said Cori. 'Maybe it's the eyes and the hair colour?'

'Maybe.'

'But tell me about the mystery woman under the tree – any news?'

'Oh, Alex thinks he's got some idea who the skeleton might be – she wasn't Georgiana, and she died from a close-range shot, but he says there's an aunt that fell off the radar around that time. Alex suggested to the forensics team it might have been a suicide, because of where she was buried.' It wasn't a lie. He had spun a jolly good tale, pretending it had been an aunt rather than the Countess; the family didn't need any more Hartsford-related scandal. It was ironic, he'd said, that he was the one now trying to cover up *their* misdemeanours.

'In those days,' continued Elodie, 'they buried suicides and witches at crossroads, so their spirits got confused when they wandered. Where she was found forms a crossroad where the drovers' routes meet. Anyway. I'm not going to talk about her. I want to look at Georgiana. I recognise the locket from the tomb.' Elodie was quite glad that the portrait was protected by a layer of bright, shiny glass. She had a huge compulsion to run her hand over the locket around the girl's neck and knew she'd probably ruin Simon's work if she started poking around. She contented herself with running a fingertip across the glass, then guiltily rubbed the resulting greasy smear off with her sleeve.

'Hasn't she come to tell you exactly what happened then?' asked Cori.

Elodie laughed. 'Not exactly. But I'm fairly sure this is her.' Cori knew all about her gift – they'd both seen a ghost the very first time they'd met at the National Theatre. It had been shortly after that when things had finally cracked with Piers, and she'd made the decision to go back to Hartsford. Cori had supported her completely.

Elodie also knew that the essence of Georgiana, the *real* Georgiana was the girl in this portrait, the girl wearing the white dress and the silver locket. The girl with the blonde hair that tumbled in ringlets from her topknot and the hint of mischief in her eyes and the slight smile on her rosy lips that looked perhaps a little bruised from a recent kiss.

Elodie studied the portrait a moment longer. 'Oh, Georgiana. What really happened to you? Do you think we'll ever know?' But of course, there was no answer.

It was difficult trying to stick to the speed limit on her way back to Suffolk. She just wanted to hurry back there and show Alex the portrait and—

Elodie's foot faltered a little on the accelerator and a car behind her tooted loudly as she dropped about fifteen miles an hour and recovered it as quickly as she could. She acknowledged the driver with a little wave, but he overtook her anyway with another loud *paaaaaaarp* on the horn. Elodie was glad he had sped past and not stopped. She hadn't considered what Alex's reaction might be about the portrait and she couldn't think about a road rage incident as well as that. She really hoped he'd like it.

Elodie acknowledged to herself that she'd been swept up in congratulations and diamond engagement rings and excited phone calls to her parents involving wedding plans, and the Delilah-and-Margaret hugs had made her partially forget the fact she had borrowed the portrait so long ago. She *really* hoped he would like it. She'd called Cassie and enthusiastically told her all about it – and she, at least, was looking forward to seeing it. It had been difficult not to confess to Alex where the portrait was, the night she'd heard Blaze in the woods; the night she'd seen Ben give the portrait to Georgiana. That was why she'd glossed over the memories. But then, Alex had other things on his mind anyway; like a very real murder mystery on his estate and a skeleton that his sister had revealed.

Ah, well. She squared her shoulders. It was a *good* thing she'd done. The main aim was to surprise Alex and make him happy, and she was certain it would. Alex knew she was friendly with Simon and Cori; she just didn't think he knew how good Simon was at what he did.

Anyway. She could see the lights of the village over the fields, glittering amongst the frosty countryside. One swing of the road on the right and down the dip and she would be off the bypass and into Hartsford. She was glad she had Georgiana's picture back before Christmas though. The police hadn't released the Countess's body to Alex yet and it seemed right that Georgiana should return in a sort of triumph first.

Lucy's evil little letter had been torn into tiny squares and tossed into the River Hartsford at twilight some weeks ago. Elodie had leaned on the Faerie Bridge and watched the fragments whirl and swirl away with the currents, and she was pleased. She could have sworn she felt a little hand touch hers, and she had smiled. She gazed across at the woods, and saw Alex and Hughie weaving their way through the trees, and she had blown a farewell kiss to Lucy and turned towards them.

It had been a perfect night.

Elodie grinned into the moonlight and pressed her foot on the accelerator just a little harder. For she knew that when she pulled up in front of the Hall, she'd be able to see the lights in the Christmas Room window, twinkling and sparkling and reminding her that Alex was waiting for her and she was almost Home.

Alex *was* waiting. He was in the Christmas Room, and it was all decked out for the festivities; they'd used some of the decorations he'd found in the marquee to bring it to life again.

But the huge, formal dining table wasn't spread with food today – it was spread with his father's genealogy papers. It was the biggest surface he could find and his father had an awful lot of papers. He'd never been interested enough to look at them properly and since he'd come back from Oxford, he'd never had the time or the inclination up until now.

The family tree went back generations and generations, to the cousin they'd found in France, Etienne Jasper Somersby Aldrich, and back again to the original Kerridge line, right the way past *Alexander, first Earl of Hartsford – Mortuus in Gloria*.

'Jasper.' Alex's lips twitched into a half-smile. His father had always simply called him Etienne Aldrich, and Alex had wondered at the strange combination of a French Christian name with an English surname. But there was the family link, right there, along with Somersby, if you only knew where to look for it. Whoever these cousins were, they'd named their child after Jasper, perhaps in the hope of currying favour with the old Earl. They obviously hadn't known about Jasper's supposedly disgraceful death.

There were some complicated documents and notes that Alex skipped over, but he understood they were from George IV, when he was the Prince Regent, resurrecting the earldom in the name of Etienne Jasper Somersby Aldrich. He had created the young man the new Earl of Hartsford as a reward for his services to the crown at Waterloo, after the king's people had discovered Etienne's link to the Kerridges in Suffolk; but the most interesting thing that Alex found was a journal: the journal of George, Earl of Hartsford – the father of Georgiana.

The Earl had written pages and pages in cramped, crabbed handwriting, telling of his hatred for his children and his wife, obsessing over minutiae, years old. Accounts of his son's gambling debts were nestled side by side with vitriol about his wife's behaviour and lists detailing the whereabouts of her empty wine bottles. He heaped blame upon the Markwell family for allowing their unstable daughter, Jane, to become his Countess. The defects in their offspring were clearly Markwell traits and he wished Markwell blood had never diluted the Hartsford stock. The family was so wide-flung that he feared most of the families in the very county were related to Jane and therefore he lived within a seething mass of in-breeds and it was no surprise ... etc etc.

Reams of notes were also available, should anyone wish to read them, about his youngest daughter's fragile mental state. He painted an unsympathetic picture of a young girl trapped in her own world, fighting demons that were beyond the average adult's ken, never mind a little child's. The greatest diatribe, however, was reserved for his ungrateful whore of a daughter, Georgiana. He speculated on murder and suicide and gleefully said that they had '*hanged a man, known to be the cur that defiled her*'. Even more joyfully, he acknowledged that the girl had disappeared, along with a pistol from the family collection, and his greatest hope was '*that the corpse is found with a hole in the skull.*'

It was nothing Alex didn't already know, but he was sickened by seeing it all there, written down by someone who was supposed to care for and protect his family.

He felt no sympathy when he found the last entry:

'*I find that I am cursed to leave this life without issue. The lunatic has died from a fever and my bloodline hath ended. Is this what was destined for me? This? For a man who has only ever had the greatness of this family at the forefront of his being?*'

'No,' growled Alex. 'Your destiny is that the world will know how vile you were, because by God I'll *make* it known!' He read down the self-pitying rhetoric, disgusted, until he came to the last few lines. Then he read them again and his heart began to pound.

'*A letter arrived today. A most unfortunate letter. The whore is abroad with the bastard who defiled her, and they have sent for the lunatic. The devil take them all to Hell – the child they urge to follow them is already there, and so too shall they be when God sees it fit. The letter has been burned and that, I pray, is an end to them all. I find myself torn – but even the continuation of my bloodline is too precious a price to pay to acknowledge them. No. It is best the world believes them dead. They are, and have been, dead to me since the night it happened. I shall marry again and father more children and they shall be my heirs.*'

The entry was dated the fifth of February 1800. Lucy had

248

died on the second. And the Earl himself had died, according to the records, quite suddenly the following month. The devilish part of Alex hoped it had been the result of an apoplexy, after he discovered his daughter had survived. Whatever it was, there was never any time for him to carry out his plan – and the title had, so it seemed, died with him. That was, until 1816, when, for services at Waterloo, the remote French cousin had been granted the Earldom and the valiant, heroic nineteen-year-old Etienne Aldrich had come to live at Hartsford Hall.

Alex stared at the papers again. He had to show Elodie this. It was proof that the experiences they'd had were real, and absolute proof that Ben had come back for Georgiana as he had promised. He put the journal and the documents to one side, and saw again the image of Georgiana as she had appeared to him in Ben's memories. The likeness to his fiancée was still startling, and he was beginning to think he needed to cast his net a little wider in the genealogy field, just to check something out.

He rummaged through the papers again – there were, he knew, some tenants' lists in amongst the documents; wages paid, rents due, that sort of thing. It wouldn't take him long at all to find out the information he wanted, thanks to the internet and the wealth of genealogy websites that were available. It would be interesting reading.

'Alex?' The door opened and he turned. Elodie was standing in the doorway, still wearing her coat and boots. 'I thought you might be in here. It looks beautiful, doesn't it? I could see it all the way from the drive.'

'We did a good job.' He smiled at her. 'I'm glad you came. I was going to search for you later anyway.'

'I should hope you were!' She walked over to him and he opened his arms. She fitted into them and rubbed her cold nose on his chest. 'I wouldn't have been far.'

He laughed and kissed the tip of her nose. 'You're cold. Was Cori okay?'

'She's great, thanks. Looking forward to the wedding. As am I.'

'Me too. But *this* is what I wanted to show you today.' He led her to the table and pointed to the book. 'Georgiana's father's journal. It doesn't make for pleasant reading, but you might like the last entry. Well – some of it. The very last bit.'

'Oh?' Elodie flicked through the book and turned to the last page. There was silence as she read it, and Alex watched her face carefully for a reaction.

He wasn't disappointed; her eyes widened and her mouth dropped open slightly, then she looked up at him. 'They survived! They sent for Lucy!'

'They did. Our only mystery now is where did they go, and did they ever come back?'

'If they're going to tell us, they'll tell us. And if not, well.' She shrugged and smiled up at him. 'The most important thing is, they were together, wherever they ended up.'

'What a way to end a love story,' Alex said with a grin.

'The only *better* way is to end it with a wedding.'

'No.' Alex shook his head. 'A wedding is the *beginning* of the biggest part of the love story. Wouldn't you agree?'

'I think, perhaps, I would.'

And they kissed, and the world beyond theirs faded until there was only Alex and Elodie in the whole universe and a promise of new beginnings.

Chapter Twenty-Five

The wedding was perfect. There was no other word to describe it. Alex turned to see Elodie walking down the aisle as the first few bars of the *Prince of Denmark's March* were punched out on the ancient organ by Margaret and, to borrow a cliché from Delilah, she took his breath away.

Elodie's dress was very different to the one she'd worn that other time, and, in Alex's opinion, even more amazing; something he hadn't thought possible. Of ivory satin, it was Regency style, very high-waisted, with a long skirt that fanned out behind her into a train, like an old-fashioned riding habit. Over the top she wore a short, winter-white spencer – a little Regency style jacket that ended just under her bust. Her bouquet was holly and ivy, studded with waxy white Christmas roses. The red and green glowed against the pale dress and her hair was loose and curled around her shoulders, with what seemed like a hundred diamond clips dotted in it. They sparkled as the candlelight caught them on her way down to the altar.

Most of the village had turned up for the wedding and they were crammed into the newly repaired church, which still smelled faintly of sawdust and cement beneath the scents of beeswax and greenery. There was a small gaggle of Elodie's non-Suffolk friends clustered in a pew; Becky and Jon had loaned them five-year-old Grace as a flower girl, and Cori and Simon passed good-natured Kitty between them, the child holding her arms out to each parent in turn. Kitty was also practising a killer smile on Lissy and Stefano, who split their time between London and Italy. The way Stef was chucking Kitty under the chin as Lissy dropped little kisses on her red hair and nibbled her tiny fingers suggested that they were being won over, slowly but surely.

Grace, dark-haired and pretty in a snowy dress trimmed with red, preceded Elodie down the aisle scattering white rose petals in front of her, enjoying the limelight before her new baby brother came to join the family – she'd shared that exciting news with Alex about ten minutes after meeting him. Horace the dog strolled proudly next to Grace, wearing a red bow ribbon instead of a collar, complemented by reindeer antlers on his freshly-shampooed head. And Cassie brought up the rear, beaming and sleek in a forest-green sheath dress. She'd finished University now, and was back home.

And when Elodie's father handed Alex's bride to him, Alex was the proudest and happiest man on the planet.

'Look after her,' said Mr Bright. 'The last one didn't. Bloody idiot.'

'Daddy!' Elodie hissed, but she was smiling as she said it and Alex hadn't missed the adoration on the older man's face as he spoke to her.

'I will,' he whispered back. 'It's what I've wanted to do for years.'

'Thank you,' Elodie's father said. 'You were always the one I hoped she'd fall for.'

And then they were into the service.

Which was perfect.

'I'm sorry your parents weren't here,' Elodie said to Alex after the ceremony was over and the guests had all gone home. It was almost midnight, almost Christmas, and they were walking hand in hand back towards the church, loath to see the end of the day. And anyway, there was something important she had to do there, and part of that task was to lay her bouquet on Georgiana's newly restored monument.

'I'm pretty sure Dad was there. But Mother? Nope. Didn't expect her to come, even with the free booze.' Alex shrugged.

'Her loss.' Elodie squeezed his hand.

'Indeed. But Delilah and Margaret and your mum were there and they've been more like mothers to me and Cass than our own dear mama ever was. Hey ho. Anyway.' It was his turn to squeeze her hand. 'It's good of Delilah to give you some time off for the honeymoon – isn't it, my darling Countess of Hartsford? Or do you prefer Elodie, Lady Hartsford?'

'Don't! That sounds weird.' She laughed. 'Elodie Aldrich will do just fine. Gosh, can you imagine a couple of generations back? I'd have been expected to stay at home and do Worthy Things. But I love the café! I don't want to give it up.'

'Nowadays, I suppose your Worthy Thing at home is called volunteering at the Hall. I mean you are technically working from home.' He was serious for a moment and stopped walking. He took both her hands in his and faced her. 'I'm sorry. It was never meant to be like this, you know. I never thought I'd be opening the doors to the paying public and having my wife doing the tours. You were supposed to float around in luxury. It was always you. Everything was for you. Do you know, I came to London to find you once?'

'Really?' Elodie looked up at him. 'All that way?'

'All that way. I discovered you were working for the National Theatre. I saw your name in an Arts magazine someone had left on a picnic table. I thought it was too much of a sign to ignore. So I got the first train down.'

Elodie shook her head, her eyes wide. 'Well I never. Why didn't you ask my parents for my address? They would have given it to you. I know you keep popping in when they're home!'

He smiled, a little lopsidedly. 'I wanted to surprise you.

Thought it would have more impact that way. Stupid, huh? So I paid a fortune for a *Hamlet* ticket and I hate Shakespeare. I sat through it, willing it to end, and all I could think about was that you'd touched those costumes. That you'd designed them. Afterwards, I went to the stage door to see if I could spot you. Talk to you. Maybe apologise to you.' He looked down at their clasped hands. 'Persuade you to dump the banker fool and come home. But you weren't there. Someone said you weren't expected in all week. I didn't leave my name. I just said it was fine and I'd catch you later. Then I came home and figured it wasn't meant to be. And that I'd blown it.'

Elodie felt her cheeks heat up. '*Hamlet*. God. In the middle of that production, I ended up in hospital. The asthma. I was signed off sick for a couple of weeks. Things move so fast in that world, nobody would have thought to tell me someone had been searching for me.' She shook her head. 'My London life seems a very long way off today.'

'I'm pleased. I don't want to lose you down there again. And we're turning a profit at the Hall now – a good one. We'll be fine. I'll do the estate proud eventually.'

'You already have. Never berate yourself for that. I know we've still got lots to do – we've lost Georgiana in the wind, that's for sure. But there's still Jane to consider. No matter what happened, you're right; she was a Countess of Hartsford and that should be recognised.'

'I'm told she's coming back next week. That's what I've been promised at any rate. We can sort out a service then – just a quiet one. I'll spin the same story about the random aunt, but inter Jane in her proper plot – say we're not sure of her name, but we know she was family, so they don't start asking questions about engraving her name on the stone.' He scowled. 'She's entitled to be buried here, whatever happened that night.'

'I still say it's more than she deserves. You're just more forgiving than me. I'm awfully glad you're not cruel like they were. It would be so nice to know what happened to Ben and Georgiana though.' Elodie often thought the rest of their story was dangling just out of reach, like a shiny bauble high up on a Christmas tree.

Speaking of shiny baubles, Georgiana's locket felt warm against her chest. It had seemed right to wear it for her wedding but she knew all along it was simply a loan. Tonight, she would put it in the church, on top of Georgiana's tomb, and then it would be placed back inside it, along with Lucy's Bible and the pewter box. They wouldn't bury the pistol again. It would go in the cabinet, safely locked away with its companion. If it was up to Elodie, she'd toss it into the River Hartsford, but she supposed its place was in the Hall with the other one. She still didn't like it, but Georgiana and Ben had handled it and it was linked to their story in some way and they were linked to the Hall. And she was pretty certain Jasper's last heroic act had been to cause it to misfire, all those years ago.

'Are you all right?' Alex spoke, interrupting her thoughts.

She sighed. 'Yes. I'm just thinking about Ben and Georgiana and wondering what happened. That way madness lies, I guess.'

'Yes.'

'I can't get a handle on where they went. I mean, spiritually.' Elodie looked up at the thin sliver of moon that glowed from between heavy-looking clouds. 'The memories have just ended. If Ben was used to being a shadow in his lifetime, who's to say he would want to be found now? He's still cloaked in darkness somewhere, waiting for the clouds to cover the moon so he can ride again. I think we have to leave it to him to tell us where he took her. If he ever wants us to know, that is. And I think they're still together.'

'I agree,' said Alex softly.

They had reached the church, and stepped inside the cool, stone building. There would be no traditional midnight mass this year – it had been incorporated with the wedding service so people didn't have to come back out. The vicar and the parishioners had seemed quite happy with that arrangement, especially since the ones who were walking home had been sent away pleasantly sozzled on mulled wine and Delilah's extremely alcoholic mince pies. Really, there should have been a health warning on those pies.

And Margaret had insisted on cooking lunch tomorrow for them after all, even deciding that she would assemble all her family just beforehand and make them bring it over to the Hall in her huge serving dishes as an extra wedding gift.

So Alex had wiggled out of making Christmas Lunch nicely again. Elodie wondered what his excuse would be next year, and the thought of next year made her smile. It would be a very different sort of Christmas, that was for sure.

In the church, there was still one candle lit beside the tomb and they walked over to the white marble, hand in hand.

'I hope you're happy, Georgiana,' Elodie told her smooth, peaceful face. The cracks and damage caused by the summer storm were all but invisible now. She let go of Alex's hand and ran her finger gently down Georgiana's cheek as she had done so many times over the years. Alex busied himself lighting more candles and soon they were in a flickering fairyland, the Lady Chapel seeming like a cave of ice crystals as the flames picked out highlights in the snowy marble and caressed the contours of the freshly white-washed stone walls.

Elodie laid her bouquet gently down at the statue's feet and undid the clasp from the chain around her own neck. She placed the locket around Georgiana's marble neck and stroked her fingers along the carved hair, as if she was brushing it back from her face.

'Sleep well, wherever you are,' she whispered.

'I think we should restore that portrait now.' Alex's voice was close to her ear. 'Our wedding gift to her.'

And despite the cold in the church, Elodie felt her cheeks burn. 'Ah. About that.'

'What about "that"?'

'I already did it. It's here. It's my wedding gift to you. Technically, it was a sorry-about-the-storm gift, but it took a bit longer than I thought. And at that point I didn't know I'd be marrying you.' She slipped away from him and scurried to the back of the Lady Chapel. A clean, white tablecloth had done a great job of disguising the framed portrait. It was currently sitting unobtrusively at the back of the chapel and she carefully took the fabric off the frame.

'There she is. All sorted.' She smiled up at him. 'Happy wedding day!'

'How on earth …?' Alex looked a little bit stunned and rather impressed. 'How did you *get* it? Was it Cassie?'

'Sort of. She gave me permission to steal it. Not that I really *stole* it.' She grinned. 'I borrowed it. It was so hard not to tell you what I'd done. She didn't put up too much of a fight when she knew I was doing it to make you happy.'

'I don't know how you did it and I don't think I really *want* to know, but …' He shook his head. 'I would have got round to it. I told you that. But typical you – no patience.' And then he held his arms out to her and smiled that beautiful smile. 'Thank you. It's a lovely gift.'

She stepped forward into his embrace, and he felt so warm and so absolutely *Alex* that she couldn't stop a little, pleasurable sigh escaping from her lips.

'Simon did it, like I knew he would,' she said comfortably into his chest, 'and he even sourced the frame and didn't charge for any of it. But I could have afforded it, you know. Piers was an idiot who couldn't keep his hands off other women, but I got a jolly good divorce settlement from him. And anyway,' she said, beating her fists gently against Alex's chest, 'I have *so* got patience. I waited for this moment for bloody *years*.'

'Me too.' He leaned down and kissed her. 'Now, shall we have a look at this portrait properly?'

'Oh, it *is* her. Definitely. Look.' She pointed at the picture, which glowed golden in the candlelight. 'Ben painted her so lovingly, didn't he? It's her locket. It's the dress she was wearing when I saw her memories, that first time with you, and it's the portrait she was holding the night they ran away. There's a little bit of red ribbon in her hair too – see it? And she looks like the statue on the tomb. It's so nice to see her in colour.'

'It is,' Alex agreed. 'She looks like she did when *I* saw her in those memories. And I still say she looks like you. Can you see the resemblance?'

'Just a little. Her hair and eye colour, perhaps? Maybe the shape of her chin? I don't know. She's rather beautiful.'

'So are you,' Alex told her with a grin. 'I'm pleased we know who painted it now. I knew it wasn't a Gainsborough or a Reynolds.'

'No. They'd have both been pushing up daisies by the time this was painted. Ben painted her like this because he wanted to.' She touched the locket on the painting. 'You could hang it in the Lady Chapel, near her tomb? Or at least hang a reproduction of it, so people could see what she was really like.'

'I agree.' Alex picked the picture up and studied it for a moment. 'It's rather a precious piece of our history. I think she needs to come back to the Hall. I've a miniature there that I think perhaps was Jasper. After that sight in the Green Dragon, I think I've got a little more idea of what he was like. You might know too – as he was in the coach the first time

Georgiana and Ben met. He's got the same colouring as this girl anyway. I can only assume little magpie Lucy pocketed that as well. It's amongst my father's genealogy stash.'

'It would be so nice to put them together again – but nowhere near their awful father!'

'Nowhere near him.'

'But poor Lucy! I *knew* it was her.'

'Lucy saw the aftermath and made the story up.' Alex still had hold of the portrait and stared down at it. 'She's the one who caused all the mischief with Cassie and the one who stashed everything in here?'

Elodie nodded. 'Yes. From the snatches Cassie remembered, Lucy was crippled with guilt and that must have been what sent her over the edge – and what kept her here. It's more peaceful now, isn't it? I think she's finally at rest, poor little thing. And that French cousin must have been named after his influential relatives; just as well they did that. It must have been relatively easy for them to trace him back here because of it. Incredible.'

'And Ben was obviously a talented man, when you look at this.' He took the painting and laid it gently on the marble. 'I think, in some way, they've brought *us* back together as well. Don't you? Thank goodness something good came of it.' He turned and pulled Elodie towards him, and she snuggled into his chest. He nuzzled into her hair for a moment and they were silent, lost in their thoughts. At length, he pulled away and looked down at her, his eyes full of love. 'Do you know, I've got a surprise for you too.'

'Oh?' Elodie pulled away and looked up at him. 'What is it?'

'Come with me.' He took her hand and led her gently outside, around the side of the Lady Chapel. Lanterns were hanging from the trees to lead the guests safely through the grounds and the moon shone brightly. There was a glint in one of the tree branches, and Elodie saw something hanging off it. Something silvery, on a chain: a locket, an identical copy of Georgiana's.

'For you.' Alex stopped in front of the tree and unhooked it. He held it up, dangling it hypnotically from his fingertips. 'I thought you might like one of your own.'

'Oh, Alex! Thank you!'

She reached out for it, but he held it up high, out of her way, and she giggled. Then he smiled and beckoned her closer. 'May I fasten it, Elodie Aldrich?'

'Of course.' She stepped forward into the space between his arms.

He reached behind her neck and did so, then trailed his fingertips along the chain, coming to rest like a butterfly on her collarbone. He weighed the locket in his hand and looked at her shyly. 'D'you like it? It's got a couple of silly pictures of us in at the moment – but I thought we could make a love-knot of our own. It was just a bit awkward to chop some hair off when you weren't looking.'

'Thank you, that would be lovely. We can use some of the ribbon from my wedding bouquet.' She dipped her head down and opened the locket, angling it towards a lantern so she could see the pictures. She laughed – the original photograph had been taken at one of their Living History weekends. Elodie had been dressed in an Edwardian evening gown and had stolen Alex's top hat. Cassie had snapped the picture of them both laughing, both looking at each other as Elodie balanced the hat on her elaborate hairstyle and Alex tried to get it back. Alex had trimmed the big photograph and fitted the smaller pictures in so they were facing each other and smiling. There was, undeniably, love between them in that photograph, and Elodie knew she was finally where she belonged. With Alex, at Hartsford.

'Perhaps it was someone called Alex Aldrich who was

drawing me back to Hartsford all along. Perhaps that's why my heart and soul are here.'

'Could be.' He smiled. 'I know my heart and soul are here too. Right in front of me, in fact. And I wouldn't have it any other way.' They leaned into one another to kiss, and as they did, the last of Georgiana and Ben's memories flooded their minds and their hearts.

She was sitting on Blaze, and Ben, standing on the ground holding the reins of the big, black animal with one hand, was keeping Georgiana steady until she settled herself in the saddle and wound her fingers in the horse's thick, coarse mane.

'We don't have long,' he told her, looking over his shoulder as if the mob were still hunting for him. 'I escaped from them once tonight, thanks to our terribly unlucky poacher friend, and we shan't be so lucky a second time.'

'Please – just get up here with me and we can leave!' begged Georgiana. 'It's all gone wrong – so wrong. We need to get as far away from here as possible!'

'That is my exact plan. I'd defend you with my life – but I think we need my life intact tonight.' In one swift movement, he was behind her on the horse and his arms came around her as he held the reins and kicked the horse onwards.

Blaze bucked and reared and set off at a canter through the woods. Georgiana hung on and narrowed her eyes, trying to see through the trees. The horse seemed to know where he was going and wove through the branches expertly. Soon, they were out on the open road, heading towards the coast. The moonlight glittered on the ocean as they headed along a little-known coastal track to Ipswich.

'Ben. What about Lucy?' she asked suddenly.

'We can't go back for her.' His breath was warm on the back of her head. 'We can send for her when it's safe. We have

to leave and we have to leave now. I'm sorry. But we'll both be hanged for what we've done if they find us. I have friends who can get us – and Blaze – passage on a ship to the continent. We can sail as soon as we reach the docks and head to France. Paris isn't the safest place at the moment, but there will be other towns. In the meantime, I have other friends in Europe who will help us, and I can earn money for us – legally, I hasten to add. I told you my vocation was in the arts. I always enjoyed painting portraits, but it does not pay so well as this.' He indicated the black outfit wryly. 'My life on the road has been a useful exercise to enable me to make my fortune, but it won't be long before the continent is clamouring for portraits by Benjamin Aldrich, I swear to you. Of course, this life is not without its moments. Like tonight.'

A sob suddenly caught in Georgiana's throat. 'Ben, I couldn't have stayed anyway. Even if you—' She couldn't finish the sentence. 'Even if you weren't here.'

'I know. Murdering one's mother, no matter what the provocation, is usually frowned upon by a judge.'

'No. No. It's not that. Although, dear God, that's bad enough.' She took a deep breath and placed her hand on one of his. Gently, she worked his fingers free from the rein. Her heart pounding, she pressed the palm of his hand against her stomach. 'I'm with child, Ben. Our child. I couldn't have stayed. It's impossible.'

'What?' Ben pulled hard on the reins and drew Blaze to a halt. 'With child?'

'Yes.' Georgiana began to panic. She turned awkwardly to try and see his face. If she could see his eyes, she could read them and see how he felt. She should have waited until they were at least on board the ship and halfway to Europe before she told him. He could throw her from the horse right now, right here on this track in the middle of nowhere. He could slit her throat and leave her for dead. He could—

'Georgiana! My love!' His voice was soft, full of emotion. 'So I have two precious bundles before me on Blaze here?' His eyes were shining in the moonlight and he dipped his head. He took her hand and kissed it tenderly. 'Three precious bundles, including my bag of gold, perhaps?' His voice was teasing again, but full of emotion. 'Then it is all the more urgent that we reach the ship and take refuge there. Are you quite well? Is it safe for you to ride?' His eyes changed and were full of concern.

Georgiana looked into the midnight blue depths and felt, insanely, a little bubble of laughter begin to gurgle up within her. She was with Ben. She was on Blaze. They had left Hartsford behind. They had a future. All of them. Together.

She was the happiest she had ever been in her entire life.

'It's a little late to wonder about that now,' she said, her voice wobbling. 'But you have saved my life tonight and to answer your question – yes. I am well. I am very well indeed. I do not think I have ever been better.'

'That is the most perfect answer.' And with a great yell of delight, knowing they were alone on that ribbon of moonlit road, Ben dug his heels into Blaze's flanks and they sped off towards their future.

Elodie drew away and stared at Alex.

'Paris!' they both said together.

'The French cousin who inherited the title,' breathed Elodie. 'And Georgiana's lover was called Benjamin Aldrich! You're related to Highwayman Ben. Alex! How romantic! No wonder your family is horse mad.'

'Related to a thief, and to a murderess who committed accidental matricide?' asked Alex wryly. 'God, you have to love family. But you, my love. You have no right to talk, anyway.' His eyes sparked in that way he had. 'I did a bit of digging through that genealogy paperwork. Georgiana's mother was originally called Jane Markwell.'

'And?'

'I do believe your grandmother was a Markle from the village, before she married the good Mr Bright, a groom in the Hartsford stables?'

'Yes. So I ask again. And?'

'They're the same name.'

'No, they're not. Markwell and Markle are different.'

'In Suffolk, over many years, Markwell has evolved into Markle. Your family has been in Suffolk for God knows how many generations. So. Who's to say you're not related to Georgiana, through her mother's side? That would explain the resemblance, wouldn't it?'

'It would indeed! How exciting!' Elodie laughed. 'My word. But you still have the best genes – a thief who looked outstanding in black. Speaking of which, come here. Come here, Highwayman Alex.'

He came to her willingly; but instead of moving into his arms, she caught his hands in hers, and moved them to her stomach. She held them there, flat against a tummy that was a little rounder and a little harder than it had been a few weeks ago. She looked up at him, a smile twitching at the corners of her mouth, waiting for him to understand.

Alex stared at her, speechless as he processed the information. 'Oh, Elodie!' he said as it sunk in. He looked down at his hands. The two sets of hands formed a little heart shape on her midriff and he leaned down as if to see it better. 'Are you sure?'

'Not one hundred percent. But maybe eighty percent I am. Okay. Ninety-eight percent. Or ninety-nine. One hundred. Yes.' She laughed and shook her head helplessly. 'Yes. Yes, I'm sure!' It was no longer possible to zip up any of her jeans, and she was only about eight weeks along by her reckoning.

It had, she knew, been the night she destroyed Lucy's letter. And she knew that her Grandmother Markle had been a twin ... the possibilities were exciting.

Then she looked up and realised with a childish thrill that snowflakes were beginning to drift past. It was going to be the most perfect Christmas. With that thought warmly in her mind like the scent of pine trees and the mulled-wine fragrances all around them, she raised her head and kissed her husband.

And the snowflakes began to fall faster, like whispers, and they settled around them and on them like angels' kisses.

Thank You

Thank you so much for reading, and hopefully enjoying, this novel – the first instalment in the *Hartsford Mysteries Series*. I hope you enjoyed meeting a new cast of characters and also enjoyed spotting the links to the *Rossetti Mysteries Series*. I hope you'll grow to love Hartsford and its inhabitants as much as I do.

Authors need to know they are doing the right thing and keeping their readers happy, because without people like yourselves, a novel like this is just a collection of words on a page. So it would be wonderful if you could find a moment just to write a quick review on Amazon or one of the other websites to let me know that you enjoyed the book. Thank you once again, and do feel free to contact me at any time on Facebook, Twitter, through my website or through my lovely publishers Choc Lit.

Thanks again, and much love to you all,

Kirsty

xx

About the Author

Kirsty Ferry is from the North East of England and lives there with her husband and son. She won the English Heritage/Belsay Hall National Creative Writing competition in 2009 and has had articles and short stories published in various magazines. Her work also appears in several anthologies, incorporating such diverse themes as vampires, crime, angels and more.

Kirsty loves writing ghostly mysteries and interweaving fact and fiction. The research is almost as much fun as writing the book itself, and if she can add a wonderful setting and a dollop of history, that's even better.

Her day job involves sharing a building with an eclectic collection of ghosts, which can often prove rather interesting.

For more information on Kirsty visit:
www.twitter.com/kirsty_ferry
www.facebook.com/Kirsty.Ferry.Author

More Choc Lit

From Kirsty Ferry

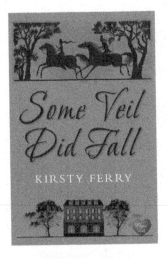

Some Veil Did Fall

Book 1 in the Rossetti
Mysteries series

**What if you recalled memories
from a life that wasn't yours,
from a life before …?**

When Becky steps into
Jonathon Nelson's atmospheric
photography studio in Whitby,
she is simply a freelance
journalist in search of a story.
But as soon as she puts on the
beautiful Victorian dress and poses for a photograph, she
becomes somebody quite different …

From that moment on, Becky is overcome with visions and
flashbacks from a life that isn't her own – some disturbing
and filled with fear.

As she and Jon begin to unravel the tragic mystery behind
her strange experiences, the natural affinity they have for
each other continues to grow and leads them to question …
have they met somewhere before? Perhaps not in this life but
in another?

Available in paperback from all good
bookshops and online stores. Visit
www.choc-lit.com for details.

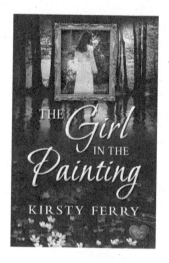

The Girl in the Painting

Book 2 in the Rossetti Mysteries series

What if you thought you knew a secret that could change history?

Whilst standing engrossed in her favourite Pre-Raphaelite painting – Millais's Ophelia – Cori catches the eye of Tate gallery worker, Simon, who is immediately struck by her resemblance to the red-haired beauty in the famous artwork.

The attraction is mutual, but Cori has other things on her mind. She has recently acquired the diary of Daisy, a Victorian woman with a shocking secret. As Cori reads, it soon becomes apparent that Daisy will stop at nothing to be heard, even outside of the pages of her diary …

Will Simon stick around when life becomes increasingly spooky for Cori, as she moves ever closer to uncovering the truth about Daisy's connection to the girl in her favourite painting?

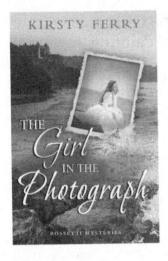

The Girl in the Photograph

Book 3 in the Rossetti Mysteries series

What if the past was trying to teach you a lesson?

Staying alone in the shadow of an abandoned manor house in Yorkshire would be madness to some, but art enthusiast Lissy de Luca can't wait. Lissy has her reasons for seeking isolation, and she wants to study the Staithes Group – an artists' commune active at the turn of the twentieth century.

Lissy is fascinated by the imposing Sea Scarr Hall – but the deeper she delves, the stranger things get. A lonely figure patrols the cove at night, whilst a hidden painting leads to a chilling realisation. And then there's the photograph of the girl; so beautiful she could be a mermaid … and so familiar.

As Lissy further immerses herself, she comes to an eerie conclusion. The occupants of Sea Scarr Hall are long gone, but they have a message for her – and they're going to make sure she gets it.

Available in paperback from all good bookshops and online stores. Visit www.choc-lit.com for details.

A Little Bit of Christmas Magic

Book 4 in the Rossetti Mysteries series

Any wish can be granted with a little bit of Christmas magic …

As a wedding planner at Carrick Park Hotel Ailsa McCormack has devoted herself to making sure couples get their perfect day, but just occasionally that comes at a price – in this case, organising a Christmas Day wedding at the expense of her own Christmas.

Not that Ailsa minds. There's something very special about Carrick Park during the festive season and she's always been fascinated by the past occupants of the place; particularly the beautiful and tragic Ella Carrick, whose striking portrait still hangs at the top of the stairs.

And then an encounter with a tall, handsome and strangely familiar man in the drawing room on Christmas Eve sets off a chain of events that transforms Ailsa's lonely Christmas into a far more magical occasion than she could have ever imagined …

Available as an eBook on all platforms.
Visit www.choc-lit.com for details.

Watch for Me by Twilight

Hartsford Mysteries series

The past is never really the past at Hartsford Hall ...

Aidan Edwards has always been fascinated by the life of his great-great uncle Robert. A trip to Hartsford Hall and an encounter with Cassie Aldrich leads him closer to the truth about Robert Edwards, as he unravels the scandalous story of a bright young poet and a beautiful spirited aristocrat in the carefree twilight of the 1930s before the Second World War.

But can Aidan find out what happened to Robert after the war – or will he have to accept that certain parts of his uncle's life will remain forever shrouded in mystery?

Available as an eBook on all platforms and in audio. Visit www.choc-lit.com for details.

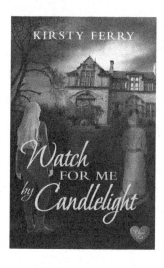

Watch for Me by Candlelight

Hartsford Mysteries series

"The stars are aligning and it's time again ..."

Working at the Folk Museum in Hartsford village means that Kate Howard is surrounded by all sorts of unusual vintage items. Of course she has her favourites; particularly the Victorian ice skates with a name – 'CAT' – mysteriously painted on the sides.

But what Kate doesn't realise is how much she has in common with Catriona Aphrodite Tredegar, the original owner of the skates, or how their lives will become strangely entwined. All Kate knows is that as soon as she bumps into farrier Theo Kent, things start getting weird: there's the vivid, disconcerting visions and then of course the overwhelming sense that she's met Theo before ...

Watch for Me at Christmas

Hartsford Mysteries series

When midwinter magic brings you home for Christmas …

When Emmy Berry arrives at Hartsford Hall to work at the Frost Fayre she immediately feels at home. Which is odd because she's never set foot in the place in her life. Then a freak blizzard leaves her stranded and things get even weirder when she bumps into Tom Howard. Tom and Emmy have never met before but neither can ignore the sense that they know each other. With Christmas fast approaching and the weather showing no sign of improving it soon becomes apparent that Hartsford Hall has a little bit of midwinter magic in store for them both …

Available as an eBook on all platforms and in audio. Visit www.choc-lit.com for details.

Every Witch Way

Book 1 in the Schubert series

Time for a Halloween road trip …

Nessa hates her full name – Agnes – which she inherited from her great-great grandmother – but is that all she inherited? Because rumour had it that Great-Great Granny Agnes was a witch, and a few unusual things have been happening to Nessa recently …

First, there's the strange book she finds in her local coffee shop, and then the invite from her next-door neighbour Ewan Grainger to accompany him on a rather supernatural research trip. What ensues is a Halloween journey through Scotland in a yellow camper van (accompanied by a big black cat called Schubert), a mystical encounter in an ancient forest and maybe just a touch of magic!

Available as an eBook on all platforms.
Visit www.choc-lit.com for details.

A little bit of black cat magic ...

A Christmas Secret

Book 2 in the Schubert series

What if a secret from Christmas past was stopping you from moving on to Christmas future?

When Hugo McCreadie steps into Isla Brodie's pet portrait studio to get a 'Festive Furball Photo Shoot' for his sister's cat Schubert, he does question his sanity. But he knows the photographs will be the perfect Christmas present for his eccentric sister, Nessa – and he finds himself quite taken with ditzy, animal-loving Isla Brodie, too.

Will a Christmas secret from long ago prevent Hugo and Isla's new friendship from going any further? Or will a certain big, black cat taking matters into his own paws lead them not only on a mad winter dash through snowy Edinburgh –but into each other's arms for Christmas as well?

KIRSTY FERRY

Summer
at
Carrick Park

Summer at Carrick Park

A summer wedding, fifty cupcakes and a man she thought she would never see again …

When Joel Leicester walks into the hotel where Rosa Tempest works, she can't believe her bad luck. Out of all the hotels in all of North Yorkshire, the man who broke her heart would have to walk into Carrick Park!

The last time Rosa saw Joel it was after a whirlwind holiday when they'd been greeted at his flat by a woman claiming to be his fiancée. Rosa never stuck around to hear Joel's side of the story but now, six years later on, Fate has another trick up its sleeve as a potentially disastrous summer wedding at Carrick Park can only be saved by Joel and Rosa working together …

Available as an eBook on all platforms and in audio. Visit www.choc-lit.com for details.

Choc Lit

Introducing Choc Lit

We're an independent publisher creating
a delicious selection of fiction.
Where heroes are like chocolate – irresistible!
Quality stories with a romance at the heart.

See our selection here:
www.choc-lit.com

We'd love to hear how you enjoyed *Watch For Me by
Moonlight*. Please visit **www.choc-lit.com** and give your
feedback or leave a review where you purchased this novel.

Choc Lit novels are selected by genuine readers like yourself.
We only publish stories our Choc Lit Tasting Panel want to
see in print. Our reviews and awards speak for themselves.

Could you be a Star Selector and join our Tasting Panel?
Would you like to play a role in choosing which novels we
decide to publish? Do you enjoy reading women's fiction?
Then you could be perfect for our Choc Lit Tasting Panel.

Visit here for more details…
www.choc-lit.com/join-the-choc-lit-tasting-panel

Keep in touch:
Sign up for our monthly newsletter Spread for all the latest
news and offers: www.spread.choc-lit.com. Follow us
on Twitter: @ChocLituk and Facebook: Choc Lit.

Where heroes are like chocolate – irresistible!